Will You
Sing to Me?

Will You Sing to Me?

T.S. Lowe

J. Kenkade
PUBLISHING®

Little Rock, Arkansas

Will You Sing to Me?
Copyright © 2022 by T.S. Lowe

J. Kenkade Publishing
 6104 Forbing Rd
Little Rock, AR 72209
www.jkenkadepublishing.com

J. Kenkade Publishing is a registered trademark.
Printed in the United States of America
ISBN: 978-1-955186-24-7

PROLOGUE

History books want to teach. Religion wants to convert. Wars are fought to promote or destroy one thing or another. All these things change the world – sometimes slowly, sometimes very quickly. But underneath all these palpable changes, there runs a dark river. A river foul and thick. It is full of decay, sorrow, and putrefaction. No one wants to look upon it. No one wants to go near it. Yet, this river has moved quietly and methodically beneath the current of all humanity. It drags the young and old, rich and poor, powerful and lowly beneath its greasy waves.

No one escapes it.

Eventually, every human will be washed away in its tide, despite their clutching, scratching, crawling, and begging. Some may temporarily escape the reach of the river by climbing out onto the other side, but these temporary survivors are never the same. Their lives are changed forever, and there is always the dread that they will fall into the river again. It is only a matter of time. They live out the remainder of their lives with the scars. Some of the scars are visible, gouging deep, ugly, painful burns into the skin and organs. Other victims are not so fortunate. They emerge with deeper scars. Scars that bend their minds, destroy their will, and haunt them daily. You've seen the river. You have friends and family who are now fighting to stay alive in the river. You may have even been in the river yourself, perhaps as a survivor, perhaps trying to claw your way out even now. Some may survive this ordeal, but others will sink beneath the river's terrifying surface.

The river has many names. It is referred to as suffering, purging, cleansing, retribution, or punishment. But you will call this river any name you want when you stand on its banks. There will not be a word that can describe its fearsomeness. You will either find religion or forsake it, but neither will change the outcome. Medicine calls this river disease, and it has destroyed more lives than all the wars in the world combined, for everyone dies from something. Everyone. Nations have changed hands and power has been won or lost because of nothing more than fevers and weakness.

Commonly referred to as "the plague," these insidious bacteria, fungi, and viruses lay dormant like sleeping tigers, waiting for their opportunity. That's all they need – an opportunity – and the great plagues of the world begin. Many people will succumb to the illness. Those who are attacked by these stealthy diseases will not be able to work or provide for their families. Rumors of riots, crime, and uncontrolled death will circulate. Some will take this as an opportunity to force their will, preaching fear and death. Pain and suffering run rampant, and whether we fall victim to the fear or the disease, we are all consumed.

But while the plagues of the world stretch their diseased hands across the world, humanity moves along as well. Struggling to survive, humanity seeks solace in the comfort of the common things. The people of Arkansas have learned to enjoy life's simple gifts, such as sunrises creeping over tree-laden hills moving the mist in the valleys and the smells of fresh earth, coffee, and smoke. Homey smells, relaxing smells, familiar smells of lives and days that bleed into each other with hard work, poverty, and great love. So much love that it can overshadow the darkness, like the sunshine trailing through those trees.

While the morning fragrances bring promise and newness, the fragrance of the evening brings a whole different variety of odors. Wafting smells of the meager resources meander through the hills, bringing with them the fiddle players, the dancers, the young, and the old. These are the fragrances of human beings: whiskey, tobacco, and smoke. Vice smells good.

1

Tiny little dust speckles were suspended in the air. Hattie could see them flitting about in rays of the setting sun coming through the barn window. There were too many to count, floating and disappearing once out of the light. They were numberless, shapeless, moving constantly, becoming part of the air she breathed. She thought how harmless they looked, and yet they could carry so many seeds of despair. She took a deep breath, knowing that some of these dusty particles would find their way into her own system, but breathing was a necessity, and people were left to the will of God. May He have mercy on their souls. "Your husband does such a fine job with the fiddle." Hattie turned toward the sound of the voice. "Yes," she answered, smiling. "Martin does possess a gift for the thing." A loud voice came from the front of the room. It was a large open area in the storekeeper's barn. Hay was moved to one side to make room for dancers and musicians. A large board was laid across two sawhorses to fashion a makeshift table. Trays containing fried catfish and barbecue meat lay on top. No one asked where the meat came from or even what kind of meat it was. It was a better thing not to know. Crock jugs were lined up on the end with clear, glass canning jars sitting nearby. Discolored corks in the jugs held the pungent smell of the content at bay, but once opened, the smell permeated through the room, and there was no doubt what lay within. Prohibition was over, and every home in the hills imbibed, some more than others.

"And now..." came a loud voice from the front of the room. "I would like to introduce you to the latest member of our musical group. He's kinda young, but he shows much promise. Please make him welcome. My son, Clemson Baker!"

The dancers moved from the floor, allowing a small pathway from the back of the room to the front. Running into the opening came a little red-haired child, grinning and running past the dancers. He stepped up onto the wooden platform on which the musicians stood. His father lifted him up into his arms.

"Now, my little man, what musical selection would you like to perform?"

The little boy smiled at his father. "D-d-daaad-dy," he stuttered. "You know I on-on-only know one s-s-song."

The crowd laughed, and the little boy blushed, hiding his face in his father's neck. His father laughed, brushing his son's hair and pulling up his chin.

"You only know one song now, but we shall surely teach ya more when the crowd hears this one. C'mon, boys, let's git this song goin'."

The banjo and mouth harp players started playing the instruments, and the dancers began clapping their hands together with the rhythm. This was a familiar song.

"Hey, farmer!" Martin and the crowd yelled out.

"Yes?!" the little boy shouted without stuttering a bit. He smiled from ear to ear.

The crowd joined in with his father in singing the song.

"You been livin' here all your life?"

The little boy leaned forward. "Not yet!" he shouted.

The crowd laughed out loud, readying themselves for the next verse by clapping and stomping their feet.

"Hey, farmer!" they shouted. "Where does this road go?"

The little boy took a deep breath, preparing for the long response. "I been livin' here all my life. It ain't gone nowhere yet!"[1]

Loud laughter echoed throughout the barn with hands clapping.

Martin kissed his little boy on the forehead and placed him on the floor. The child walked back through the dancers, so proud of himself for not stuttering. He felt happy, and his little face beamed with self-satisfaction. As he walked through the crowd, the partiers tousled his hair and patted his back, telling him how well he did, that he was a natural born entertainer like his father, and how much they loved his red hair.

"One more announcement, please, and then we'll go back to the dancin'. I wanna take this time and raise a glass...to me!" Martin raised his mason jar, which was half full of a clear, thick liquid. "For today I been given some good news that well deserves a congratulatory draught. Today, my fine wife and mother of my three lovely children did tell me we are to be blessed with another child!"

He smiled at his wife, while the others raised their glasses and shouted their well-wishes, although no words were truly distinguishable from the loud, fuddled crowd. One woman's voice, however, did reach out over the noise. "We should be toastin' the mother, then!"

Martin wiped his mouth with the back of his hand. "Why so? Everyone knows it's the man that does all the work!"

The women in the crowd bellowed, and the men all shouted in agreement. Hattie smiled, and other women came close to hug her and ask how she felt and the other things women speak of when such news is announced. Hattie told them how the morning sickness was not too bad, but the fatigue was much worse this time than with her other three children. The two younger children, Clemson and Eulalie, came close, and their little heads were tousled by the adults. They were warned of the new baby and all the changes.

"But not so many changes that we can't spare some licorice whips for these two," the woman said, handing the two young children candy from a jar.

"Oh, Mrs. McCrary, you spoil these children rotten." Their mother kissed their heads as they ran towards the other children with enough candy for all.

"Will you dance with your husband, Mrs. Baker?"

Hattie looked up and smiled at the man. "I would love to."

The remaining musicians played a waltz, slow and rhythmic.

Dancing with him was like wearing comfortable clothing. He had a natural rhythm to his walk and voice. Like the waltz, both were slow and familiar. Comfortable. He still had the gift of moving the soul with his eyes. Deep, dark pools of unrealized dreams. His black curls were too long, and he could use a shave, but it did not matter. People did not come to admire him; they came to dance, drink, and forget their problems, at least for a short time. And Martin Baker could take them to places where they were not so poor or pitiful, and he did so with a simple fiddle.

The crowd clapped when the couple finished their dance. Martin kissed his bride on the forehead and returned to the little musical group. Hattie found the closest chair. She was so tired, and there was this tickle in the back of her throat. It caused a chronic irritation with a slight burning in the chest. She was sure it was nothing. Perhaps it was only pleurisy or maybe a sickening of the stomach from the pregnancy. She was not a doctor, nor did she have any training as a nurse, but she had real-life education as a midwife in these hills. Her mother and grandmother had both been midwives, and they passed down their knowledge and skills to her.

She tried to take a deep breath, but the coughing sensation and fluttering pain were nagging. She saw Martin packing his fiddle into the case. She enjoyed these dances but was ready to leave. She stood slowly, trying to catch her breath.

"Are you well?" Mrs. McCrary asked as she brought the two smaller children to their mother.

"Yes," she lied. "I'm just tired." She placed her hand on her abdomen. "This doesn't get any easier when you get older."

Mrs. McCrary smiled. She had no children but doted on Hattie's three, especially the oldest, Jack, who had a creative talent. He was able to carve wood, tool leather, and build with the slimmest of materials. He was talented like his father, full of dreams and "what ifs." The McCrarys allowed him to have access to tools and supplies at no cost. If they could, they would give him more. Their hearts were empty, and he helped fill that void.

Hattie placed the two smaller children into the wagon while Jack made his way through the dancers. Hattie placed the blanket down on the bottom of the wagon. She tucked them in. It was warm enough, but lying quietly in the outside air could bring on a chill.

"And where have you been all evening?" She asked as the oldest child ran up to the wagon.

The boy jumped up and twisted himself to sit solidly beside his brother and sister. The two smaller children were already closing their eyes. They would be asleep before they got home.

"I was over at the workshop. Mr. McCrary unlocked it for me, and I was working on a hog trap. I used some old traps he had back in the shed, and I think if I can get Ol' Joe the blacksmith to rework the hinges—"

His father cut him short. "It all sounds like a fine idea, son, but now we must be on our way. The younger ones are nearly sleepin', and I reckon you will be, too, once we git goin."

The boy did as he was told while his parents lifted themselves up into the wagon and made their way through the resting children. The wagon was a simple hay wagon with the rails placed on the sides. It creaked and crackled, rocked from side to side as the plow horse pulled it along the dirt road. Despite its unholy appearance, the hay wagon was soothing. The rocking was calming, and the children fell asleep quickly. Hattie and Martin stood at the front of the wagon. He put his arm around her, holding the reins of the horse with the other. He was warm and sweaty and smelled of fresh-mown hay and whiskey. Like the wagon, he was soothing. Even the warm smell of the whiskey was comforting. It was all familiar, and it made her feel safe. She did not like change. Martin liked new ideas and new inventions. He and Jack could talk for hours about the things they could create and what they could do with them, but Hattie liked the familiar. She liked the big, old hardwood trees that surrounded their house. She liked the wooden cabin Martin's grandfather built so many years ago. The sounds of the wind, rain, and horses' hooves on a dirt road reminded her why she loved it here. This was where her children were born. This was where her family was buried. This was home.

"Are you well, dear?" Martin asked his wife as they made their way home. She was quiet, and her breathing was rather shallow.

"Yes, I'm just tired, fretfully tired." She leaned her head onto his shoulder.

"You go straight away to bed when we git home. I'll bring the children in and put them to bed."

She put her arm around him. The night was cool, and he was warm. "Oh, I'll be all right. I just need to rest. I'll help with putting the children to bed."

Martin turned his head and looked at her. She was older than he, but not by much. He liked to imagine great things. She could do great things. While he could create with his hands and dream with his mind, she had such knowledge. Perhaps not appreciated by the outside world, but here in these hills, she was a godsend. She left the comfort of their bedtime and time over to assist with another woman's childbirth, or sick infant, or dying parent. She was never too tired, never too busy, never too vain to help others. Her eyes were just as bright as they were the night they wed. He could remember her shyness and uncertainty. She was quiet in a crowd unless it had to do with healing. Then, she was certain and secure. It pained him to see her feeling ill herself. He kissed her forehead and held her close. They would be home soon, and she could rest. He would try to make it easier for her. Perhaps it was her age or the fact that this was the fourth child, but he knew she was not well. She was too tired, too pale, and her breathing was short with spells of coughing. She pushed it off, but he knew this was not normal, and he was concerned for her.

"Go on into the cabin, Hattie, and I'll bring in the little 'uns." Martin said as he pulled the reins of the horse to stop the wagon.

Hattie turned to see her three children. All three were deep asleep, mouths open, and slow, deep breathing. All were sounds of little people filled with happy exhaustion. Martin jumped down out of the wagon and helped his wife down also. She did not walk into the cabin but followed her husband to the back of the wagon.

"Go on now, Hattie. I'll git these children. You look bone tired and need to lie down." Martin picked up Clemson and shook Jack. The boy stretched and yawned. Sitting up, he made loud groaning sounds.

"Jack, be still, you'll wake up these other two," his mother scolded him as she rubbed his face. "Get to bed now. I'll take Eulalie."

She went to pick up the smallest child but found she had no

strength. Her arms gave way, and her knees would not even hold her own weight. She quickly laid the child back into the wagon as Martin grabbed her about the waist to keep her from falling. She leaned on the wagon for a short time. The little girl was awakened by the sudden jolt of her mother's near fall. She twisted her face and began to cry softly.

"Are you all right, 'Lalie?" Her mother asked quickly, composing herself and checking the little girl.

"'Lalie good, Momma," the child cried, rubbing her eyes.

"Come to me, 'Lalie," her father said, releasing his hold on his wife and reaching for the child. "Are you able to walk, Hattie?" He asked as they started to make their way towards the house.

"Yes, I just lost my balance."

"Jack, help your mother."

Jack jumped down off the wagon and held his mother's hand. She was weak, but it was improving. She felt so tired, as if she had already walked a thousand miles.

"Momma," the young boy whispered. "Is this somethin' we should worry 'bout?"

She smiled at him. "No need to worry 'bout nothin'. Don't do no good, anyway." She smiled at her oldest son again. "It'll all be fine, son. One way or t'other, it'll all be fine."

Hattie woke the next morning. The sun was already shining through the milky glass windows. Ivory-colored muslin hung as curtains and moved gently in the breeze. She closed her eyes again. She'd slept all night but still felt exhausted. She could hear Martin and Jack outside doing chores. Farm sounds such as hogs squealing and cows bellowing drifted through the open window. Maybe it was the cool night air that was giving her this cough or the wind kicking up the dust. She opened her eyes to see her smallest child standing beside her bed. The little girl's eyes were watching her mother.

"I'm whisperin', Momma, so not to wake you."

Hattie smiled. "You did a good job. I can't hardly hear you. You whisper so soft."

The child smiled. "Is you wakin' up now, Momma?"

Hattie pulled her arms out from beneath the comforter. She pulled the child close to her. "Yes, I'm wakin' up now. You must be hungry."

The child nodded.

"Eu-uu-lalie Ja-jannneee!" came another small voice trying desperately to whisper, but not very successfully. "D-d-daddy told you n-n-not to wake M-m-momma."

Hattie rolled over to see Clemson creeping in. "It's all right, Clemson. Momma's awake. You two needin' some breakfast?"

Clemson climbed up into the bed with his mother, quickly followed by Eulalie, who needed a little help from her big brother. "I am r-r-ready for b-breakfast, M-momma. I ain't t-t-too hungry, th-though. M-m-maybe just some ham, b-b-biscuits with b-b-butter and j-j-jelly, eggs, m-m-milk, and s-s-some g-g-grits this m-m-morning."

Hattie laughed out loud. She hugged them both. "Well, Clemson, I'm glad you're not too hungry this morning or else I'd have to butcher another hog just to feed you."

The two children laughed and wrestled each other as Hattie got out of the bed. She could feel the urge to cough but was able to calm it. She knew if she relented, it would bring on the chest pain and shortness of breath. Best to keep all that for another time. Right now, she needed to fix breakfast for her children. Then there were the people she told she would come to see today. She especially needed to visit Jessica Pike. She was a young woman expecting her first child. She'd been having trouble with headaches and leg cramping. Hattie was concerned for both the mother and the baby. It was a far piece to walk, but the girl needed to be watched carefully. Hattie wished often that she had been able to attend school, to be a nurse or some kind of educated person who could help these people. They were often forgotten or ignored, but they were wonderful people, kind and pure in spirit. Although they didn't necessarily trust strangers, Hattie thought she could do so much more if she had some education, but that was not to be. She'd need to be satisfied with the little knowledge she'd been given by her mother and grandmother. That knowledge alone had helped a lot of people, birthed a lot of babies, and comforted the dying. So, today she would command all the strength she could to get her work done. People depended upon her, and she did not want to disappoint anyone.

"Momma..." came a pitiful little voice from across the room. "Dis butt'n."

Hattie turned away from the cabinet and wiped the flour from her hands. Her apron was worn from the thousands of biscuits she'd made in the past. Her dress was old, and she was barefoot, but it was getting hot outside, and the thin material of her clothing and bare feet against the cool dirt floors were relieving.

"Come here, darlin', and Momma will fix it fer ya."

The little girl walked up to her mother, holding the two sides of her dress forward for her mother to fix her.

"These little bitty buttons are hard for you, ain't they?" Hattie asked the child as she watched intently as her mother demonstrated the process of buttoning clothing. The child nodded in agreement then smiled up at her mother. "I'll sew on some bigger buttons for you, Eulalie, and then you can do it yerself."

"Thank ye, Momma." The child turned and bounded out of the room, letting the screen door slam shut behind her as she went outside.

Hattie watched the child scamper from the room. She was a delightful little girl, bouncing blonde curls with freckles sprinkled over her nose. Her pudgy cheeks were begging to be squeezed. Hattie unconsciously rubbed her hands across the small bump in her belly. It was a small thing, barely noticeable. There were no signs of life yet, but she hadn't felt life until four or five months along with the other three children. She wasn't worried. She was always concerned, though. Life was not easy in these Arkansas hills. It was beautiful with cold, blue lakes, river falls, mountains, and gigantic hardwood trees. But it wasn't easy. For every blessing, there was a price to pay. Sometimes, the price was high.

Martin came through the door, leaving it open behind him. "It is already gettin' so hot out there. It's gonna be warm today, and I need to git to the bottom land today. Is breakfast ready?"

He kissed his wife on the forehead and picked up the coffee pot. He poured himself a cup of coffee and threw its contents down his throat.

"Yes," she replied, leaning over the oven and pulling out the biscuits. Their fragrance filled the house, and it brought three children into the room, ready for food. She placed the biscuits along with the meat and grits onto the wooden table. They all sat down and folded their hands.

"Clemson," Martin said in his fatherly tone. "Will ya please say the blessin'?"

The little boy looked frightened. He licked his lips and bowed his head. He could feel the terror well up inside him. It was this feeling that caused the words to stop. He knew what he wanted to say, but the words got stuck. His mother placed her hand on his leg, patting him gently and winking. He took a breath.

"B-Bless this f-f-food..."

He was starting to sweat. It was warm, and he felt as if all eyes were upon him. Everyone was waiting on him. Everyone was watching him. His mother patted his leg again and smiled. He tried to remember what she taught him, that he was a good person, worthy of everyone's praise and respect, take your time, breathe, and find peace in your mind.

"Dear Lord, we thank ye for the fine food before us. Bless this house, these fine people, and forgive us of our sins. In Your Son's name. Amen."

The rest of the family looked at him and smiled.

"Amen," they said together.

His father rubbed the boy's cheeks. "Good job, my son."

"Can we eat now?" Jack said as he reached across the table for the biscuits.

"Yes, let's eat now 'cause we got work to do today," His father said as he picked up the platter of ham and passed it to his wife. "And you prob'ly got people to visit?"

Hattie nodded as she put food on the younger children's plates.

"Hattie," Martin said quietly. "Do ya think that wise?"

Hattie smiled her best "don't fret" smile and nodded. "I feel better today. I'll be fine."

Martin nodded and began eating his food. He covered his biscuits with molasses and drank down the strong, chicory coffee in his cup. He wiped his mouth with the back of his hand as he pushed his chair away from the table.

"I think I'll start bustin' up the ground in the lower forty today. I'm hopin' the last of the big rains is over and there won't be no more flooding down there. That land is rich, but it floods like a son of a..." His voice trailed off as his wife gave him a side eye stare. "It floods," he said flatly as he placed his dirty black hat on his head.

Hattie picked up the plates from the table. "That sounds good, Martin. That ground is some of the best we got. What are you wantin' to plant down there?"

"Too late for wheat and too wet for soybeans, so I guess I'll try corn. Hope it grows fast down there. The price of corn is pretty good right now, and we can use the money. There seems to be a lot more call for corn these days," he answered and smiled.

"You mean there's more call for the squeezins, don't ya?" Jack laughed as he grabbed his hat and went outside.

Hattie wiped the faces of her two smallest children. They pulled away but relinquished their rights when she gave them that familiar motherly look. She managed a few successful swipes, wiping the molasses and milk away from their little faces. She helped them both down from the large, wooden chairs as they both tore off for the outdoors, letting the screen door slam behind them. Hattie looked at her husband. "Corn's gonna be hard to grow down there. It's so hot. What about sorghum or tobacco?"

"Nope," came the short answer. "Jack's right. It's gonna be corn." With that, Martin kissed his wife on the forehead and left the house.

"You gonna be back for supper?" she hollered after him.

Martin turned around on the porch. She could see him through the screen door, despite its dirty screen and dead flies.

"I'll stay in the field until supper time. Tell Jack to feed for me tonight and watch that white sow. She's gonna farrow any day. She ate her young before, and I don't want her to eat these. I paid good money for that service."

Martin made his way to the barn to obtain the tools he would need for the day. He placed them into the back of the hay wagon and guided the horse to the front where he harnessed the animal and slowly moved out of the barn, towards the field.

Jack called his dog, and the two went towards the barn. He believed he had a great idea on reworking that hog trap and was anxious to determine if it could work. He'd still need some blacksmithing, but his wooden trap would be good enough for a trial run. It still had the sharp, metal teeth he procured from another trap. It was just a matter of getting the tension correct so when the hog stepped on the trigger, the teeth would snap closed so fast that the hog would be unable to escape. And if the trap was secured to something stable, like a tree, the hog would be unable to get away. He'd thought about this for some time and thought he figured out a way to catch more of those wild animals than they were able to in the past.

Wild hogs ran through the hills around their house, tearing up the earth, rooting up gardens, and ruining the hunting of other animals. But they made for good eating. Smoked or barbecued, these wild animals could feed a family for weeks, and if his trap worked, it removed some of the danger of hunting the angry beasts. It wasn't meant to kill them, just hold them until someone could get to them and shoot them. These wild animals had an ugly strip of unruly hair straight down their backs and possessed razor sharp teeth, which earned them the nickname "razorbacks." They were not easily frightened. They would fight viciously anything that threatened them: wolves, bears, and men.

"Jack!" his mother shouted, but she soon realized that shouting was a bad idea.

There was a sharp pain in her chest, a welling of pressure up into her throat. She attempted to calm the fury that was building within her lungs. She swallowed hard, breathing slowly, using all her power to keep this under control. Jack walked up to the porch. He could tell his mother was not well.

"Momma," he said very quietly as he approached her. "You all right?"

Hattie grinned, keeping her lips tight in an attempt to keep from coughing. She nodded in the affirmative, taking her time to answer.

Her voice was very soft, almost a whisper, as she answered her son. "Your father wants you to feed tonight and keep an eye on that white sow."

Jack stood very still, slightly confused but certain his mother was ill. "I know, Momma. The sow will farrow real soon, and she's bad news when it comes to babies."

Hattie nodded in agreement, desperately trying to contain this unbelievable urge to cough. But she knew how it would be. It would start off as a slight hacking, unquenchable, and then become increasingly deep. The coughing would become so deep and violent that the tiny, little, fragile vessels in her lungs would rupture, causing blood to spill from her mouth. She did not want her children to see that.

"I'll take care of it, Momma. I'll do the milkin', too. That way maybe you can rest a bit."

The boy returned to the barn and wrapped his contraption in a burlap sack. He slung the whole thing over his shoulder and took off for the hills with his dog, Amos, close behind. The two started up the steep embankment behind the house. The hill was rocky and slippery as the ground beneath Jack's feet slipped and rolled away, but he'd been up here a thousand times and knew how to maneuver himself to climb this hill. He'd place the trap between two large trees and hope to catch one of those hogs tonight. His dog sniffed the ground, yelping when he smelled the sign of the wild animals. They weren't difficult to find. They left destruction and hog waste everywhere they wandered. Jack noticed his dog circling between two big oak trees. The ground beneath was rooted all to pieces with a dank smell of hog manure mingled with the fresh-turned earth. He wedged his wooden trap between the trees and pushed one side back and away, allowing the springs to pop, barely holding the sharp teeth of the trap apart. The slightest movement in this trap would release the springs and the two sides of the machine would tear apart anything within its mouth. Jack smiled as he stood upright and witnessed his creation. It was wonderful and fearful at the same time.

Jack scratched the back of his dog, "You keep your ears peeled, Amos. We might have a hog by nightfall."

Hattie packed some little lunches for her two youngest children and picked up Eulalie's rag doll and Clemson's mouth harp. She placed both children into the little wooden wagon Martin built for them years ago when they were just babies. Hattie was younger and healthier at that time. Back then, she pulled the little wagon up and down these hills without a second thought. In fact, she rather enjoyed it. She could visit the people she helped and keep her children close by. They enjoyed the ride and playing with the neighbor's babies. But now, this wagon with its little passengers seemed like pulling a barge across these hills. She walked more slowly and became so tired in the afternoons. She wasn't able to visit with all the people she wanted to see, but she still saw the people she could. They relied on her, just as they had her mother and grandmother. Many of these people never saw a doctor. They had no money and no transportation into town. There was only one doctor within miles of here, and he did not make house calls. Hattie was sure he was satisfied with the patients he treated in his office in the town, in his big house with his servant and his family.

There was no love lost between the doctors and the women who worked with these hill people. Hattie saw her work as a calling, a continuation of a job started by her ancestors. A job that helped others and kept them alive and comfortable as long as they could be. The doctor in town saw these women as unlicensed quacks. Hattie wasn't sure if he disliked her because she was not professionally educated or because she was a woman. She was sure he thought she was infringing upon his vocation.

It didn't matter much, though.

Hattie didn't really care what the doctor thought of her. She didn't think much of him, either. Although they'd never met, she was sure with all of his education and money, the doctor had lost his first love – the love of helping people. These people couldn't pay with hard cash, but their lives were not to be thrown away and discarded. They paid with chickens, handwoven blankets, and moonshine. On a cold evening in these hills, eating fried chicken, sitting in your rocking chair on the front porch wrapped in the blanket, while drinking some of that moonshine... It was something money could not buy.

Hattie's first visit was to an expectant mother, Jessica Pike. She lived with her husband's family, as did most of the people in this area. It was cheaper and more convenient that way. The whole family could help each other. Jessica needed her mother-in-law's help. The girl wasn't very old and had a bad heart. Hattie had known the girl's mother who also had a bad heart and died at a young age. It was good for the girl to be with family. So far, though, the pregnancy had been normal, which was more than Hattie could say for her own. She unconsciously looked down at her own unborn child. Her own abdomen was not very big. The child would be small. Perhaps that was a good thing. In Hattie's present state of health, short labor and easy birth would be blessings. Hattie rubbed her abdomen with her free hand as she pulled the little wagon behind her. Clemson and Eulalie were singing the ABCs. Most children didn't attend school until they were older, and most quit when they got old enough to work. So, the education was not very long or very good. Hattie was taught to read and write by her mother. She, in turn, taught her own children. Jack attended school for a couple of years but left when he could help his father. Hattie wished him to go on. He was a bright young lad and could do many things with the proper education, but he was needed to help the others survive. So, he left school and worked the farm.

"Good morning," came a chipper greeting as the little wagon band came upon a wooden cabin.

"It is good to see you this morning, Miss Hattie."

An older woman was standing outside, hanging up laundry. The smell of fresh clean cotton washed in lye soap permeated the air. The fragrance was clean and homey.

"Good morning, Mrs. Pike," Hattie responded. The children cut short their song and began to wave at the woman.

"And it looks like your helpers are here, too."

The woman finished her laundry and picked up the basket. "Looks like time for some ho-daddies for these two."

Hattie stopped the wagon, and the two children jumped out. "Yes, ma'am!" they both shouted as they ran to her side.

The woman smiled down upon them. "I can hardly wait 'til we have babies like these. It's been a long time since we heard little voices 'round here. C'mon in and let's see what we can find."

The children followed Mrs. Pike with Hattie close behind. She carried a satchel across her body filled with supplies she thought she'd need in her rounds: cotton bandages, herbs, tonics, and salve. Upon entering the house, Hattie removed the satchel and began searching through it for a small, clear jar.

"Where is Jessica this morning, Mrs. Pike?" she asked after finding the jar.

Mrs. Pike was pulling out the baked pie crust she kept on hand. It was dusted with sugar and a little cinnamon. Commonly referred to as ho-daddies, for an unknown reason, it was a sweet treat for children and not too bad for adults along with a cup of cold milk or hot coffee.

"She's in the other room. She was kinda tired this morning, so I told her she could rest while I did the warsh."

Mrs. Pike always put an "r" in the word "wash." Clemson had asked his mother in the past why Mrs. Pike added an "r" to certain words, and Hattie told him it was just her way. Clemson liked that and thought he'd do the same, but Hattie explained to him that it was Mrs. Pike's way, not his, so he should speak as well as he could. Hattie thought her little boy had enough problems with the stuttering and didn't need to be adding extra letters to make a difficult situation even worse. Even so, when Mrs. Pike spoke, Clemson giggled and laughed at her vocabulary. Fortunately, the older woman thought it was an endearing quality in the child and laughed along with him.

Hattie took her satchel and jar into the other room where the young Mrs. Pike was found lying on the bed.

"How are you today, Miss Jessica?"

The younger Mrs. Pike looked at her visitor and smiled, rubbing the large mound protruding from her abdomen.

"I'm good this morning, Miss Hattie. Mother Pike let me sleep in a bit, and I feel pretty good now."

Hattie sat down on the bed beside the expectant mother. "Glad to hear it. You look pretty good, too. How's the baby?"

"Wonderful," the young woman replied. "He's movin' around in there like he's at the rodeo."

Both women laughed. Hattie placed her hand on Jessica's abdomen. She could feel the unborn child moving. Jessica was right. The child moved a lot.

"Are you hungry?" Hattie asked as she stood up and began pushing gently on Jessica's abdomen.

"Yes, ma'am. I ain't hand nothin' to eat yet this morning. I suspect that's why he's so active this morning. He's probably hungry, too."

Hattie smiled as she moved the covers from the young woman's feet and legs. She applied gentle pressure to both.

"Good," she said after a few moments. "No swellin'. That's a good sign. Have you had any more fast heartbeats, can't catch your breath, or chest pain?"

"No, ma'am. Just tired." She rubbed her belly. "He's a heavy load to carry, Miss Hattie." She smiled. "I 'spect you know all about it, though, with your baby."

Hattie smiled back at the woman as she repacked her satchel. "Here's some lard for you to rub on your belly. It will keep your skin soft so you don't end up with so many purple streaks after the baby comes."

"Thank you," the young girl answered as she accepted the jar. "How much longer you got, Miss Hattie? I mean, with your baby?"

Hattie stood up straight. She was embarrassed to say. She knew the growth of the child was questionable. There was no large protuberance. In fact, she was barely showing.

"Oh, I got a long way to go yet," she said, smiling. "Keep your feet up as much as you can and watch the salt. Get word to me as quick as you can if you have any problems. The baby's doin' fine, and I think everything will go real good."

Hattie gathered up her children who, by now, had consumed multiple ho-daddies and several cups of milk. They would be tired now and probably sleep in the wagon as Hattie made her way to the next person. Mrs. Pike kissed the two little ones on their heads and waved goodbye as Hattie and her little wagon of travelers made their way to the next visit.

Hattie was correct. The slow, rhythmic movements of the wagon and full bellies soon put both children to sleep. They lay cuddled together, their skin so soft and delicate.

Like angels, she thought.

She unconsciously looked down at the unborn child. She could not bear to think of losing it. She shook her head and thought of something else – the next patient, Mrs. Lowery. A dear, old widow who lost her husband in the first world war. He'd been in Europe, but no one knew where. They were never able to recover his body. Mrs. Lowery was just told he was missing in action, and that was the end of it. The poor, old thing never remarried. She had no children but managed her own little farm with only the help of a part-time farm hand. There were rumors, of course, about Mrs. Lowery and the farm hand, but Hattie believed they were simply that – rumors. Rumors spread by people who had nothing else to do but create mischief. The rumors didn't seem to bother Mrs. Lowery, either. She held her head as high as anyone and attended church every time the doors were open. She could play the dulcimer, and, on really still nights, you could hear that dulcimer music sounding through the hills. It was a lovely sound but melancholy, too. Hattie tried to visit Mrs. Lowery at least once per week. She thought the visit with the children was uplifting to the older woman, and the woman had dropsy, which needed Hattie's attention.

Dropsy, a condition of the heart, was incurable but could be managed with the proper treatment. Mrs. Lowery grew foxgloves, as did Hattie, and the dried leaves of the plant caused the heart to beat more efficiently, thereby allowing the woman to live a better life. Mrs. Lowery was very careful about her foxglove regimen, and she had been able to manage her chronic illness without too much difficulty. Still, Hattie thought the woman should have someone check on her regularly. Without a husband or children, only neighbors and church brethren were available to assist.

"Good morning," came a familiar voice.

Hattie looked up and saw Mrs. Lowery in her garden. She waved and made her way towards the woman.

"How are you today, Mrs. Lowery?" Hattie asked when she was closer.

The woman came to the garden gate, opened it, walked through, and closed it tight behind her. Mrs. Lowery built a little wooden picket fence around her garden, no doubt to protect her precious foxgloves. The gate latched behind her and now secured her flowers. She walked towards Hattie, hugged her, and looked down into the wagon.

"They are both sound asleep." She smiled.

"Yes, we just came from Mrs. Pike's..."

Mrs. Lowery stopped her short. "And she had ho-daddies for 'em."

Hattie smiled and nodded. "She did, and I'm afraid they are out for a while. But this will give us time to visit and see how you're doin'."

The two women walked to Mrs. Lowery's front porch. Hattie parked the wagon beneath a large oak tree in its shade. There was a soft breeze there, and the children would be comfortable even if they were sleeping so close together. Mrs. Lowery entered her house and then came out with two cups of water.

"I hope a cool cup of water is sufficient for you, Miss Hattie," she said as she handed the liquid to her visitor.

Hattie took the cup and drank it greedily. "My..." she said after a moment. "I didn't know how thirsty I was."

"Would you like another?"

Hattie looked down into the empty cup. "Yes, I think I would. I am powerful thirsty for some reason."

Mrs. Lowery took the cup back into the cabin while Hattie sat down in one of the rocking chairs on the porch. She always thought it odd that Mrs. Lowery lived alone but had two rocking chairs on her front porch. Mrs. Lowery told her that it was for her dear, missing husband. That way, if he ever came back, he would know she was waiting for him, and he had never really left her life.

"Here, Miss Hattie, drink up. There's always more where that came from. I'm sorry I can't offer you anything more."

Hattie drank several cups of the fresh spring water. She felt so thirsty, as if she hadn't drunk anything for days. She always had that nagging feeling of chest tightness with the constant urge to cough, but she could still control it.

"Breathe softly," she told herself. "Relax and calm yourself."

So far, she was able to keep the wicked beast at bay. She chewed hoarhound candy and peppermint to squelch the cough and disguise the putrid smell of blood that lingered on her breath. But now, there was this unquenchable thirst. This was new, and she didn't like it.

"Miss Hattie, would you like an apple?" the older woman offered as she sat in the rocking chair next to Hattie. "I always keep a few apples around in case my husband shows up. He loved apples. I 'spect when he comes to fetch me home, I'll be sittin' right here, eatin' an apple."

Hattie smiled. "No, thank ye. Just the water will be fine."

"I had a visitor yesterday, Miss Hattie," Mrs. Lowery said softly as she rocked in her rocking chair.

Hattie turned her attention to the woman. "Oh? Who was it?" she asked as she drank down the last of the water.

"Her name was Mamie Starkweather. She is a nurse from the Department of Health."

Hattie said nothing. She just looked blankly at the woman. After a few moments, she asked,

"What did she want?"

The woman stopped rocking and leaned forward as if she held a great secret and didn't want anyone to hear, although she and Hattie were alone on the porch and the two children were yards away under a tree, sleeping. "She said my name was on a list of Dr. Tucker's patients and that she would stop by every week to check up on me. She said my records showed I had heart failure, and she had some pills for me."

Hattie thought for a moment. "What did you tell her?"

"I was hospitable to her. I asked her in the house, gave her some tea, and let her listen to my heart and lungs. She had a long-handled contraption that she held up to my chest. She said she could hear my heart beating and air going in and out of my lungs. It was the darnedest thing. You got one of those things, Miss Hattie?"

Hattie shook her head. She had no such equipment. She listened to the heart and lungs by simply placing her ear to their chest. She listened to her breathing by holding a drinking glass or canning jar to their chest. She looked into their ears and throats by taking them to the window where the best light was found. She had no tools other than those nature and her mother provided for her.

"So," Mrs. Lowery continued. "She gave me these pills."

She pulled a small amber bottle from her apron pocket. She handed it to Hattie, who turned it around and read the paper taped onto it.

"I don't know what these words mean, Mrs. Lowery." She handed the bottle back to the woman.

"Are you gonna take those pills?"

The woman shook her head. "No, ma'am, Miss Hattie." She leaned back in her chair and began to rock again. "I'm an old widder woman. I have no children and no one to mourn my passin'. All the people I loved are dead." She hesitated. "...or missin'."

She smiled and laughed quietly. "I don't mean to make it sound so depressin'. I have had a good life and the people 'round here have been kind, but I don't want to prolong my life any more than necessary. So, even if Dr. Tucker and his nurse, Mamie Starkweather, have suddenly taken an interest in me, I'm happy where I am. You been takin' care of me for many years. Before you, it was your ma that came to see me. She was a good woman, your ma. Always smilin' and happy, no matter what came down the pike." Her voice trailed off.

When the older woman began to speak again, her voice was soft. "Miss Hattie, it seems you're looking a-might peeked these days. Are you ailin'?"

Hattie sat up straight in her chair. "No, ma'am, Mrs. Lowery. Just havin' a lot of mornin' sickness with this one." She rubbed her belly.

Mrs. Lowery did not move, nor did she smile. She wasn't fooled. "Much blood?" she asked after a few silent moments.

Hattie could feel a great weight press down on her. Unconsciously, her eyes began to tear. She couldn't control it. This burden was crushing.

"Some," Hattie answered, closing her eyes.

"What did your mother do with her people who had this?"

Hattie shook her head. "I tried. I been tryin'. Nothin' seems to help. I can't get out from under this."

"And you're powerful tired?"

Hattie nodded. In a way, it was a great relief to talk honestly about this condition, but it was also dreadful. The old widow knew. Regardless of how hard Hattie was trying, her appearance was deceiving her. She wasn't sure how much longer she could keep her illness a secret. And now, with this new public health nurse showing up, she wasn't sure if she could hide it at all. Mrs. Lowery seemed to read her mind.

"I told the public health nurse that I was doin' fine. I didn't say nothin' about you, but keep low, Miss Hattie. Stay near your home and don't go no farther than you need. You know what that nurse will do if she finds you."

Hattie looked out across the old woman's yard. Her vision lingered on those large trees that cast shade onto her two little children. A soft breeze blew her hair and brought the fragrance of confederate jasmine along with it. Hattie knew what would happen if that nurse knew about the coughing and the blood. All of this would disappear. Everything here would disappear. It was almost too much to believe, too much to absorb. Mrs. Lowery placed her hand on Hattie's knee.

"Thank you, Mrs. Lowery. I shall heed your warnin'. You are very kind."

Hattie turned to the woman and forced a smile. The woman nodded.

"If you decide to take those pills, don't use the foxglove. I don't know what those pills are, and it could cause you harm if you take both."

Mrs. Lowery helped Hattie down the steps and toward the little wagon. The two children were awakening, stretching, and yawning as they tried to shake their sleep.

"Well, you finally decided to wake up and give me a hug," Mrs. Lowery bent over and hugged each child.

"We g-g-goin already, M-momma?" Clemson asked as he stretched again in the wagon.

"Already?" she laughed. "We been here almost an hour, and you two slept straight through it. Say goodbye to Mrs. Lowery."

The children waved and shouted their goodbyes.

Mrs. Lowery hugged Hattie. "I'll say a prayer for you, girl," she said as they parted.

Hattie forced a smile and nodded. At this time, prayer was about the only thing anyone could do. Events were spinning out of control, and it was all because of one person – that public health nurse, Mamie Starkweather. Hattie would have to avoid her. Hopefully, the woman was not familiar with these hills and wouldn't find Hattie until she could heal herself...if she could heal herself.

Hattie made her way slowly through the trees and hills towards her home. It was late afternoon, and it was time for her to fix supper for her family. The two children in the wagon were now walking alongside her. She was walking as slowly as they were. They picked the wildflowers along the rocky path and made up rhymes as they went their way. She was so tired, and that nagging feeling to cough was becoming worse as the day progressed. She attributed it to the dust of the road, the hot sunshine, and her weariness. She refused to admit defeat, but there would be a time when she would need to face reality. But it wasn't today.

"Momma," Jack yelled from the barn. "I finished milkin'. Are we gonna eat soon?"

"Yes," she replied as she unloaded her little wagon and the other two children climbed up the front porch steps. "Did you check that sow?"

Jack nodded and shouted, "Yes, ma'am," as he ran past her into the cabin.

"Would you start some coffee, Jack? I think I need to lie down just for a few minutes, and then I'll fix supper."

Hattie was beyond tired. She was exhausted on the inside. Her body would no longer obey her. Her legs were melting beneath her, and this overwhelming urge to cough had taken on a life of its own. Her lungs demanded to be released from this pain. She went into the room she and her husband shared. She closed the door behind her and sat on the edge of the bed. She coughed slightly and took a breath. The next cough was deeper and harsher. She took another breath. The next cough was overpowering, pulling fluid and tissue from the depths of her chest, so deep inside she could feel her diaphragm spasm. She was unable to take a breath for a moment afterward. She sat up straight, knowing she could breathe, but the sensation of lack of air was frightening. She unconsciously placed her hands on her chest, desperately trying to pull in air. She could feel her lungs tearing, ripping with each breath, and bleeding out with each cough.

She placed her hand over her mouth.

She pulled it away.

There it was.

The bright red fluid with strings of phlegm in the palm of her hand. She coughed again, and the pain was the same. There was more blood in her hand. She tried to stand to grab a towel to wipe her mouth, but her legs were gone. She collapsed back onto the bed, trying to breathe in between the coughing. She lay there and felt herself floating, out of body. She wasn't sure if she was still breathing, but she was relaxing and drifting.

She heard a great noise and sat up quickly. It was dark outside. The blood on her hands had dried, and she had a metallic taste in her mouth. She saw a streak of lightning and heard the thunder. She got up and walked out of the room. Martin sat in his chair with Clemson and Eulalie in his lap. Jack sat on the floor in front of the fire, whittling a stick with his knife.

"Well, there's Momma." Martin smiled as his two children climbed down from his lap and went to hug their mother.

She leaned over and kissed their heads.

They were in their nightclothes.

"We was waiting for you, Momma," the little girl said.

"M-momma, I'm g-getting t-tired," her son stammered.

"Yes, I'm sure you are." Hattie was confused. "Have I been asleep all

29

this time?"

Martin nodded his head.

"Did you have supper? Why did you let me sleep so long?"

Martin stood, picked up Eulalie, and touched the back of Clemson's head, gently urging him into the bedroom.

"Everyone's taken care of, Hattie. We ate some leftover ham and biscuits. Jack fixed coffee and brought in the milk. You looked so tired." He looked at her.

She could see the concern in his face. His eyes focused on her hands, still stained from the blood. Unconsciously, she folded them and moved them towards her back.

"C'mon, children, let's get to bed. Mornin' comes early."

The two children laid down quietly, yawning and rubbing their eyes. They cuddled close to one another in their shared bed. Martin covered them and kissed their heads.

"Say your prayers, children. Nothin' makes for a good night's sleep like a little talk with God."

He could see their mouths moving, but no words were heard. They were falling asleep while praying.

Martin turned back towards Hattie. She was making her way towards the coffee pot.

"Eat some of that left over ham, Hattie." Martin came up behind her, placing his hands on her shoulders and kissing the back of her head.

"I'm not hungry right now. Maybe later. I am powerful thirsty, though." She tried to be discreet in washing her hands, but the water in the basin turned pink, and she had to scrub her hands with the soap. The dried blood was sticky and difficult to remove.

"You need to eat something, Hattie. I bet you ain't ate all day. At least drink some milk."

She nodded and removed the pitcher of milk from the cold water bucket.

"Daddy," Jack said as he rose from the floor and made his way towards the door. "I'm goin' out to check on that sow. She was rootin' around earlier."

"I'll go with you. It's stormin' pretty good out there. It might take two of us to keep her in that pen."

Jack wrapped a blanket over his head and around his shoulders. Martin grabbed his hat, pulling it tight over his head. He looked back at his wife, who was now walking towards her chair next to the fireplace.

"You stay in here. Me and Jack might be a bit. With this storm, that sow might be pretty cantankerous, and I want her in that pen."

Hattie nodded, sitting back in her chair, still weary and trying to ignore that metal taste in her mouth.

Martin and Jack stepped off the porch. The ground was soggy. Puddles of water lay in low-lying areas of the ground. The tops of the trees were moving dangerously in the wind, making a creaking noise. It was loud out here. The sound of the thunder and the blowing limbs made it nearly impossible to hear the other speak.

Jack was the first to arrive at the hog pen. "She's not in here, Daddy!" he yelled as he looked frantically around the little hog house and the wooden fence. "She's not in the hog house or the pen."

Martin pulled his hat down tighter. The wind was kicking up, and debris was falling off the trees.

He looked closely at the wooden fence. "She's broke out, son. She's goin' up the hill. C'mon, we gotta find her. If she has them pigs up in those hills, none of 'em will last 'til mornin'."

Jack nodded. He whistled, and the dog came running out of the barn.

"It'll be hard for Amos to smell her tracks in this rain, but we should be able to see where she's runnin'. She's leavin' some deep tracks in the mud."

Martin bent down closer to the earth. "See here, Jack, she's headin' up that way." He pointed with his fingers up towards the top of the hill behind their house. "You take Amos up that way, and I'll get my gun. We might need it up there."

Jack nodded and moved up the hill. The hog's tracks were difficult to see. It was dark, and the water from the rain was running down the hill, filling the tracks and washing them away before he could see them. The dog's head was down, trying to smell anything, but the water was washing away the scent. Jack held onto the trees and little saplings as he climbed the steep embankment. The earth gave way under him, and he slid backward several times. He'd been up this hill a thousand times. He knew the terrain, but now, under these conditions, the area seemed strange and foreign. He was trembling, although he was not sure why. He couldn't decide if he was cold or scared.

Probably both, he thought to himself.

The dog stopped and looked towards the ridge of the hill, ears up and alert. He began barking and ran. Jack pulled himself up, clutching anything that he could find to help him maneuver this hill. Lightning flashed, and he could see the outline of something moving in a hollow place on the side of the hill. The dog was barking constantly, and he could hear him running through the wet leaves and underbrush. Jack looked around. This was where he placed his hog trap. Those trees in front of him, now bending and swaying in the storm, were the very trees he lashed that trap to earlier today. He heard grunting and squealing. The ground was a little more level now, and Jack was able to stand upright. He walked carefully towards the noises. He could not tell if it was the sow in that hollow or a feral hog. Either way, Jack knew to watch himself. Those tusks on hogs could kill a dog or a young boy.

The noises from the dog became vicious, guttural, and life-threatening. The other sounds were barbaric. High-pitched squealing that bled into an eerie scream, filling the night with dreadful sounds followed by flashes of light from the sky. Dark creatures ran back and forth with the intermittent lightning reflecting off their white tusks. Fiery eyes glistened in and out of the brush as the dog chased the white sow from her nest with tiny, crying young left rolling in the leaves.

Jack tried desperately to make his way to the little pigs, to move them out of the way. He bent over to pick up one of the newborn pigs. The rain was pelting his face, partially blinding him with water. He felt something heavy push against his back, nearly knocking him down. The thing was hot and large. He heard heavy breathing from behind him. He grabbed the piglet, stuffing it inside his shirt. It made a desperate, crying sound. Jack heard the heavy breathing now over him and felt a terrible, ripping pain on the back of his leg. He heard someone cry out. He suddenly felt dizzy, and a loud rushing sound filled his ears. He thought he heard his father's voice calling his name, but Jack was unable to answer. There was someone screaming, and then there was this burning sensation to the back of his leg. He could see the lightning, but nothing else, and he felt his spirit moving away from him. It wasn't frightening. It was relieving and gentle, and he could hear the rain.

Martin held his son close, sliding down the hillside that was now wet and washing away under the pouring rain. The ground gave way beneath him, causing him to fall onto his back, slipping farther down the path. Martin managed to gather himself together, still clutching his unconscious son to his chest. The boy's body was limp in his father's arms with his left leg torn apart, bleeding onto Martin's pantleg, washed away by the rain and onto the dirt. It made red ribbon rivulets down the hill. Martin cried out in fear and anguish. He tried to run, but the path was slick. He leaned forward, holding his son to his heart, feeling sick inside, knowing he could do nothing to save him.

"Let me help you!" a loud voice shouted over the thunder. "We can both carry him inside."

Hattie put her arms out to grab the boy's legs. She pulled her hand away. She had seen this so many times, but it had always been her own blood. Now, it was the blood of her son. She wrapped his pantleg tight around the wound and moved him quickly towards the cabin. She and Martin entered their home, placing their son onto the table. He remained unconscious. Hattie checked his breathing.

"Heat some water, Martin, and tear some cloths into bandages. I'll need some fresh milk and bread."

Martin did as was requested, moving quickly as Hattie tore the pantleg away from Jack's leg. She moved him slightly, exposing the torn flesh. Muscles were exposed, and vessels leaked blood onto the table, where only a few hours ago, they sat and ate together. Martin brought the clean bandages to her, and she packed them deep inside the wound, applying pressure to cause the vessels to clot. Martin brought her the satchel she carried with her when she went on her visits. She pulled the needle and fine twine from the bag, cleaning the wound with whiskey, then carefully sewing muscle and tendon back together. There were pieces missing where the hog had pulled its teeth through, removing the flesh and muscle. Martin brought over the hot water and began washing and rinsing the wound. They said nothing to each other.

Each innately seemed to know what needed to be done next. Once the wound was cleansed and rinsed and portions mended, Hattie began to lay the milk-soaked bread inside the wound, gently patting it into place. She then wrapped the long, jagged wound with the bandages, leaving the bread and wet gauze in the wound. She stood up straight.

"That's about all we can do for him now. We'll need to redress that wound every day. Hopefully, he won't get blood poisonin'." Hattie dried her hands on the towel Martin brought to her.

Martin placed his hands beneath his son. "I'll carry him to the bed."

"Let him sleep in our bed, Martin. It is bigger and will give him more room to move."

Martin carried his son into the other room. Hattie began cleaning up the bandages and blood from the front room. Her weariness was returning. She had been lying down when she heard the gunshot and screaming. Her heart stopped, and she knew instantly what was happening. She ran outside to see Martin bringing Jack down the hill. She could not remove that sight of Martin carrying their wounded son down that hill. It was a terrible sight that made her nauseated and weak. She still was not sure where she found the energy to run up that hill or treat her son, but, wherever it came from, it was gone now. In its place, was left sheer exhaustion. She was not sure she had the energy to even make it to her chair.

"He is resting. I think he lost consciousness right after that hog got him. The pain must've been too much," Martin said quietly as he re-entered the room.

Hattie nodded. She was soaking wet. Her clothes hung on her. Martin could see her collarbone protruding from beneath her nightgown, and her arms were small and frail.

"You better go get some dry clothes on, Hattie. You don't need to catch cold." He took a breath.

"I'm gonna see if I can drag that dead hog down and maybe save some of the little pigs. The dog's dead." He lowered his head. "He tried to save Jack, but that hog turned on him and killed him."

Hattie said nothing. She knew Jack would be heartbroken. Maybe it would be better not to say anything for a while, at least until he healed a bit.

Martin looked at his wife. "Do you think he'll heal?"

She swallowed hard. "I think we done all we could. I'm hopeful."

Martin walked to her, hugging her and kissing her forehead. "Go get dried off and lay down. I'll take care of all this."

Hattie smiled softly at her husband. "He will survive, Martin, and he will walk. I have a hundred years' worth of knowledge that I can use, and I will use all of it for him. He will be fine."

Martin smiled back. He wanted to believe her. She knew a lot of things and was stronger emotionally than he. Her body was deceiving her, but her mind was quick. He wanted desperately to believe her.

The rain had stopped. There was just the soft dripping of the water from the leaves. It was a comforting sound, but Martin didn't notice. He had to save little pigs, butcher a hog, bury their dog, and clean the blood from the floor before he could rest. It had already been a long night, and it was going to get longer, but in these hills, you had to do what you had to do every day, every minute, every time.

2

Mamie Starkweather grew up in the delta of southwest Arkansas. Her mother and father owned the general store in town, along with the feed store and the funeral home. There was plenty of money at Mamie's home. Plenty of fresh fruit, vegetables, and hot ham with boiled potatoes. She grew up knowing very little of poverty or want or hunger. The most desperation she knew was not having new hair ribbons at Easter. She was an only child, naive to the ways of the world, but her family insisted she have an education. Although this was unusual for the people of that region of that age, Mamie was excited. She went to nursing school nearby, graduating near the top of her class. She was intelligent and now educated with enough knowledge that she could perform basic nursing care for her patients. Her first job, now, was as public health nurse. She was orientated with other nurses and was proud that she obtained this position, although somewhat surprised. It was unusual for a new graduate to be accepted into this position, but she had worked hard and devoted much of her time to study and clinical experience. She would do her best to prove the committee had made the right decision in entrusting her with this job. She wanted to help people, and this was the best way she knew how to do that.

She rode the train from Helena to Russellville, making several transfers and keeping her little, black bag close by. It held her nursing equipment. She had to purchase everything she used with her own money. Her father provided the funds, and she would be too embarrassed to ask him for more money if she lost the black bag. He could be an irritable man but also had moments of gentleness. Her mother was quiet, never crossing the man. It was his way, always. Mamie thought they both acted as if they had different people living inside them. Her father had this angry man, and her mother had a woman with a voice. But both her parents kept these people hidden away.

She met with a doctor in Russellville, Dr. Tucker. She thought him a handsome man – tall and slender with a touch of graying hair near his face. His eyes were dark, and his voice was very low. She pictured him as one of the leading men in one of those new talking pictures. She and some of her friends had seen such a moving picture show. It was such an amazing thing. To watch handsome men and beautiful women in worlds far away from the hot, dreary days of Southern Arkansas. She could see Dr. Tucker as the dashing, swashbuckling hero, whisking leading ladies off their feet and riding off into the closing credits. He asked if she understood her obligations.

"Yes," she remembered saying, not actually hearing one single word the doctor said.

He smiled at her and showed her out of the house. He pointed to a large, burly mule eating from an oat bag. This was her transportation. Every day, she would come to his office, receive her assignments, and pack up this mule. Her nursing instructor never mentioned this part of the profession. She had never ridden a mule in her life. While he was gentle, he was stubborn. She placed the saddle on his back and cinched the saddle. The mule inflated his stomach and then released the added air, causing the saddle to roll onto the side of the animal and then underneath his belly. The mule stood stone-still, chewing on the oats remaining in its mouth, oblivious to anything else.

Mamie stood silent for a moment, looking at the saddle now dangling beneath the mule. The mule made no movement but continued to eat from the feed bag. Mamie released the saddle, and it fell onto the ground. She attempted to saddle the beast once more, and, again, he inflated his stomach, causing the tightened cinches to lose their grip, and the saddle slid over the side and beneath his stomach. Mamie sighed. She knew a lost cause when she saw one.

She placed the saddle onto the rail and threw a blanket onto the mule's back. On top of the blanket, she sat her black bag. Tying a rope around the mule's neck, she led him out of the barn. He obeyed willingly. Apparently, he knew a lost cause, too.

The land before her was hot, baked in the steaming southern sun. Humidity high enough to fizzle the best hairdo. Sweat would run down the neck and take a long, leisurely journey down the spine, leaving all clothing damp and uncomfortable. The hills were high with rugged terrain, much like the people who lived among them. They were a surly bunch, as hot as the weather and as rough as the land. She didn't know any of them but heard the stories. The fables of moonshine runners and backwoods witches, toothless farmers and barefoot women. Mamie wasn't sure if she disliked them or feared them, but this was her position. She was hired to bring knowledge and health to these poor mountain folk. Perhaps this would be a great challenge. A challenge she was sure she could overcome. After all, she had the education and perseverance to accomplish any mission. She was a Starkweather. A daughter of people who had land, shops, and money. She may not be able to ride this dumb beast, but she was a good nurse.

Her first assignment was to visit several people along a certain road with an especially urgent visit to an older widow who visited Dr. Tucker some time ago. He diagnosed her with heart failure and prescribed medicine, but she never returned. Mamie wasn't even sure if the woman was still living. Dr. Tucker provided her with a hand-drawn map of the area where the old woman lived. The young nurse made her way along the dirt road and took a turn to the path. It was not a very long ride, but it was a long walk. She pulled the mule up next to a fallen tree and positioned him parallel. She stood upon the dead tree and tried to throw her leg over the animal's back, but the mule moved slightly to the side, and Mamie stepped hard onto the ground, failing to mount the beast at all. After several attempts, she turned the mule around so she was facing his eyes.

"Now, listen here, you stubborn mule. You and I are stuck with each other, and we must make the best of this. At this moment, I need you, and you will need me later when you want food and water. So, I suggest we each try to give in a little bit so we can both survive this hardship."

Mamie pulled the mule towards the fallen tree. She pulled the rope tight.

"Remember," she said sternly as she adjusted the blanket. "If you want to survive this journey, you're going to have to work with me."

She threw her leg across the back of the animal, placing the handle of the black bag between her teeth and the rope in her hands. The mule did not move. He stood as still as stone, as if he understood her words and decided to cooperate.

She positioned herself on the blanket, slightly surprised that she was successful. Perhaps the mule didn't mind the load but objected to the restriction. Maybe the cinching of the saddle, the loss of freedom and control bothered him. At any rate, she was riding this animal. He knew who was in control, at least for the moment. She tapped him with her heels, and he began to move, slowly at first and then with more purpose.

This was her first expedition into the hills. She met with the people Dr. Tucker wrote on the list. They were not hostile but leery. She could sense they did not trust her. They allowed her to listen to their breathing with her stethoscope, a device with which most of them were totally unaccustomed. They kept her at arm's length otherwise, offering her a cup of water or tea on the porch, never asking her into their homes. She was surprised by their wariness but assumed it was their custom with all strangers. After all, she was sent to help them. It was unfortunate that they did not understand. This, she decided, would also be her mission. To educate these poor, unfortunate souls about the world beyond the hills and valleys in which they lived. She believed that education was what they needed most of all. To be brought out of their dark shadows and into the light.

At the end of the day, she returned to Dr. Tucker's office.

"Well?" he asked as she unburdened the mule in the barn and curried his coat. "How was your first day?"

Mamie placed the mule into his stall and filled his feed bag.

"Surprisingly well," she responded, not wanting the doctor to think she could not handle her assignments. "I was surprised by the kindness the people had for me."

The doctor looked surprised. "Really? The last nurse I had said they were almost hostile, not at all forthcoming with their illnesses and even avoiding her if possible."

Mamie tidied up her bundle and bag, trying to avoid direct eye contact. "Perhaps she was mistaken. They do have their odd ways, but I believe it is because they know no better."

"Possible," he replied. "But I am glad you got along so well with them. That will make your job so much easier. If they trust you, they will tell more things concerning their illnesses. We have had such a problem getting them to be honest, especially concerning the communicable diseases."

"Hmm," she replied as she placed her bag beneath her arm. "I am surprised. One would think they would want to know how to prevent and treat such diseases."

"Yes, one would think that, but, as you said, I believe they are uneducated and don't understand such things."

He smiled at her. It was the first time she'd noticed how kind his facial features were when he smiled. He looked gentle and understanding. Neither of them said anything for a few moments, until Mamie noticed there was this odd quietness between them.

"I suppose I should be going." She repositioned her bag nervously.

"Yes," he replied in the same nervous voice. "Yes, of course. Where are you staying?"

"In the boarding house across town. I rent a room there."

He nodded. "Yes, I know it." The smile faded from his face as he looked in the direction of the boarding house. "I had dealings down there once."

"Nothing tragic, I hope, Dr. Tucker."

He reclaimed himself, shook his head, and smiled again. "No, nothing tragic. Just old memories."

"Well, then, sir, I will be on my way. I will stop by your office in the morning for my instructions."

"Very well. I will see you in the morning."

Mamie smiled and walked past him. He smelled of camphor and mercurochrome. To most people, the fragrance may have been noxious, but to Mamie, it was a delight. A fragrance of a smart man, with graying hair and a kind smile.

It would be nice if they would make an aftershave with those fragrances, she thought to herself as she walked down the street. That way, you could always think of that doctor.

"Good afternoon, Miss Mamie."

The landlady was sweeping the front porch of the big, old house.

Mamie imagined that at one time it was a single-family dwelling, possibly owned by one of the wealthy families in the area, but this old home, like many in the south, had been carved into multiple dwelling places for travelers and renters. Done out of desperation, Mamie understood the rationale but was saddened that so many of these beautiful homes had fallen into disrepair. This home was not too badly in need of repair, although the single bathroom on the second floor was prone to backup with water from the tub and take forever for the water to become warm. But, all in all, it was a suitable place. The landlady was especially nice. She fixed supper for everyone every evening, which was included in the rent. It was usually a simple meal: chicken or pork with potatoes or rice. Lots of gravy, lots of bread. Mamie thought this was an inexpensive way to fill up the guests without looking too obvious, and the gravy and bread were good, so no harm done.

"Good afternoon, Mrs. Stuckmeyer," Mamie replied, climbing the multiple steps that lead to the front door.

"How is Dr. Tucker?" the landlady asked as she completed her sweeping and walked in the house behind Mamie.

"He is well. He does seem to have a lot of patients, though. He appears to work very hard."

Mamie began the climb up the stairs to her second story room.

Mrs. Stuckmeyer nodded. "Yes, he does. How is his sister?"

"His sister?" she asked. "I did not know he had a sister. I have never seen her."

The landlady smiled coyly, as if she believed she spoke out of order. "She is sometimes ill. I am sure you will meet her by and by."

"That is odd, though, that he has never mentioned a sister or any family at all for that matter."

"He is a man of few words, Miss Mamie. Don't take it personally. I don't believe he likes to discuss his personal matters with the help."

Mamie was not sure if she should be relieved or insulted. She understood that she had no business knowing the doctor's personal life, but to be referred to as "help" was demeaning in her eyes. She said nothing as the landlady smoothed her hair and apron from the vigorous sweeping she'd performed.

"I suppose I should get busy fixing supper now, Miss Mamie. Fried chicken with mashed potatoes sound good?"

Despite the fact that they had this same food every other day, Mamie managed a faint smile. "It sounds wonderful, Mrs. Stuckmeyer. I shall be down to help set the table if that is all right."

"That would be very helpful, girl. Thank you."

Mamie turned and climbed the stairs. Now she was "girl." She felt insulted but again realized this old woman was from another time. A time when women were either someone's wealthy wife or their "girl." Mamie was glad those times were over and she could define her own destiny. Although, the thought of becoming someone's wife, perhaps someone who smelled of camphor and mercurochrome, could be a fine thing.

3

Martin placed his hat upon his head as headed out the door of the little cabin. "I'm going to the store. Hattie!" he hollered through the house. "What supplies did you need?" Hattie came out of the bedroom. "Shh," she said, placing a finger to her lips. "Not so loud. Jack's resting. I need more gauze and salve. If she has any, ask Mrs. McCrary if they will be gettin' any rubbin' alcohol." "What if she says they won't be gettin' any rubbin' alcohol?" "Then you'll need to go up to your sister's house and ask your brother-in-law for some whiskey from his still." Martin smiled devilishly. "What if we just forego the rubbin' alcohol and I'll go get the whiskey?" Hattie walked across the room and hugged her husband. He kissed her head. He could feel her thin arms about him. Her body was so frail. The bump that was growing in her belly was no bigger than a small mound. While he meant to be joking, the reality was so severe. "Perhaps..." Hattie said as she pulled away, trying to force a smile. "...even if they have the rubbin' alcohol, you could go see your brother-in-law." He nodded and touched her face. It was pale and gaunt, but the eyes were still bright. "I will try not to be too long."

Hattie nodded. "Thank you, Jack will need those dressings changed before too long, and I need those bandages. Most of mine are either dirty or still dryin' on the line."

Martin left the cabin and saddled the farm horse. He made his way down the mountain towards the store.

"Good morning, Martin!" Mrs. McCrary shouted as soon as she saw Martin emerging from the trees.

Martin nodded. "Good mornin', Mrs. McCrary."

"What's new up on the mountain today, sir?" she asked as she welcomed him into their store and home.

"Hattie's in need of a few things. She sent me down here to pick 'em up."

"Of course. What is it she needs?"

"Bandages, mostly, but also salve and if you have some rubbin' alcohol."

Mrs. McCrary began to look through her supplies for the needed items. "Sounds like someone has a bad wound. Anything I can do to help her? I know she doesn't always feel that perky. I'd be glad to help her if she needs."

"Thank you, ma'am, but I think she'd rather do this one herself. It's Jack, the boy – he got pretty tore up the other night tryin' to save that sow."

Mrs. McCrary stopped her packing and looked at Martin. She seemed genuinely worried about the boy.

"What happened? Is he all right?"

Martin nodded, looking down at the floor. He could feel a flood of emotions trying to overwhelm him. He thought all along that he was in control of these feelings. It was unbecoming of a man to break down, and he was surprised that this sadness rose up from the deepest regions of his body and was so difficult to push back. He swallowed hard, giving his best effort to overcome the urge to cry and fall to his knees. He nodded, holding his hat in front of him.

"I don't rightly know..." he began after a few moments. "He put a hog trap up there earlier that day. I don't know if the sow got caught or the razorback, but either way, the sow had her pigs up there, and Jack went up there to try to git 'em. Somehow, that razorback got ahold of him and tore up his leg." There was a pause. "Hattie says he'll be fine, though."

Mrs. McCrary could hear the man's voice breaking. Martin was not a man to show his emotions lightly. She understood how difficult this must be for him and how serious the situation would have to be for him to react this way.

"Of course," she said hurriedly, trying to alleviate the awkward situation. "If your wife says he'll be fine, then he'll be fine. She is a smart woman and knows her healin'. Now, let me gather the rest of your things. I do not have any rubbing alcohol today, but the salesman should be through this week, and I'll get her some. Can she make do with what she has?"

Martin nodded again, feeling better and beginning to control his emotions.

"Yes, she said she can use whiskey until you get the alcohol."

Mrs. McCrary smiled. "Aye, one alcohol in place of the other."

Martin smiled, choking backing any trace of his prior emotions.

"Thank you, Mrs. McCrary," he said as he turned to leave the store. "Pardon me, ma'am," he said to the young woman who was entering the store. He placed his hat back on his head and unleashed his horse from the railing.

The woman watched him. She looked up at him when he spoke to her. She could see his eyes were red, as if he had been crying.

"Is that man all right?" she asked Mrs. McCrary.

Mrs. McCrary nodded. "Yes, he's just had some bad news. His son was badly hurt a few nights ago, and he's just concerned."

The young woman looked intently at the storekeeper. "What is his name? Perhaps I could help. I'm a nurse."

Before Mrs. McCrary could think about it, she spoke. "Baker. Martin Baker. His wife is Hattie Baker."

Mrs. McCrary could see the facial features of the young woman turn sour. "Is that the same Hattie Baker who does midwifery around here and practices medicine without a license?"

Mrs. McCrary stood back, understanding that perhaps she had said too much. "She is Hattie Baker, who helps these people with their ailments and does assist with childbirthin', but she does not practice anythin' and certainly needs no license to help others in need."

Mamie took a deep breath. Perhaps she had been rude to the woman. After all, she did not know her nor the man who left the building. This was certainly no way to cultivate goodwill among these people.

"I beg your pardon, ma'am. I was out of line. I apologize. My name is Mamie Starkweather, and I am a public health nurse. Perhaps I could help Mrs. Baker with her son."

Mrs. McCrary continued to be skeptical but decided to be mannerly. "It is nice to meet you, Mrs. Starkweather. I am Mrs. McCrary. My husband and I own this store. I suppose you work with Dr. Tucker?"

Mamie smiled. "Yes, I do."

"Pity," the older woman smiled.

Mamie seemed confused. "What do you mean? Dr. Tucker is a very knowledgeable physician."

Mrs. McCrary continued with her granite expression. "I'm sure he is. But he lacks an essential element to be a successful physician."

"What is that?"

"His first love," Mrs. McCrary continued. "If a body is goin' to be a good healer or teacher or preacher, they must have a first love. That first love must be the compassion for others. A genuine carin' must be there. I'm afraid your Dr. Tucker lacks the compassion and understandin' to be a good doctor. I believe that is why he hired you. I know you work for the state, but he is still your boss. He wants to use you to reach these people." Mrs. McCrary waved her hand. "But they are not as unknowin' as you might think. These people, my people. have learned to live with hardship and deprivation all their lives and it will take more than a pretty, young nurse to convince them to trust an outsider. Especially when she works for the state and Dr. Tucker."

Mrs. McCrary leaned back. "Would you like some tea?"

Mamie was bewildered. No one in her life had ever spoken to her like this before. She was not sure if she should be angry or beg for forgiveness. She had no idea that these people felt this way towards Dr. Tucker. She was confused how his philanthropic ideas could be so misunderstood to the point of the people distrusting him and going so far as to distrust her, even though most of them had never met her. Part of her was frightened. She wondered how she could make a difference the lives of these people if they did not trust her, and without that trust, she could lose her job.

"Please," she responded softly.

Mrs. McCrary showed her into the back of the store. The store was the McCrarys' home. She and Mr. McCray lived in the back while the front portion of the building served as the store, post office, and general meeting house. Mamie thought it a smart little place, with chintz curtains and pictures hung on the wall. No newspaper insulation seen and no tobacco stains on the floor. Mamie sat down at the little kitchen table as Mrs. McCrary rambled on about the weather and politics. Mamie was still stunned by their earlier conversation and not paying much attention to the woman's current remarks.

"Do you take sugar or cream?" Mrs. McCrary asked as she sat down across from Mamie.

"Neither, ma'am."

"Well, then, your family wasn't British, were they?"

Mamie took a drink of her tea. "Ma'am?"

Mrs. McCrary poured a small amount of milk into her cup, then slowly added the hot tea from the pot. "True British people drink a little milk in their tea, but others drink it without anything. So, your family is not originally from any of the United Kingdom."

"No, ma'am. I'm not sure where my family originated from. My father and mother never spoke of their ancestry. I suppose I have no other family since they were never mentioned."

Ms. McCrary smiled faintly over her cup of tea. "I have often noticed that people who do not speak of the past have somethin' to hide."

"Well, I can assure you, ma'am, that simply because we did not discuss past ventures and exploits does not mean there is anything to hide. My father and mother simply did not find it necessary to talk about their family."

Mrs. McCrary nodded and placed her teacup back in the saucer. "Then they are successful."

"How so?"

"Whatever it was that they need to hide, remains hidden."

Mamie sat very still. Again, she was not sure how to interpret this conversation. Part of her was insulted, but the other part was curious.

Mrs. McCrary had a point. Now, thinking about it, there was never a conversation regarding her grandparents, or cousins, or any other members of their family. It was as if her parents had been dropped into the middle of the delta with no lineage at all.

"I didn't mean to unnerve you, dear," the older woman stated, seeing the uncomfortable look on Mamie's face. "I just meant to say that there are skeletons in everyone's closets, whether we know them or not. Some families feel it belittlin' to discuss such matters, where others decide to bring it into the light and deal with it. My family brings it out, sometimes too much into the light." She smiled. "My husband would tell you I sometimes talk too much."

Mamie laughed, placing her cup and saucer on the table. "You have a lovely home."

"Thank you. My husband, Mr. McCrary, and I live here alone."

"You have no children of your own?"

The old woman looked down and shook her head. "No. The Good Lord did not see fit to bless us. 'Tis probably the greatest burden I bear. Childless and now too old to even consider it. But I shan't cry about it. Mr. McCrary and I have a good life. We been blessed with a good livin' and health, so I can't complain." She laughed. "I do complain, but it gets me nowhere."

"Is this how you spend your time, woman?" came a blustery voice from a blustery man as he entered the room. "Well, what do we have here?"

"This is the new public health nurse, Mamie Starkweather."

He held out his hand, and she shook it. "Well, 'tis a pleasure to meet ya."

He had a slight Irish accent, and his words were mixed between Old Irish and English, sometimes a bit difficult to understand but always a slight lilt to the words. Mamie found this entertaining. She liked to hear him speak. It was like listening to a poet.

"Likewise," she responded.

He looked at his wife. "My fine wife, there be customers in the store. Would you be so kind as to help them, or need I hire another to do the work so you can occupy your days drinking tea?"

Mrs. McCrary stood, patting his shoulder. "I'll get out there, Mr.

McCrary. No need to hire another. I can always come back to the kitchen for more tea." She smiled as she left the room.

"So, you be the new nurse then? You workin' fer Dr. Tucker?"

Mamie was afraid to go down this road again. "Yes, sir, I am."

The man gave her a sideways glance.

"I do not know him well, sir," she continued.

Mr. McCrary nodded his head. "Come speak to me in a few months, after ye know him better. Then we talk."

He sounded so ominous. His jovial countenance was more serious. She was unsettled. He smiled slightly and offered to escort her from the kitchen.

"Thank you for the tea, Mrs. McCrary," she said as she passed by the woman.

Mrs. McCrary said nothing as she was assisting other customers but nodded her head and smiled. Mamie thought this was an odd encounter, not the kind she envisioned when she started her day. She walked outside, pulled the mule alongside the rail, and stood upon the railing.

"What in the world are you doin', girl?" a man shouted as he came down the road.

"I'm getting on the mule," she responded, standing on the rail with the rope in her hand.

"What kind of a method is that?" he continued as he came near and grabbed the rope from her hands. "You're gonna fall and hurt yourself doin' it that way."

Mamie remained standing on the rail. He was right. She was teetering from side to side on this rounded surface.

"This is the only way I can get on him. He pulls away, and I can't reach him. He also blows up his belly so I can't cinch the saddle, so now I'm forced to ride on this blanket."

The man laughed. "You been outsmarted by the animal. He's smarter than he looks. He learned a long time ago that the best way to get out of a thing is to stay quiet but be so disobedient that you will eventually give up. And it looks like he may win."

"What do you suggest, then?" she asked with a tone of arrogance.

"Here, get down off the railin' and let me show you."

The man assisted Mamie from her perch and brought her up along the left side of the mule. He positioned her blanket. He then took off his own vest. The man spoke softly, assuring the animal he was in no danger, gently placing the vest over the animal's eyes. The mule stood very still. The man bent over and made a cup with his hands, motioning for Mamie to let him assist her onto the animal. She did so, and the animal remained still. The man handed the rope to her. He then calmly and slowly removed his vest, continuing to speak softly to the mule.

"That's amazing," she said in disbelief as the man back away slowly. The mule remained calm and obedient.

"Not so amazin', ma'am. Kindly words gain their trust. Then they don't balk at the reins if they don't see them comin'."

"Thank you," she said. "Sir, can you tell me how to get to Hattie Baker's home?"

The man pointed up the dirt road. "You take this road as far as it goes. When it forks, go the left. She lives about half a mile to your right, kinda up in the hills there. You might have to walk a bit right up to the house. The rains washed out some of that road, but it be passable."

"Thank you again," she said as she nudged the mule forward.

She was not sure if this was the correct action to take but felt she must see this woman who was so trusted by these people. Dr. Tucker spoke of Hattie Baker as if she rode on a broom. He referred to her as a hillbilly witch. Mamie was told the woman was doing so much damage to these people, filling their heads with old wives' tales, and using toxic concoctions to pretend to heal disease. She didn't practice safe hygiene, and who knew what poisons she gave to these people? They needed proper medical care, the kind an untrained midwife could not provide. He was convinced that as long as Hattie Baker remained in these hills, the people would refuse to see him for appropriate care. It was time for Hattie Baker to move along with the wheels of change – either with them or beneath them.

Mamie rode the mule up the road, following the directions of the man at the store. He was right. The rain had washed out the road. There were gullies ripped through the terrain, and pieces of the road were pulled away from the bluff. Deep ravines separated the road from the woods. There was no way up into the hills where the man said to turn. The crevice was too deep, and the dirt gave way beneath the mule. Mamie threw her leg over the mule and landed on the muddy surface. Her feet sank in the mud, but she was able to climb up the embankment pulling the rope on the mule behind her. The ground was soft, and she sank into it several times, but the directions she was given were accurate. She looked up and saw a small cabin ahead, just up the hill. There was a little barn and some animal pens. There was a slight breeze blowing through the tops of the trees. The storm from the night before left behind scattered limbs and leaves, but it was still a peaceful setting.

"Good afternoon, sir," she called up when she saw a man walking out of the barn.

"Good afternoon," the man replied, stopping. He took off his hat and wiped his forehead with his sleeve. He began to walk towards her.

She struggled a bit walking up the steep hill in the soft earth. She pulled the mule, but he was pulling against her.

"Here," the man said as he grabbed the rope from her and helped her through the mud.

"My goodness," she said breathlessly. "That rain really did some damage to the road. It was terribly difficult to get up here."

The man nodded, continuing to help her towards the cabin.

"Thank you," she said as they neared the steps.

"I'll take the mule to the barn, ma'am. He looks like he could use some tendin'."

"Oh, that would be wonderful. Thank you so much."

"Hattie!" the man shouted as he helped Mamie up the steps. "We got a visitor."

He released her hand and took the mule to the barn.

Hattie saw a slight shadow on the other side of the screen door. She could smell familiar scents, meat, potatoes, whiskey, and smoke. Fragrances that reminded her of her own home with her mother and father. A place where she was loved and protected. Although, after the conversation with Mrs. McCrary, she had doubts concerning her own family. The screen door opened, revealing a very thin, pale woman with two small children at her skirt. The little boy was adorable with curly red hair and bright eyes. The little girl had the long curls, pudgy cheeks, and an adorable smile with tiny, white teeth.

"Hello," the woman said as she moved the children aside. "Please come in."

Mamie smiled and nodded. "And who are these little wonders?"

"C-C-Clemson, m-m-ma'am," the little boy said as he held out his hand.

"It is very nice to meet you, Clemson. My name is Mamie Starkweather."

"And me," the little girl chirped as she partially hid behind her mother's skirt.

"Oh, yes. Such a lovely little girl, too. What is your name?"

The little girl buried her face into her mother's garment.

"Eulalie," the child's mother answered flatly. "Babies," she continued. "Go play in the barn. Daddy's out there."

The children released their mother and ran outside, yelling and shouting as they jumped off the front porch. Mamie watched them, smiling. They seemed so happy and healthy. Their complexions clean and beaming. Their little bodies strong and able as they jumped and ran. It was not at all what she expected. She turned back towards Hattie.

"My name is—"

Hattie cut her off before she could finish the sentence. "I know who you are."

Mamie stood very still. This small, frail woman was intimidating. Even with her pale skin and hollow eyes, she was a force to be reckoned with. "I'm here to—"

And again she was cut off.

"I also know why you are here."

The two women stood silently in the doorway. The sounds of the children could still be heard.

"Your children are beautiful."

Hattie softened a bit. The woman had hit upon the one thing to which a mother has no defense – her children. To compliment a parent on their children softens the heart and causes them to remember the meaning of life and that most things in this world are of little importance compared to those children.

"Come in," Hattie said softly. "Please, sit down."

Mamie pulled out one of the chairs and sat down. Hattie went to the stove and poured them each some coffee. There was an awkward silence. Mamie noticed the woman's bare feet and dirt floors. She wore an old dress, threadbare and stained, but washed a thousand times in hot, sudsy water. The house was small, two rooms only, with a large stone fireplace made from hand-hewn wood and stones. Although it was humble, it seemed to envelop all emotions: love, fear, hate, hopefulness, thankfulness. Mamie did not recall any of this in her own home with her parents. It took a lifetime to imprint those types of emotions onto solid objects.

"Do you take milk or sugar?

Mamie shook her head. "No, thank you." She took a sip. It was bitter and extremely strong.

Hattie saw the repulsive look on Mamie's face. "It is chicory," she said as she sipped her own coffee.

Mamie smiled, trying to choke down the distasteful brew.

"Now then," Hattie began. "You came here to find me out, see how the hillbilly witch lives, and report back to Dr. Tucker."

Mamie choked on her coffee. Hattie's words were so abrupt. She was caught off-guard.

"Well, ma'am..." she began.

Hattie laughed. It was a weak laugh, not with much breath or feeling. "I didn't mean to startle you. I'm afraid in our neck of the woods we have ways of comin' straight to the point. There's not always time to be polite and kind, sometimes the grim reaper comes a' creepin' without our knowledge. So, we say what needs to be said straight away."

Mamie nodded, still a little unsettled. "There's also not always time to get to the doctor, and the public health nurse only makes rounds as she sees fit, so what are these people to do?"

Mamie took another drink of her coffee. She wasn't sure which was more bitter to swallow – the coffee or this conversation.

Hattie continued, "My family has lived up here for generations. The women have been helping the sick, childbirthin', and easin' the dyin' to their great reward. Where have you been?"

Mamie said nothing.

"Where has Dr. Tucker been? Where has anybody been? Most folks up here live and die without ever seein' a real doctor. And now... now you come along and want everyone to make their way down the mountain and into the office or let you come by once in a blue moon to give 'em pills and concoctions with no idea what effects they have and not care for it either. I will gladly give their care to you, for, as you can see, I am not well myself, but I do not believe you or Dr. Tucker will see to their health."

Mamie finally found her bravery and took a deep breath. "Mrs. Baker, what you have done up here has been wonderful for the services it provided, but now there are more resources available to these people besides just you. As you said, you do not seem well. As far as the medicine Dr. Tucker prescribes, it is approved and tested for safe human consumption."

"And you believe a once a month visit to their homes is sufficient to treat 'em? Do you know their histories, their families, their stories?" Hattie leaned forward across the table, giving Mamie a stern look.

Mamie was learning that even though this woman was small and frail, there was a deep emotion within to safeguard these people. Mamie was a little impressed by the woman's devotion. She had not seen this in Dr. Tucker. He said he wanted to help people, but he lacked the heated compassion this woman expressed. In fact, neither he nor the other public health physicians allowed the field nurses to administer basic care, not even vaccinations for common diseases. The diseases the rest of the country overcame but were still seen in these hills, all because the people were not vaccinated or offered the appropriate care.

Mamie took a breath. Perhaps it would be better to change the subject. She knew she was fighting a losing battle. Hattie Baker had all the answers on her side. There was no good argument Mamie could bring. Science was wonderful, and it could heal and cure many things, but this common person knew the human side of disease, and science was a cold suitor compared to her.

"How is your son, Mrs. Baker?" Mamie asked more out of desperation than concern.

Hattie sat back in her chair, a little surprised. Mamie could see the woman's bones protruding through her cotton dress. Hattie's face was thin and pale. Mamie had seen this face before. There were hundreds of them, in the TB sanitorium.

"He is improving," Hattie said after a few moments.

"I heard you did some amazing wound care on the boy. I must say that in nursing school, wound care was my shortfall. Would you share with me your method for handling such a wound as your son has?"

Hattie smiled mischievously. She was old enough to know a diversion when she saw one. She drank the last of her coffee and stood up. She motioned for Mamie to follow her into the bedroom. Hattie knocked quietly on the door, opened it slightly, and stepped inside the room. Mamie followed her to see a young man lying on his side, facing the wall. The room was bright with the windows open. A soft breeze blew the ragged curtains gently. Fresh foxgloves and lavender filled a glass jar sitting by the bed. There was a strange fragrance, however, that permeated the air. It smelled strangely warm and noxious at the same time. The boy turned his face towards the two women. He had a soft, boyish look with large eyes. It was apparent he was ill as his face was flushed, but he smiled politely.

"Jack," his mother said as she drew close to him. "This is Mamie Starkweather. She is a public health nurse. She would like to see if I dressed your wound in a healin' way."

Mamie stood very still. Her method to look at the boy's wound was not very deceptive. Hattie knew exactly why Mamie asked to see the boy. She did not believe Hattie had the knowledge or expertise to take care of the terrible wound that the boy suffered. Hattie understood that this public health nurse believed her care was inferior, dirty, and of no benefit. The boy lay his head back down on the pillow and closed his eyes. Hattie gently moved the newspaper that lay across him to expose the gaping wound on the back of his leg. The leg was propped up on pillows. Mamie could see the discoloration, blue and gray flesh, but there was something moving. Something writhing within the deep tissue that gave the wound an eerie, fluid look. Mamie could not help herself. She walked close to the boy, peering deeply at the wound, seeking to find the cause of this silky flesh. There was a foul smell emanating from the wound. Mamie stood silent as she watched the wound move.

"Maggots," Hattie said.

Mamie looked closer, repulsed and amazed at the same time.

"Maggots eat the dead and diseased flesh, leaving behind the clean flesh. It keeps down infection and stops blood poisonin'."

Mamie looked deep into the wound. Hattie was correct. Small, white gelatinous orbs moved from side to side, consuming the dark, dead flesh and leaving behind them pink tissue. The smell was repulsive, decay and putrid flesh, but the results were indisputable. The boy had no fever, and the remainder of his leg was pink and warm. There was no packing or wrapping of this wound. The entire site was left open to the air and sunshine.

"How long do you leave them in there?" Mamie asked, pointing to the maggot-infested wound.

"A couple of hours a day. Then I take them out and bury them outside. Every day I put new maggots in there, and every day I bury them."

"How long does this treatment last?"

"I start it a day or two after the injury. It depends on the wound as to how long I keep doin' it. How the skin looks and how the person is doin' determine if I do it again. I don't like to do it too much. Too much of good thing, as you know, can also be bad. The maggots can eat too far down into the flesh. You don't want 'em to get too close to the bone or eat too deep into the good flesh. That's why a few hours every day is usually enough. Once I'm satisfied that most or all of the damaged flesh is gone, I'll start to sew it up. I start in the deep tissue and work my way towards the skin. That way, I can keep an eye on how each layer is healin'." It takes a lot of time and care. Is that how they do it at Dr. Tucker's office?" she asked, casting a sideways glance at the young nurse.

"No," Mamie responded, still staring at the maggot-infested wound.

"I thought not," Hattie responded quietly.

Hattie looked at Mamie, who was enthralled with this wound care. It sounded like something from the Middle Ages, but it made sense.

The boy's wound was healthy, and he was not infected, even several days after the attack.

"What did you use to cleanse the wound?" Mamie asked, still amazed at this medical intervention.

"Corn squeezins."

"Whiskey?" she asked again in disbelief.

"I use squeezins to clean it and burn sage in the room to keep the air clean."

Mamie looked at her in total amazement. These were the sources of the strange odors in the room. The strong odor of whiskey, the rancid smell of maggots, and the warm waft of burning sage. Mamie looked at the bedside table where a bowl of milk-soaked bread lay.

Hattie smiled, silently knowing what the younger woman was thinking. "It ain't for eatin'," she said quietly. "I place the wet bread around the edges of the wound to draw out the dirt. I don't know why all this works, but it does many times. I lost a few but saved a few, too. How would you treat such a wound?"

Mamie stood up straight. "I don't know."

Hattie said nothing further to the young nurse but spoke to her son. "I'll be back shortly, sweetheart, to clean your leg."

The boy nodded, still with eyes closed. Mamie understood this was her cue to leave as Hattie covered the boy's leg with the newspaper. Mamie was dumbfounded. She had expected dirt and filth, ignorant methods followed by poor results. But the boy's leg was still healthy. These backwoods methods were all these people had. They had been forced to use whatever they could find to accomplish cures, and they were able to do so with more success than Mamie imagined.

"I owe you an apology," Mamie began as she gathered her bag and began to leave the cabin. "I judged you and your ways very harshly, and I was wrong. You have done what you could whenever these people needed you, but I must urge you to consider helping me to get them to the doctor's office and allowing me to help them."

Hattie said nothing. She was becoming tired and could feel the terrible urge to cough beginning. If this nurse would leave now, Hattie could spare herself the diagnosis of this young woman. For Hattie knew that if the nurse saw the blood and heard the deep, raspy cough

Hattie now possessed, there would be no question in the young nurse's mind as to Hattie's disease, and there would be the devil to pay.

"Perhaps we can come to a compromise, you and I. Perhaps if Dr. Tucker knew that you were trying to help these people..."

Her voice trailed off.

Hattie stood very still, saying nothing. Mamie knew enough to know that the conversation was over. Dr. Tucker would not agree to help this mountain woman with her work, and there was no way Hattie would relent to the doctor. Unlike Dr. Tucker, with Hattie, these people were not her patients; they were her people.

"Thank you for the coffee, Mrs. Baker," she said as she lowered her head and made her way to the door.

"You are welcome," Hattie replied as she followed Mamie out the door.

Martin saw the two women come out of the cabin. He grabbed the rope on the mule and led him towards the porch.

"Your mule has been watered, but where is your saddle?" he asked as he handed her the rope.

"He rebels against constraint," she answered as she positioned the mule alongside the steps. She placed her cloak over the animal's eyes as the stranger showed her earlier. She climbed up the steps and threw her leg over the mule and grabbed the cloak away. The mule stood still as she settled herself.

"Goodbye, Mrs. Baker." she said over her shoulder. "Thank you for the coffee and the education."

"Goodbye," Hattie answered as she went back into the house. That sensation to cough was becoming unbearable, and she began to choke as soon as she got back into the cabin. She breathed in, and the coughing began. The coughing was shallow at first, but with each breath, the choking became deeper, more painful, and those tiny vessels in her lungs began to rupture, releasing their precious blood into the throat. Hattie could feel that iron taste boil up into her mouth and the thick, sticky fluid layer her tongue. She wiped it away with her sleeve. It was bright red with streaks of phlegm. Ugly and foul, it was expelled from her lungs, and she walked to the wash bowl, pouring water into the basin. She washed her hands and wiped her mouth with water. She coughed again and was forced to spit into the basin, leaving red spots and blood-tinged strings in the water. She continued to cough until she bent over, trying desperately to pull in enough air to stay conscious.

Mamie heard the severe sounds outside. Martin stood very still and said nothing.

"How far along is she?" Mamie asked, cutting through the uncomfortable silence.

"I don't rightly know. She won't say," he replied staring at the cabin as his wife's near-death experience occurred on the other side of the door.

"What are your intentions?" Martin asked, turning his head to look directly in Mamie's eyes.

"I don't know," she answered as Hattie's coughing subsided.

She turned the mule down towards the hill. It would be easier riding him down the hill than it was coming up. He would obey when he was going down the hill, not fighting to pull himself up. He would submit to her will and maneuver through the ditches and gullies until he found himself where she led. It would be fine, once they were on the road. The mule would be fine, and she would be fine. The dumb beast just needed to relax and let her guide him.

Mamie rode down the road and towards her next patient. Martin's last statement was embedding itself into her mind. What would she do? Martin knew she was obligated to report Hattie's illness. Although not diagnosed by a physician, there was no denying she had tuberculosis, or "consumption" as they referred to it up here. The government set up sanitoriums throughout the country to quarantine those with the disease. It was in an attempt to keep the disease from spreading, but the act was not without opposition. Families were forced to divide, sometimes for the rest of their lives. Husbands were forced to leave their families with no means of support. Children were removed from their parents, never to see them again. Wives were taken away from their loved ones to live out their time among strangers. She rode to the next house in silence, thinking about what she would have to do.

"That lady nurse is comin'!" Mamie heard a shrill, little voice shout.

She looked up and saw the backside of a small child running up to another cabin. This home, too, had the garden of foxglove, lavender, herbs, and vegetables. Homemade bird feeders hung from many low branches. As Mamie passed by them, small colorful birds flew in all directions. An old mother cat lay sleeping on the front porch, nursing her newborn kittens. They nuzzled her, but she did not open her eyes. She lay in the sunshine, and this was her enjoyment for the day. Two yellow dogs came barking out of the barn. Too late, she thought, to warn anyone of danger, but the dogs soon stopped barking and started wagging their tails and switching their heads back and forth. They were not as much watch dogs as happy greeters.

"Good morning to ya!" a thin, older woman shouted from the doorway as Mamie rode near the house.

"Good morning, Mrs. Pike," Mamie answered as she drew the mule near the steps so she could dismount.

"Still ain't got him used to the saddle, I see," Mrs. Pike noted as she held the mule's rope for Mamie.

"No, and I think I'll just learn to live with it. If he's so stubborn as to give me grief over such a thing as cinching a saddle onto him, then I'll not push him too far. He lets me ride him all day and obeys me in every other aspect, so I'll learn to work with what I have."

Mrs. Pike smiled and nodded. "Probably best."

She ushered Mamie into the house.

"Can I git ya some coffee or a cool glass of water?"

Mamie followed Mrs. PIke into the house and began to walk towards the daughter-in-law, Jessica.

"No, thank you, ma'am, I just had some coffee at Mrs. Baker's house."

The older woman stopped shortly and turned on her heel. "You went to see Hattie Baker?"

Mamie knelt near the younger Mrs. Pike, who sat in a rocking chair with her feet elevated on a little chair. Mamie began to unpack her bag, pulling out her stethoscope and a piece of twine.

"Yes, ma'am. I just left there."

Mrs. Pike came close to the two women. In a very low voice, she whispered to Mamie, "You shouldn't a-gone over there."

Mamie turned to her, unnerved by the woman's comment. Mrs. Pike's voice was low, almost threatening.

"Why?" she asked in a tone just as low as Mrs. Pike's.

"These people up here need her, and I 'spect she needs us, too. You're just gonna cause trouble and heartache fer us up here. I don't think ya should be here anymore."

The older Mrs. Pike grabbed the young nurse by her arm and began lifting her up.

"Mrs. Pike," Mamie said quickly, resisting these attempts to move. "Mrs. Pike, please, I am here to tend to your daughter-in-law. I wish to only help her with this childbirth."

Mrs. Pike did not release her grip on Mamie but pulled her aside. "This is no place fer us to argue. Step out on the porch with me."

"No need," the younger Mrs. Pike said, lowering her feet to the floor. "I know you think I'm a bit muddle-minded, but I know what's going on, and I have somethin' to say 'bout it."

Mamie and the older Mrs. Pike stood still as the very pregnant younger woman maneuvered herself to a standing position.

"I want this child to be borned as healthy as it can be. If that means Nurse Mamie looks after me or Miss Hattie, I don't care. In fact, I want 'em both. What one don't know, the other might. I know there's somethin' wrong with my heart, and I'm feelin' dizzy sometimes, but I don't want my ailment to affect this baby." She rubbed her protruding abdomen and took a deep breath. "So, now, Mother Pike, if you will let this nurse do what she will, you can ask Miss Hattie to come over, too. There..." she said abruptly. "I spoke my piece and believe my wishes should be respected."

With that, the young woman sat back in her rocking chair and put her feet up onto the little chair, leaning her head back.

Mamie and the older Mrs. Pike released their holds on each other and nodded.

"I am sorry, Nurse Mamie," Mrs. Pike said softly.

Mamie softened her tone. "I, too, am sorry, Mrs. Pike. I didn't mean to cause conflict. I will just examine Jessica and see what needs to be done."

The older Mrs. Pike sat in a chair across the room from the nurse and her daughter-in-law. Mamie listened to Jessica's heart and lungs, then turned her attention to the unborn child.

"You do certainly have a heart murmur, Miss Jessica," Mamie began. "But many women do, especially while they are pregnant. It could just be due to the added stress from the baby."

Mamie then took the twine and wrapped it around the young woman's legs. Once around, she held it out in front her, measuring it visually. Mamie pressed her fingertip into the young woman's extended leg. A deep impression was made into the skin which lingered for a few moments.

"Your legs are very swollen. Let me see your hands."

The expectant mother held out both of her hands. Her thin, gold wedding band was nearly buried by the skin of her fingers. "Your hands are very swollen, too."

"Yes," the young woman responded. "Miss Hattie told me to stop eatin' too much salt and keep my feet up as much as I could, but I got work to do and can't just sit around all the time."

Mamie nodded in agreement. "I have some water pills here that might help you. Take one of these every day and let's see if that doesn't help. These will make you..." she hesitated, trying to find a sensitive method of saying what needed to be said. "These will make you pass water more often. That will help alleviate some of this swelling."

"And the baby?" the older Mrs. Pike asked. "What about the child?"

Mamie began to pack up her bag, placing her stethoscope inside followed by rolling the twine. "Fetal heart tones are good. The child seems to be doing fine. I'll stop in again next week."

Jessica nodded but said nothing. She kept her head back on the chair, both hands holding the unborn child in the front. The older Mrs. Pike pulled herself up out of her chair and escorted the nurse out of the cabin.

"I prob'ly owe you an apology, Miss Mamie," she began as they crossed the porch towards Mamie's mule. "But I'm not gonna give it to ya."

Mamie turned to her host, but said nothing, allowing the woman to finish her thought.

"I don't like the way ya come in here and think ya know it all. Miss Hattie lives amongst us, and I trust her. I'm not so sure I trust you or your Dr. Tucker. Folks up here can be a peculiar people. We trust our own more so than outsiders."

"But Mrs. Pike," Mamie began. "I don't want to be looked upon as an outsider. I would like to be your friend."

Mamie touched the older woman's folded hands. Mrs. Pike did not respond. She did not move, nor did she believe.

Mamie removed her hands and pulled the mule close to the steps, tossing her cloak over his eyes. She climbed onto his back and removed the cloak.

"Ya know, Miss Mamie, folks 'round here aren't as dumb as you might think. Ya can't throw a blanket over our eyes and think ya fooled us no more than ya can fool that poor beast ya ride. When he has had enough, he'll let ya know who's boss. Be careful, Miss Mamie, people git hurt when they think they have the upper hand."

Mamie didn't know how to respond. She nodded politely and pulled the rope of the mule so he would head back down the road. So far, her day had been nothing as she'd hoped. She was making more enemies than friends. She was disillusioned and frustrated. She had one more visit to make. It was just a checkup and should not be as difficult as these last two visits – at least, she hoped not as difficult. After that, she thought, she had some soul searching to do.

Mamie rode the mule towards her final appointment. It was the home of a little boy. He'd been kicked in the mouth by a horse, causing several teeth to be knocked out and his lips cut. The unfortunate side effect of all this was that the little boy was unable to eat or drink anything due to the pain and swelling. Although he was not mortally wounded, these little injuries could become something greater, especially when the body was not able to get enough fluid.

As Mamie rode towards the child's house, she found herself wondering, How would Mrs. Baker handle this? Mamie shook her head, trying to remove herself from such thoughts. She was a trained nurse, not some mountain quack. Although Mamie admitted to herself that she was impressed with the way Hattie treated her own son's wounds, it certainly wasn't medically sound. The idea of using maggots and wet bread was appalling. Now that Mamie had time to think about it, the whole treatment was ridiculous. Burning sage, cleansing with whiskey, and keeping the wound open to air were all barbaric ideas.

But yet, she had to remember, Hattie's outcomes were good. Mamie had not spoken to one person in these hills that said Hattie had not helped them, in one way or another. This was more than any of them said about her or Dr. Tucker.

Mamie looked up and saw a woman sweeping the porch of her cabin. "Excuse me, ma'am!" she shouted to the woman.

The woman stopped her sweeping and looked up at her visitor, nodding.

"Can you tell me how to get to the home of Edgar Mudd? I'm the public health nurse, and I need to see him."

The woman pointed up the road. "Go 'bout a quarter mile and turn left on a little path. It's not far."

The woman turned her attention back to Mamie. "Don't know why ya need to go up there, though. Hattie's already been there and took care of him."

Mamie stopped her mule. "Really?" she asked with some frustration in her voice.

"Yes 'm," the woman responded, continuing her sweeping.

"Thank you," Mamie answered as the woman waved but never stopped sweeping.

Mamie followed the directions to the little boy's house. It was a small cabin, perched on the edge of the bluff overlooking a deep ravine. Multiple children ran and hollered in the yard. They all began to shout that they had company when they saw Mamie riding up. Several of them came towards her, patting the old mule, looking up at Mamie and smiling.

"Hey," one child said loudly. "Who you be and what you want?"

Mamie smiled down at him. He was barefoot and had several teeth missing. His face was dirty, but his eyes were bright, and he was full of mischief.

"I am Mamie Starkweather, the public health nurse. Are you Edgar Mudd?"

The little boy laughed loudly and ran off. "Nope. Edgar!" he shouted. "Edgar, there's a punkin' head nurse out here to see you."

Mamie laughed to herself. After today, she might agree with the child. She was the punkin' head nurse.

A woman came out of the cabin, calling loudly to these children, "Billy, Nancy, Caleb..."

She continued with multiple other names, and the children were rounded up in the yard like baby chicks. One little boy came tearing out of the barn. His face was bruised and his lips swollen, but he ran as if nothing was ailing him as he gathered with his brothers and sisters.

"Good afternoon, " the woman said, smiling a friendly smile at Mamie.

This was friendliest welcome Mamie had received so far today. "Good afternoon, ma'am."

Mamie responded, "I'm Mamie Starkweather—"

Her introduction was cut short.

"She's the punkin head nurse here to see Edgar."

"Daniel, " the woman said nervously. "'Tis not a polite thing to say 'bout a lady."

"She said it," the child answered, twisting his face.

"Public health nurse, ma'am," Mamie intervened.

"'Course," the woman answered.

Mamie dismounted from the mule and held out her hand to shake.

"I be Dorothy Mudd," the woman said, smiling. "Come on in. Would you like some coffee or anythin'?"

"No, thank you," Mamie answered as she tied the mule to the porch post and followed the woman into the house. "I'm here to see Edgar, ma'am. How is he doing?"

"Please have a chair." The woman pulled out a kitchen chair from the table as Mamie unpacked her black bag. "He's doin' good. Edgar!" she shouted out the door. "Come on in here and let this nurse see your mouth."

The little boy Mamie saw earlier running from the barn came into the cabin. His face was discolored, his eye blackened but in a healing state. His mouth was still swollen but not actively bleeding, and the skin surrounding it was pink and fleshy.

"Hello, Edgar," Mamie introduced herself. "I'm nurse Mamie, and I'd like to look into your mouth. I understand a horse kicked you."

"Yes'm," he answered as he drew close and opened his mouth slightly.

Mamie used a thin, wooden tongue depressor to move the child's lips. He winced slightly but made no other sign of pain. He had certainly lost several teeth, but they were baby teeth. Mamie could see the buds of his adult teeth peeping through his gums. There were cuts to the inside of his cheek and lips, but Mamie could see they had been stitched.

"Stand over here by the window, Edgar." She moved his body slightly to use the natural light to get a closer look into his mouth. "Did someone stitch these cuts?"

The little boy closed his mouth and pulled away. "Yes, ma'am," he answered with some difficulty speaking. "Mrs. Baker. She came right after Daddy went and got her. That horse is gun-shy, and when he heard that gunshot, he kicked me right in the mouth. So, Daddy went and got 'er. She came up right then. She washed my mouth out with somethin' nasty, burned like hellfire."

"Edgar!" his mother said sharply.

"Sorry, ma'am. It did burn, though. And then she got out her needle and thread and sewed up my mouth."

"And how does it feel now?" Mamie asked, releasing the child.

"It's still powerful sore, but it's gettin' better."

The child's mother spoke up. "Mrs. Baker told us to rinse his mouth out after he ate. He had trouble chewing, so she said to fix him milk with bread and honey. He's been doin' real good with that. I think the swellin' is goin' down. He can talk better, and Miss Hattie said nothing was broke."

Mamie gently felt the child's face. She believed Hattie was correct, again. The bones seemed to all be intact, tender to touch, but not broken. The boy's eye was clear, and his vision was not affected.

"Well, then," Mamie began as she replaced her equipment back into the bag. "It seems Mrs. Baker has done a fine job here. You seem to be doing very well, Edgar. I suggest you stay away from the backside of that horse, though."

"Yes ma'am," he answered, wincing as he gave her a half-smile with the unaffected section of his mouth.

"Thank you, ma'am," Mrs. Mudd stated as the two women arose from the table and Mamie walked towards the door.

Mamie nodded, feeling totally useless. She threw her cloak over the mule's eyes and positioned the animal close to the steps. The mule was becoming accustomed to this routine. He stood very still as Mamie threw her leg across his back, and she removed the cloak.

"Looks like you be a waste," Edgar said as he ran across the porch to join his brothers and sisters in the yard.

"Yes," she answered as she waved goodbye and rode down the path. Under her breath, she whispered to herself, "That seems to be the way of the punkin' head nurse."

Mamie tried to make the mule move faster. She wanted to speak to Dr. Tucker. She knew he would be upset when he found out Hattie Baker was still practicing medicine on these people in the hills. She decided not to tell him of Hattie's unorthodox methods, of the maggots, the wet bread, and the stitching of the little boy's mouth. It would just make him angry, but her results were impressive. She also did not know if she should tell him about her suspicions. Hattie had all the signs of TB, but the ramifications of such a diagnosis were severe. Mamie was required to disclose any suspected case of the disease to the doctor. It was a mandate from the Public Health Department. They deemed it a matter of public safety. The diseased person must be removed from their homes, placed into one of the TB sanitoriums, and remain there until they were cured or died.

So far, no one had ever been cured.

The thought of forcing this woman to leave her family and home, to live and die alone among strangers seemed unbelievably cruel. On the other hand, Hattie was still going out among the people, possibly exposing others to the disease she carried.

The mule plodded along at his regular rate, and there was nothing Mamie could do to make him move faster. By the time she reached the doctor's office, it was getting dark. She knew his office was closed. After settling the mule in the barn, she walked to the front door of the doctor's home. Lights were still on, so she knew they were still awake. She knocked on the front door and could hear hard footsteps coming down the hall. The door opened slowly, revealing a small woman on the other side.

"Good evening, ma'am," the woman said softly.

"Pardon me," Hattie began. "I'm Dr. Tucker's nurse and need to speak with him. Is he here?"

"He is, ma'am, but he is at supper and can't be disturbed."

Hattie continued, "But I have urgent information and need to speak with him now. It concerns one of his patients."

"Who is at the door, Celeste?" came a harsh voice from another room.

Celeste turned slightly to answer the voice. The door opened slightly more behind her. "It is the doctor's nurse, Miss Flora."

Mamie heard heels on hardwood coming from that room, soon followed by a tall, gaunt woman standing in the hallway. Her hair was tied back severely, and she wore a plain, cotton dress.

"Excuse me, ma'am," Mamie began as she gently pushed herself past the servant. "I am—"

"I know who you are," Flora said sharply, cutting off Mamie's sentence. "The doctor is eating his supper and does not take calls during that time. Whatever it is will have to wait until tomorrow."

"Please, ma'am," Mamie said more forcefully as she walked up to the doctor's sister. She stood directly in front of her as they stared at each other in the hallway.

"Flora, who is there and what do they want?" A man's voice was heard from the other room.

Mamie started towards the door where the doctor's voice was coming from but was stopped short by Flora's hand. "It is your nurse, Mamie Starkweather."

Mamie heard the screeching of wooden chair legs against the floor. Shortly, the doctor appeared in the doorway between the hallway and the adjoining room.

Mamie expected the doctor to be livid, but he smiled and offered his hand. "Nurse Mamie, have you eaten? Would you like some coffee?"

Flora turned and walked away, sighing in disgust.

The doctor motioned Mamie towards a door on the far side of the hallway. He opened the door for her, and she walked into his office. "Please forgive my sister. She has not been feeling well lately, and I'm afraid it has made her a bit of a shrew."

Mamie wasn't sure how to answer but smiled a bit and nodded.

"Now," the doctor began. "What is it I can do for you?"

"Well, sir, in my travels today, I came across several of your patients that I believe require your attention."

"Of course, " he answered. "What are your concerns?"

They walked into his office. He sat down behind his desk, removing a cigar from the drawer and lighting it. He leaned back into the chair, stretching his legs beneath the desk.

Mamie was slightly taken aback by his actions. She expected a cooler reception from him. It was not every day a nurse would be so bold to disturb a doctor's supper and attempt to direct the medical care of his patients. Most physicians expected nurses to be handmaidens, to follow orders, and to have no thoughts of their own. Mamie was trained this way, but the reality of the condition of these people forced her to disregard the social norms of her vocation and speak directly to the doctor now.

She drew a deep breath. "The first is the young, pregnant woman, Jessica Pike. Her blood pressure continues to be elevated with increased edema in the lower extremities. She says at times, she suffers from palpitations and shortness of breath."

The doctor removed the cigar from his mouth. "What treatment was prescribed?"

"According to her file, nothing. She did not come to see you. She's had no prenatal visits at all."

There was a brief silence, and then Mamie continued, "There is also Mrs. Lowery who seems to be experiencing a flareup of her heart failure. She calls it dropsy."

The doctor nodded his head. "Many of the older people still use that archaic term. Is she under my care?"

"Yes, sir. You prescribed furosemide as a pill some time ago."

"Is it helping?"

Mamie stammered a bit. "Well, sir, it might help if she actually took it."

The doctor nodded, mulling his cigar between his teeth.

"The last patient is a little boy, Edgard Mudd. He was kicked in the mouth by a horse. It knocked out several teeth and blackened his eye."

"Were there any broken bones, any sign of brain involvement?" the doctor asked as he crushed out his cigar and rose to stand. He then moved towards a cabinet in the back of the room. He withdrew a delicate crystal vase and two small glasses.

"Not that I can tell," Mamie responded, watching cautiously as the doctor returned to the desk and poured the dark, red liquid into the glasses.

"That is good news, then." He offered Mamie one of the glasses. "Do you indulge, Miss Mamie?"

Mamie took the glass. She was unfamiliar with spirits. Prohibition had been the law for most of her life. Only recently had she even tried beer. She thought it nasty and distasteful, but this looked like wine. It was a clear, ruby red and sparkled in the lovely crystal glass. Perhaps she would find it more pleasing than the beer. She accepted the glass and lifted it slowly to her lips, sipping gently.

The doctor downed his glass and sat down into his chair. "So, then, Miss Mamie, what is your real concern? I cannot treat people who are not my patients. I cannot force those who are my patients to adhere to their treatments, and I cannot treat children with no ailments. So, what can I do for you?"

Mamie downed the rest of the alcohol. It tasted sweet on the tongue but became strong and bitter once swallowed. She felt a little swimmy-headed but decided she may need this feeling of euphoria to say what she wanted to say.

"Dr. Tucker. I know how you feel about the people in the hills who look to their own for healing."

The doctor spoke up quickly, "You mean Mrs. Baker."

His tone was deep and low. She halted her speech, but the results of the alcohol kept her moving forward.

"Yes, Mrs. Baker. She has made a great difference to these people, though, Dr. Tucker. Her methods may be archaic and not scientific, but they do have a line of common sense. You certainly do have better medicine, better treatments, and much more knowledge of the human body. You have access to the most modern equipment and accessibility to the most recent discoveries, but she has a way."

Mamie became silent.

The doctor sat very still, saying nothing, leaning back in his chair. He took a deep breath. "I am sure there was a time when those people needed her help and the help of her ancestors before her. But it does all those people a disservice now to continue to treat their ailments and illnesses with herbs and tonics that have no basis in real medicine. She could actually be doing those people harm. What she does may be good for a short-term treatment, but without real medical care, they could succumb to infection and die. They need to come to my office and let me treat them. Then, they need to follow the treatment plan and allow you to follow up with their care. Is that not what real medicine does?"

She could not argue with him. He said all the things she was taught in school. He made perfect sense.

"There is one more thing, Dr. Tucker," she said, lowering her head and her voice.

Dr. Tucker arose from behind his desk and walked around, sitting on the corner of that piece of furniture. He folded his arms in front of him. He sat directly in front of her. She was not sure if he meant to intimidate her, but he did.

Mamie summoned up the last of her courage. "Mrs. Baker seems to be unwell."

"Yes," he said quietly.

"She is pale and cachectic."

Dr. Tucker said nothing but remained motionless, sitting on the edge of his desk.

Mamie raised her head, meeting his eyes. "She is coughing up blood."

The doctor looked away, far beyond the nurse, over her shoulder. He leaned his head back and nodded slowly.

"Did she say anything?" he asked.

"Nothing to do with her illness."

"I see," he responded. "Well, we will need her to come in to make a definitive diagnosis, then."

The room was silent for a time. Mamie could hear footsteps outside the office door. A soft knock was heard.

"Yes," the doctor answered.

The door opened, revealing Flora. She leaned her thin, pale face into the room. She glared at Mamie and then focused her attention onto her brother.

"Your supper is getting cold, Doctor," she said sternly.

The doctor smiled back and nodded. "Thank you, Flora. I'll be with you shortly. We are about done here."

Flora nodded and closed the door behind her.

"It would be best if you could have all of those people come to see me. It is difficult for me to help them when I cannot lay eyes on them. It sounds as if they are all in need of a good workup, but it will be necessary for them to come into my office. See if you can make appointments with them as soon as possible."

He hesitated.

"...And as for Mrs. Baker, that is a sad story. Although I do not agree with or condone her methods of practicing medicine without a license or even any rudimentary education, I can see that the people near her have come to depend upon her. They will be upset when she must leave. That is why it is so important for you to gain their trust so you can step into her place when she is gone. In this way, I believe you and I can make a great team in delivering the needed care these people need. Isn't that what you want, too, Miss Mamie, for us to be a successful team?"

Mamie looked the doctor in the eye. This is what she wanted, for them to be a successful team, in more ways than one, and she wanted to believe he was sympathetic and caring, but there was something in his delivery that overshadowed his compassion.

"Must she be taken away?"

The doctor shrugged his shoulders. "If she has a positive diagnosis of TB, then that is the law. The state has provided sanitoriums to quarantine those inflicted. It protects the rest of the community."

"But aren't the numbers of TB decreasing, even before the sanitoriums were built? Is it not true that as the overcrowding of houses lessens and clean water and proper hygiene are available, TB cases are becoming more and more rare? Is there still a need to quarantine every single person who has this disease? Do you not believe removing the infected person may do more harm than good?"

Mamie knew the wine was taking over. She was losing control of her mouth and her mind, either of which could cost her position.

"The law currently says that you and I are to report every single case of TB we encounter. Failure to do so is a failure of us to uphold our oaths. We promised to 'do no harm,' which includes knowingly allowing a person with a deadly, contagious disease to continue to visit the elderly, the ill, and the newborns. She could be doing them a great disservice if we do not remove her from the community. Until we have a cure for this disease, these are the measures we must take. It is for their own good."

Mamie was adamant in her argument. "But if you take Mrs. Baker away, who will tend to her children? Who will help with the chores on their farm? What will become of her unborn child?"

"Although these are sad side effects, she must be examined, diagnosed, and, if found to have TB, she will be sent to a sanitorium. Her family, like all the other families afflicted with this disease, will need to make other arrangements or do what they must to survive."

"And you condone this?"

The doctor took a deep breath. Mamie knew she was pushing too far. He was tired and hungry. She could tell he was running out of patience with her arguing.

"It doesn't matter if I condone this. It is the law. If you and I do not follow the law, we will lose our licenses. Are you willing to risk that to help Mrs. Baker? And, besides, if she has TB, the sanitorium is the best place for her. They will tend to her, help her, take care of her, and see that she is comfortable for the remaining days of her life."

He stopped, straightened his shirt, and continued. "Now, Miss Mamie, if you will excuse me. I believe I have answered all your questions. You have your orders, and I don't believe there can be any misunderstanding between us. I will talk to you again in the morning."

Mamie knew this was her cue to leave. She was unimpressed with the doctor's explanation of his orders. Her heart ached, and she wasn't sure she could do as he instructed. The doctor, though, did have a point. This was the law, and to break the law meant losing everything. All the education, all the clinical experience, all the opportunities to help any other ill people would be thrown aside for one patient, Hattie Baker.

"Mamie," the doctor said softly as he approached her. He placed his hands on her shoulders and looked into her eyes. "I realize this puts you in a difficult position, and I can appreciate your sympathy for these people, especially Mrs. Baker. But I know I can count on you to do the right thing." He drew near her. "You will do the right thing, won't you?"

Mamie was caught off-guard, bewildered but entranced by his nearness. She nodded in agreement, unsure if she could speak at this time. He smiled, and she smiled shyly in return. She was a bit embarrassed by her actions. She was a grown woman and felt weak-kneed and fluttery at this moment.

The doctor released her, still smiling at her. Mamie turned to walk out of the office. She didn't remember leaving his office but then found herself walking down the hallway and out the front door where Celeste waited to lock the door behind her. Mamie walked down the front steps and across the street. She could barely feel the pavement beneath her feet as she made her way towards the boarding house. She made a promise with which she disagreed. She knew she would regret it, but at this moment, she was as light as air, flying over the ground with wings made of gossamer and angel hair. There would be a price to pay, she was sure, but not tonight. Tonight, she would think only of that touch, that smile, and that sly glance by that doctor.

Celeste closed the door behind Mamie, bolted it, and turned to go into the kitchen.

Flora spoke from the dining room. "Celeste, make sure when that woman returns, she uses the servant's entrance. It is unseemly to have the help enter by way of the front door."

"Yes, ma'am," Celeste replied as she began her nightly duties.

The doctor unbuttoned his shirt cuffs as he began to climb the steps leading up the stairs. "Must you be so crass, Flora? The woman is my nurse. She is educated and deserving of your respect."

Flora folded her arms across her chest. "You speak to me of respect when I saw you touching her just a few moments ago? You, who have no room for emotion in your life, speak to me of respect and compassion?"

The doctor turned his face towards his sister, who remained on the lower level of the hallway.

"Have I not shown you compassion through all of your troubles? Perhaps my lack of emotion is only a façade to hide my great disappointment in you. Perhaps I could care for another if I did not have all these burdens weighing me down."

"And whose fault is that, brother?" Flora's voice was loud. "Or is it easier just to blame me than face the truth of the matter?"

"What truth would that be, Flora?" he asked with his voice also raised.

"That you were wrong. You destroyed my happiness, my chance to have a family, and ruined my life," she answered flatly, lowering her arms to her sides and staring defiantly at her brother.

He did not reply but glared at her from the higher platform. There was a long silence.

He eventually softened his look. "Let me wash up, and I'll be in to help you with your medicines."

He turned and climbed the remaining stairs and disappeared into the darkness. Flora stood very still.

"Good night, ma'am," Celeste said as she donned her hat and walked into the hallway.

"Good night, Celeste," Flora replied.

The servant turned to leave out the back door through the kitchen.

"Celeste," Flora called quietly after her. "Please let me know if that nurse come back. I'm not sure what her motives are, but I believe she has her cap set for Dr. Tucker, as many other women have done in the past, but if I cannot marry whom I want, then neither can he."

"Yes, ma'am," Celeste answered as she tied her hat and left the house. "Strange folks," she said under her breath. "Money and secrets can make some folks mean."

4

Hattie prepared a pallet on the front porch of the cabin. The house was hot, and Jack needed some air. It was cooler outside, and he was able to get in and out of the cabin with his father's help. Jack lay flat on his stomach on the pallet, propping his head up with elbows bent beneath him. "There," his father said as he smoothed the wrinkles from the pallet beneath his son. "That's better, don't ya think?" "Yes, sir, it is better." Martin rubbed his son's head. "What's wrong, son? Your leg is gettin' better every day. You'll be able to walk again, so your momma says." "Yes, I know," the boy responded. "Then what's botherin' you?" Jack leaned on one arm to face his father. "When I used to lay out here, Amos was always with me. He ain't here no more." Martin sat down beside his son and touched the boy's face. He was so innocent and had so much to learn, so many heartaches and disappointments. Martin hoped those naïve eyes would be strong enough to handle whatever the future held for him. "This is true, my boy. What was once here is no longer with us, but we have their memories. So, are they really ever gone from us?"

"Is that the way it's gonna be with Momma?"

The boy's face did not flinch. There were no tears. The boy was asking a sincere question. He was old enough to know what was happening. In fact, the boy could look upon this unhappy situation with more calmness than his father.

"What do you mean?" Martin asked his son, trying to bide his time in answering, giving himself a chance to control his own feelings and think of a good answer.

"When they come to take her. Will we remember her, too?"

Martin could not bear to speak. He turned his face away from his son. He was fighting back tears. Martin simply nodded. The boy lay down on the pallet, his face turned away, and closed his eyes. Martin patted his son's back until the boy fell asleep.

"D-d-daddy," came a soft little voice from inside the screen door.

Martin turned to see the little face of his younger son. Martin patted his leg, and Clemson came out to sit on his father's lap. They sat together on the step, listening to the crickets and tree frogs.

"D-d-do you think that b-b-b-big c-c-cut hurts real b-b-bad?" the little boy asked quietly, pointing to the gaping wound on the back of Jack's leg.

"I don't think it hurts too bad, son. Jack said it's feeling better every day. Your momma is takin' real good care of it."

"G-g-g-good, c-cause it l-looks l-like it hurts s-s-somethin' awful. It's all r-red and p-purple." The little boy looked closer at the wound. "And I th-think I c-c-can see the t-t-teeth m-marks of the hog."

"Oh, don't say that." His father smiled, holding him closer. "You can't see the teeth marks of that hog. Your momma says the discoloration is a sign of its healin'. Come along, now. I'll carry you into the bed."

The child held onto his father's neck. "When c-can I s-sleep on the p-porch, Daddy?"

His father looked him in the eyes. "When you stop stutterin'. Deal?"

The little boy shook his father's hand. "Deal," the child said as clearly and plainly as anyone.

His father smiled at him and kissed his head.

Enjoy these moments, he thought to himself, for they will be fewer and further between. Jack awoke the next morning, still lying on the front porch. Clemson stood over him with the fly swatter, moving it from side to side to keep the flies away from his brother's leg.

"D-d-daddy said your c-cut don't hurt. D-d-does it hurt, Jack?" the little boy asked.

Jack leaned onto one arm to face his little brother. "Sometimes, but Momma puts salve on it so it don't dry out or get too dirty."

The little boy continued, "I t-t-told D-d-daddy I could see the t-teeth marks of the hog in your l-l-leg. Th-there m-might even be some t-teeth still in your l-leg, b-but D-d-daddy said there was no t-teeth in your l-l-leg. D-d-do you see t-teeth marks, Jack?"

The little boy bent over closer to the wound, desperately searching with his eyes for signs of lost teeth or marks from that hog. He stopped waving the fly swatter and was peering at Jack's leg.

Hattie and Eulalie were in the yard, feeding the chickens and ducks.

"Clemson!" his mother shouted. "Don't say such things. There's no teeth marks in Jack's leg, and I can guarantee there's no hog's teeth there, either. You keep your eyes on the flies and watch what you're doin'."

The little boy groaned and began waving the fly swatter over his brother. He began singing his ABC song, keeping his fly swatter swinging in time with his song.

"Here, chicky, chicky, chick," said a little voice.

"Come on over here, 'Lalie," her mother encouraged.

Hattie handed the little girl a small handful of crushed corn. "Toss it over there to those new little chicks."

"Here, chicky, chick. Come and git you b'fast." Eulalie tossed little bits of ground grain onto the grass. "Look, Momma," she said, pointing to the new little chicks. "Mr. Yeller Britches has babies."

Hattie smiled and laughed quietly. She knew better than to laugh out loud; it brought on coughing, and coughing brought on blood.

"I think Mr. Yeller Britches is Mrs. Yeller Britches," she said as she kissed her daughter's head.

Eulalie's eyes grew wide with amazement. "Why, Miss'r Yeller Britches. You be a momma."

The little girl crouched down and cupped her hands. "Come here, babies," she said in her sweetest voice. "'Lalie won't hurt'cha. I be you fweind."

The little chicks followed the hen in an attempt to gather more food. None came to the child.

"Why don't they come, Momma?"

Hattie waved her skirt slightly to rid herself of the last of the corn crumbs. "They need their momma, just like you. She makes sure they eat good food, sleep in warm beds, and say their prayers every night."

Eulalie stood straight up, tilting her head to the side and placing her hands on her hips.

"Momma," the child began in an irritated tone. "Chickies don't say dem pwayers."

"They don't?"

The child shook her head, curls bouncing.

"No, chickies can't fowd dem hands to pway."

Hattie could not help herself. She began to laugh out loud. She felt the fluid deep in her lungs, waiting to be released. Her cough was slight at first, but she knew it would not be sufficient. She took a breath, and then a hard, deep cough took advantage of the opening. It wrenched her body and forced the bloody mucus from deep inside her chest. She turned away from her children, holding onto a small sapling tree to keep from falling to her knees. Jack elevated himself on his pallet, watching his mother struggle to breathe. Clemson stopped singing and watched, too. Eulalie stood silent, fear and disbelief in her little, innocent eyes. She saw the blood leaking from her mother's mouth and dripping between her fingers as Hattie tried to contain it.

"You all right, Momma?!" Jack shouted as he tried to raise himself from his pallet.

Hattie waved a bloody hand, nodding and gasping for air. She knew she was frightening her children. Somewhere, she had to find the strength to raise herself upright. She drew in a short, shallow breath, and the great beast that lived within her was satisfied for now.

Eulalie began to cry.

Hattie shook her head, wiping her blood-stained hands on her dress. "No need to cry, 'Lalie," she managed to say, rasping and short-winded. Her voice was barely above a whisper. "Momma's fine. I just got choked, but I'm fine." But the little girl would not be comforted. The sight and smell of her mother's blood were traumatic for the child. She ran towards the porch and quickly took a seat next to Clemson. He put his arm around her, looking with disbelief at his mother as they watched her stagger toward them, dried blood on her clothing and face. Clemon's eyes began to fill with tears, and Eulalie made whimpering sounds.

Jack repositioned himself so he could see his younger siblings. He reached his hand out and touched Eulalie's arm.

"Momma's fine. She just got choked, but she's fine now. Stop your cryin'. Here, come over here and sit closer to me so Momma can git through. She needs to lay down."

The two younger children scooted themselves closer to Jack as their mother staggered past them. They watched with fear in their eyes. This was the stuff that produced nightmares.

Hattie managed to make it to her bedroom and laid down on the bed. Her chest was on fire. She could hear her heart beating in her ears. The sound of it was deafening. The horrible taste of metal was in her mouth, a souvenir of the blood that spewed from her mouth only moments before. Her lips were sticky from its passage. She tried to take short breaths, not enough to fill her lungs with air, but only inspiring enough to keep her from losing consciousness. For loss of consciousness was not far off. She could see the large, black dots before her. A lack of air, she thought, causing this feeling, but she could manage it. She had to manage it.

"Hattie," a came a soft voice. "Hattie," the voice said again.

She opened her eyes slowly. Martin stood directly over her, his face near hers and eyes full of concern. She nodded, opening her eyes wider to see him. The burning in her chest subsided, but the metallic taste in her mouth persisted.

"Martin," she managed to say quietly with a hoarseness she had not heard before.

"Shh," he answered as he repositioned her in the bed and smoothed back her hair.

"My babies," she whispered.

"They are fine. I brought them in. Jack's back in his bed."

Hattie opened her eyes. It was dark.

"Oh, Martin," she tried to say with more force. "I left them outside. I couldn't stop coughin'."

He placed his finger on her lips. "Sshh, my dear. The children are fine. They were all on the porch when I got home. Clemson and 'Lalie made jelly sandwiches with leftover biscuits. They took it to the porch, and Jack helped 'em, so I just put 'em to bed when I got home."

"Oh, Martin. I'm such a bad momma. I take care of other people, but now I can't even take care of my own babies." She could feel hot tears rolling down the sides of her face.

Martin lay quietly down beside her, holding her in his arms. "You are not a bad momma. You are the best momma in the world. No momma could love her babies anymore 'an you, but we must face it, my dear. You are ailin', and we must look it in the face."

Hattie moved her face to look her husband in the eye. "I know, Martin, but I don't want to look it in the face. It is too frightenin'. I don't want to leave you and my children. I don't want to die."

He pulled her closer and could feel her tears drop onto his chest. She wasn't crying. She hadn't the strength to cry, but the emotions so long held at bay within her now seeped out of her eyes, creating warm lines of despair on her face.

"You ain't goin' nowhere, and you ain't gonna die. Just hold onto me, and it'll all be fine. It'll all be fine."

He held her until she went to sleep. He could hear her breathing, ragged and frothy. She was ailin', ailin' terribly, but he did not want to think on it now. She was right. She was weary, and he was tired to the bone. So, he would listen to his wife for now. They would sleep and face tomorrow's problems tomorrow. He held her in his arms, listening to her uneven breathing until it lulled him into sleep, too.

Mamie started each day by preparing the mule and then her little black bag of equipment with gauze, bandages, salves, and pills from Dr. Tucker. She obtained her list from the doctor. Each day, Dr. Tucker asked her about Mrs. Baker, but Mamie told him she had not been back to the Bakers' house. In truth, she did not want to go back to the Bakers' house. And, besides, there were other people who needed a nurse's care. Hattie was staying close to home, not going out to practice her skills, leaving all these people without any type of care. Mamie saw as many people as she could, but she was unable to see all of them. Mamie began to have some sympathy for Mrs. Baker. Taking care of so many people was a great burden, and Mamie was thinking she was in over her head. Despite all her training, there were so many ailments and injuries that she had no idea what they were or how to treat them. She secretly wished Hattie was with her.

Hattie had her own set of problems, though. She stayed close to home so as to avoid running into Mamie. But, also, she was becoming so weak, and the coughing was almost uncontrollable. It was ever present, always lurking deep in her lungs, ready to come screaming into the air, bringing with it putrid fluids.

She found herself becoming short of breath just walking from one room to another. Mrs. McCrary visited often. She often brought little candies or trinkets for the children. Jack's leg was healing, but he was still not able to bear much weight on it. Martin fashioned a type of walking cane from a hickory limb allowing the boy to lean on it. He was then able to slowly make his way across the house and out onto the porch. He was still not able to help Martin, leaving more and more work for his father. Hattie was concerned for both of them. Jack, because he should be able to bear weight on that leg by now, and Martin, who was becoming so weary. The entire lot of her family looked a sorry sight: thin, tired, and worried.

Jack whittled penny whistles for Clemson and Eulalie, and they played outside with their new toys. Mrs. McCrary fixed food and did some housework as well as laundry. Hattie hated the fact that she was no longer able to do all she needed to do, but the older woman seemed to enjoy having a family to fend for. The woman brought the latest news and gossip. She knew more about the community than anyone else.

"...and then old Mr. Peterson came by and said he's gonna sell that cabin he has. Says he can't find anyone to rent it anymore. Since that last lady was there, there ain't been no one stay there more than a couple of days. Mr Peterson said folks that stay there say they hear a baby cryin' and smell tobacco."

"Like a haint?" Hattie asked in her quiet voice as she sat drinking warm tea. "Oh, I don't know 'bout that."

Mrs. McCrary smiled and shook her head, "Oh, you know how people talk."

The woman continued her sweeping. "You been up there, ain't'cha, Hattie?"

Hattie nodded. It seemed like a lifetime ago. "There weren't no haints when I was there. Mr. Peterson found that young woman all alone and near death. That's when he came and got me."

She took another sip of her warm tea. "She almost died, and why? I don't know. She had a miscarriage, but it wasn't that bad." Hattie remembered the little amber bottle she found on the floor next to the bed. She was unsure what had been in it but had suspicions it was the reason the woman was so ill.

"I stayed with her fer a little while. Martin's sister came down and helped him, but that woman didn't die. I don't know what happened to her. The next time I went up there to check on her, she was gone, but she didn't die in that cabin."

Mrs. McCrary temporarily stopped her sweeping. "I don't know, either. I never saw her. I saw the man, though. He came in for supplies. He was a looker if I do say so myself."

Hattie smiled slightly at the older woman. "Why, Mrs. McCrary, I do believe you were quite taken with the man."

Mrs. McCrary gave a sly smile as she moved the broom from side to side. "Well not at my age, but a few years younger and few less wrinkles, and I most certainly would've been tempted."

Both women laughed quietly.

"He had the most beautiful eyes," she continued as she went back to her work.

Mrs. McCrary changed the subject but continued talking. "I hear Jessica Pike's near her time. She should be havin' that baby any day now."

Hattie nodded, leaning her head back and closing her eyes.

"I believe that public health nurse has been by a couple of times to see her."

Hattie opened her eyes but did not respond.

"…but then I think they'd rather have you at the time of the birthin'.

They feel more comfortable with you. Why, I bet, you birthed half the babies up here. Do you rightly recollect how may babies you birthed?" the woman asked as she leaned on her broom.

"No," Hattie answered flatly. "I never counted. I know them all by name, but never kept a tally. They were all like special little blessins."

"Did you ever lose any, Miss Hattie? Not that that's a pleasant subject, but sometimes sweet Jesus takes those little angels a'fore they draw a breath."

Hattie's eyes glossed over. "Yes, I remember them, too. Some I lost before they had a chance to even see the light a' day. Sometimes, I think Jesus didn't take them, but their mommas gave them up to him. It pains me when I know anybody's end is so near, and all I can do is offer 'em a cool cloth and a soft word."

Mrs. McCrary resumed her sweeping. "You might be surprised how much good a cool cloth and a soft word does in easin' 'em across Jordan. Even if they were unwanted, unloved, or unforgiven. Poor little creatures, old or young. Well, they have a good home in heaven. Maybe no one wanted 'em here on Earth, but Jesus holds 'em all in His arms, singin' soft words and keepin' 'em close."

"You think they sing in heaven, Mrs. McCrary?"

The old woman smiled. "I surely do. What else they got to do? They don't sweep floors or bake bread."

Hattie laughed slightly. Her voice was barely a whisper. "I hope they sing up there."

"If it's all right with you, Miss Hattie, I'd like to fix your family some supper before I leave. I saw you have ham and potatoes. I'll fry us up some, and we'll have a nice meal together. Would you like that?"

Hattie smiled. "That would be nice, Mrs. McCrary, but I don't want you to feel you must do everything. I feel bad enough you have to help so often."

Mrs. McCrary waved her off. "Nonsense, I enjoy it. I like to cook, and the sounds of those babies laughin' and talkin' does my heart good. I feel useful."

"Well," Hattie continued. "You are truly useful and needed here right now, Mrs. McCrary."

Hattie noticed Mrs. McCrary going towards the door, drying her hands on a towel. She could hear voices outside. They were not calm voices.

The older woman opened the screen door and leaned out. "Stay seated, Miss Hattie. I'm going to call the children in," Mrs. McCrary said as she motioned for the children to come in.

Jack moved slowly with his walking stick, but Clemson and Eulalie came running. Mrs. McCrary took all the children into the adjoining room.

"Come along, little 'uns," she said as she urged them into the next room. "It looks like Daddy has some business to tend to."

Hattie could not see outside, but she could hear Martin's angry voice. "I don't want you on this property, ma'am."

There was a woman's voice answering from farther away. Hattie could not make out exactly what the woman said, but she heard Martin again.

"You ain't got no business up here, Miss Starkweather. This is my property, and no one comes on it that I don't want."

Hattie could feel her heart sink. She knew who their unwanted visitor was. Hattie wanted to get up, go outside, and join in the argument, but she had not the energy. Her lungs would not sustain the conflict. She would give herself away. The walk itself from the chair to the porch would bring on shortness of breath, and shouting would certainly bring about the severe coughing.

"I must see Mrs. Baker. It is my duty and obligation to report anyone who may have it. She must be evaluated and diagnosed."

Hattie could hear the nurse shouting, although she was closer to the house now. She could hear Martin's voice becoming louder and angrier.

"I don't usually shout and holler commands at women, Miss Starkweather, but 1 will surely throw you off your mule if you come one step closer. This is my farm, and you are not welcomed on it. So, turn that animal around and don't come back no more. Or else, I will have to git violent, and that won't do either of us any good."

Hattie heard no reply. The house was quiet. She knew Mrs. McCrary and the children were listening in earnest in the other room. After a brief silence, she could hear the nurse's voice again. This time, though, it was closer and softer.

"Mr. Baker, I only want to help your wife. She is very ill, and perhaps there is something I can do. They have treatments."

Martin cut her off. "At the TB sanitorium? I never knowed nobody to come back from that place. No babies, neither. I hear tell they have a cemetery up there just for buryin' their patients. I'll not let you take her from here and let her die alone with no family at her side. And my child, do you think I'd let you carry that unborn babe away, and I never even know when it was borned?"

Hattie could hear the straining of his voice, the anguish he was suffering. He was not an emotional man, but this was bringing him down to his knees. She knew he had tears in his eyes for she could hear the sorrow in his words. She wanted to get out of her chair, go to him, hold him, comfort him. She could feel warm, wet tears moving down her face. Facing this was more difficult than she anticipated. There was no good way out. There was no redemption, and the truth came with a young woman riding a mule.

"I will leave your property, Mr. Baker, but I will have to return. Your wife must seek medical care."

"Then you best bring the sheriff, 'cause that'll be the only way you take her from me, and tell him to bring his guns, 'cause I'll be bringin' mine."

Hattie did not hear a reply. She was hopeful the nurse had given up. She opened her eyes, wiping away the tears. Martin came walking into the cabin. He did not stop to speak to Hattie but opened the door to the adjoining room. Mrs. McCrary quickly ushered the children from the room as Martin walked past them, saying nothing. He closed the door hard behind them.

"Well," Mrs. McCrary began in an awkwardly cheerful tone. "Let's see 'bout gettin' supper on the table. Jack, if you want to sit here, and I'll let you cut this ham, and Clemson and Eulalie, you can help me with the potatoes."

No one said anything. The children did as they were told. Martin remained in the bedroom, and Hattie sat in her chair. Only the nervous chattering of Mrs. McCrary was heard in the house.

When Mrs. McCrary finished preparing the meal, she knocked on the bedroom door, asking if Martin would like to eat. He emerged from the room, avoiding Hattie's eyes and saying nothing. He sat at the table with his children.

"Miss Hattie, would you like to eat with us?" Mrs. McCrary asked, quietly.

"No, thank you," she replied, leaning forward in her chair.

"If you want to lie down, I'll bring you some broth, soon as I git the children fed."

Hattie moved towards the edge of her chair. Seeing her struggle, Martin got up from the table and assisted his wife into the bedroom. She lay down, saying nothing about the prior scene between her husband and the nurse. Martin placed a blanket to cover her. She closed her eyes. Martin stood over her, looking down upon his wife. She was gaunt, pale. Lying so still, she resembled a corpse. If it had not been for the sound of her ragged breathing, he would have thought she was already deceased. He could feel a deep, solemn feeling rising from his chest. An overwhelming feeling of sadness enveloped him. He swallowed hard, fighting back emotions that could barely be controlled. They crowded out all other thoughts, all other emotions, and blinded him with watery mirrors in his eyes.

He felt a warm hand on his shoulder. He turned to see Mrs. McCrary with a small bowl of broth.

"I'll stay in here with her, Martin. You go eat your supper with your children."

Martin nodded, afraid to speak. Afraid that if he opened his mouth, his voice would betray his sorrow. He left the room and joined the rest of his family at the table. Somehow, though, his appetite had vanished.

"When you gonna pway music 'gain, Daddy?" his daughter asked as she took a bite of her potatoes.

"Well," he began, clearing his voice, trying to diminish any hint of sadness. "Maybe I'll play some tonight for us. We could use a bit of music, don't ya think?"

"M-me t-t-too," Clemson began. "I c-can s-sing with ya."

His father leaned over, tousling the little boy's hair. "You surely can, son. And 'Lalie can sing, and Jack can play the mouth harp."

Eulalie clapped her hands, and Jack smiled. It had been a long time since they'd played music together. It would be a welcome diversion from the sorrow that seemed to wrap itself around them recently. Perhaps the sounds of the fiddle playing and children singing would help their mother. Before she was ill, Jack remembered a time when she would sit outside with them and sing. Her voice was never strong, nor even very good, but she could carry a tune and always knew all the words to the songs that her husband played.

Jack remembered those days as happy and peaceful. But he knew those days were gone. A new normal would now need to be discovered, but it would take time, and Jack was afraid that more drastic changes were on the way before any sense of normal could be achieved. He saw that same look in his father's eyes. That look of quiet desperation and fear, regardless of how much his father tried to hide his feelings. Jack could see the change in his demeanor. Lying on his pallet or sitting in his chair, he had time to observe his father's actions. The way the man stared blankly into the distance, held his coffee cup in front of him but never took a drink, and ran his hands through his hair in frustration. Clemson and Eulalie were too young to notice these things, but Jack had seen them over and over since his mother became ill. He knew she would not recover. He could already see the loss in his father's eyes and smell the odor of death on his mother's breath.

"Eat your supper, son," his father said as he patted his hand. "You can't play in the band on an empty stomach. We need you fed and watered so you can hold your own against your old man."

His father smiled.

Jack had not seen him smile in a long time. He was learning more than farming from his father. He learned to do what you must, every day, every time. Push the pain aside if you want to survive. Jack finished his supper and grabbed the mouth harp. It was time to pretend nothing was wrong, that nothing would change. It was time to perform.

Mrs. McCrary spoon-fed the warm broth to Hattie. The younger woman ate sparsely, like a bird. She swallowed slowly, deliberately, so as not to provoke the vicious coughing that was waiting at any moment to arise and take over. She forced the soup down her throat. She could actually feel its warmth slide down her throat and into her stomach. It was an odd feeling, unnerving, but she forced several spoonfuls down.

"There," Mrs. McCrary said softly as she sat the bowl down onto the bedside table. "I'll let you rest now. Martin and the children are out on the porch. Perhaps you can hear them singing. Martin's brought down his fiddle. He plays a fine fiddle, don't he? I wished I'd learnt to play the fiddle or piano or anythin'. Music is so calming. It seems to lift one's spirit right out of the body. I s'pose that's why God likes us to sing in church. So our spirits can be lifted up to him."

Mrs. McCrary turned back around to see Hattie. She lay there, quietly, breathing in short, shallow breaths. Mrs. McCrary picked up the soup bowl and quietly removed herself from the room. Hattie could hear the woman leave the room but did not open her eyes or say anything. She wanted to thank the woman, but her body would not let her. It lay there, floating, moving away from her as if it was no longer a part of her. She wasn't sure if she was awake or asleep or somewhere in between, but it was peaceful, and, in her mind, she was not struggling to breathe. She could hear Martin playing the fiddle, a soft, somber tune, and her children were humming along. She was not sure if she was sleeping or dreaming. No matter. Her body was drifting away again. She imagined she could see the face of her unborn child. A girl, with dark curls like her father and a cherub face. The child was sleeping peacefully – too peacefully.

Soon, Hattie thought to herself, I shall join you. Sleep, now, my child. Wait for me. I'll join you by and by.

And then she floated away, and it became dark.

5

⚜

Mamie made multiple trips into the hills over the next several
weeks. She avoided the Bakers' home, though. Dr. Tucker
asked about them regularly. Mamie informed him of the
argument she and Mr. Baker had the last time she approached the
house. Since then, she'd made excuses for why she had not returned.
She knew Dr. Tucker was wise to her, and he was becoming impatient
with her. Each morning, he would greet her as she packed her supplies,
obtained her orders, and prepared the mule. Each day, Dr. Tucker
would have "visit the Bakers" on her list, but somehow, she just never
seemed to get to it. Despite this thorn between them, Mamie thought
her relationship with the doctor a good one. He came out to visit with
her every morning, smiling and civil. His sister, however, had not
softened. She remained distant and aloof. Flora did not acknowledge
Mamie's presence in the least, except to scowl at her from a distance
when she was seen with the doctor. But Mamie knew her time was
running out. Despite the doctor's patience with her, she knew Hattie

would need to be brought in, but she would put it off as long as she could.

"Good afternoon, Mrs. Pike," Mamie shouted as she came close to the cabin. The woman was sweeping the yard. No grass grew near the cabin. Sandy white dirt as hard as brick surrounded the place, and the old woman swept the dirt each day to rid it of leaves, sticks, and anything else that cluttered the soil. Upon hearing the nurse's voice, she stopped sweeping and waved her hand as Mamie pulled the mule near the porch to use it as a step in dismounting the beast.

"Still fightin' that mule, are you, Miss Mamie?" she asked as Mamie grabbed her bag and made her way into the cabin.

"I think he and I have accepted one another, Mrs. Pike. I know how far he will go, and he knows how far I will go. So, currently, we have learned to live with each other. Not friends, but no longer enemies. How is your daughter-in-law this morning?"

Mrs. Pike followed the nurse into the cabin. "She's havin' some pain, mostly in her back. So, I'm not sure if they be birthin' pains or just resettlin'."

Mrs. Pike and Mamie walked into the bedroom where the younger woman lay.

"Good afternoon, Nurse Mamie," the young woman said, rubbing her swollen belly.

"Good afternoon, Miss Jessica. Your mother-in-law tells me you are having some pain. May I examine you?"

The young woman nodded, closing her eyes and wincing. Mamie placed her palms on the pregnant woman's abdomen. Hattie could feel the contraction. It was high, not very strong but enough to indicate the beginning of the woman's travail.

Mamie smiled. "Well, Miss Jessica, I believe by this time tomorrow you will be a new momma."

Jessica laughed nervously and winced again. "These pains come quickly, but they ain't too strong."

Mamie nodded as she unpacked her bag. "Yes. You know they will become stronger and stronger as well as closer together. Now, Miss Jessica, I'm going to check on the progress. This is a bit embarrassing, but we are all ladies in here and all subject to the same condition. So, don't be shy. Everything I do is for your safety and the safe delivery of your baby. Do I have your trust?"

Jessica looked at her mother-in-law. "I do trust you, Miss Mamie, but how many babies have you delivered?"

Mamie hesitated. "Not very many, but all of them were delivered without difficulty and produced fine, healthy babies."

Jessica smiled and closed her eyes against another contraction. "Then I trust you."

Mamie moved the blankets and began preparing the bed for the delivery. She avoided the older Mrs. Pike's eyes. Mamie was afraid that the older woman would see through her thin lie. Mamie had assisted with childbirth but never delivered a child on her own. Her hands were shaking, and she was trying desperately to remember the multitude of things that must be done. In her mind, she recited the stages of childbirth, what to watch for in each stage, and what must be done in each. She could feel her knees becoming weak, but she would make it through. She was determined to make it through.

While Mamie fussed around with linens and tools, the older Mrs. Pike saw the trembling hands, the frightened facial expressions, and the fastidiousness of unnecessary work. The two women stayed close to the laboring girl for most of the afternoon. Her contractions grew closer together but no stronger. Mamie checked the progress of the descending baby but was unsure why the labor was taking so long.

"I'm going to draw some water and boil it. I'll also find some clean cloths for you," Mrs. Pike said as she left the room.

Mamie nodded in agreement, not really hearing anything the older woman said.

Once outside the room, Mrs. Pike went outside to draw water from the well but called to her son.

"Jessica seems to be havin' some trouble. I think she might need Mrs. Baker. Take the wagon and go git her. I know she cain't ride this far, but I think she can ride in the wagon. Take some blankets for the woman. Make haste, son, I don't know how long we got."

The young man did as he was instructed, hitching up the horse to the wagon and heading down the road towards the Bakers'. Mamie was so involved in her own dilemma that she did not notice the activity outside. Mrs. Pike finished drawing the water and began to boil a pot on the fire. She pulled cloths from the pantry and checked them to make sure they were clean.

Martin heard a hard knock on the door. He had just laid down close to Hattie. His children were comfortably sleeping nearby with Jack in the next room. Martin started to get up when he heard voices coming from the other room.

"Daddy," came Jack's voice as he quietly opened the door to the bedroom. "Mr. Pike's out here to see ya. He says he needs Momma."

"I'm gettin' up," Martin said as he grabbed his pants.

He pushed back his hair and rubbed his eyes as he left the bedroom and entered the main room.

"I'm sorry, Mr. Baker," the young man said, desperation in his voice. "But my wife's givin' birth, and that public health nurse is with her, but Momma said to fetch Mrs. Baker."

Martin looked at the young man in surprise. "Mrs. Baker's ailin'.

"Daddy," Jack spoke up. "This here is Andrew Pike, Jessica's husband. Momma's been treatin' her all this time."

Martin shook his head. "I don't care. Mrs. Baker cain't go with you, son. I'm sorry, but she ain't in any shape to leave this house."

The door behind them opened. Hattie stood, weak but dressed.

"Martin," she began in a soft voice. "Please fetch my bag." She looked at Andrew. "I am ill, but if you brought the wagon, I can lie down in it and get to your house."

Martin turned to his wife. His face was betraying his emotions. "No, I won't have this. You ain't well. Not this time, Hattie. You should be in bed right now. You're as thin as a rake and pale. You ain't ate nothin' of substance in days. You're weak, and your breathin's bad. Please, if you care for me and your own babies, you'll go lay back down. Let that nurse help his wife. She's been trained and should be able to deliver his child without your help."

She walked up to him, bent but moving forward. She placed her hand on his shoulder. "This may well be the last person I can help. Let me go. I won't be long, then you can do with me as you need."

Martin placed his hands on her shoulders. "Hattie, sweetheart, how many times have they come and fetched you in the middle of the night and you always went? But not this time, not this time. I beg you."

Martin stood very still. Tears filled his eyes as his wife kissed him gently on the check. She took the arm of the young man and wrapped a shawl around her shoulders and left the house. He watched as the young man helped her into the back of the wagon. It was getting dark outside, but he could see his wife smile at him before she lay down inside the wagon, and the young man drove away with her.

The ride was rough as Andrew Pike was trying to hurry back to his expecting wife. He said nothing, and Hattie lay quietly in the back of the wagon. She knew she was not well and should not be out in the night air, but it felt cool to her skin. She began to drift back to sleep or unconsciousness. She was not sure which, but it didn't matter. They arrived at the Pikes' house sooner than she thought, and Andrew was helping her out of the wagon and up the steps into the cabin. He ushered her past the little pallets that lay on the floor containing his little brothers and sisters. They remained sleeping as the two walked between them.

"Momma," the young man whispered as he opened the door into the next room. "I brung Mrs. Baker."

Andrew could see inside the room. His wife lay in their bed, arching her back and tears rolling from her eyes. His mother stood nervously at her side. The nurse was digging through her bag for something.

The older Mrs. Pike quickly came around the bed and assisted Hattie to a rocking chair located at the end of bed. Andrew could see the look of surprise on the face of the young nurse.

"We'll be fine now, son," his mother said as she gently forced the door closed. He turned and found a chair to sit in. He sat alone, in the dark, waiting and praying.

Hattie leaned back into the rocking chair, closing her eyes slightly. She said nothing, just catching her breath.

Mamie looked at the older Mrs. Pike but said nothing. The only sound was made by Jessica moaning.

"Tell me the child's story," Hattie said quietly.

Mamie was not sure if Hattie was speaking to her. She was insulted that the Pikes brought Hattie here but relieved, too.

Hattie opened her eyes and looked squarely at Mamie. "Tell me the child's story."

"I don't know what you mean," Mamie answered.

"When did the pains begin? How fast are the contractions? How fast is the heartbeat?"

"Oh, you mean the stages of labor?" Mamie answered.

"You may call them whatever you wish, but they are the story of a child coming into the world. Now, tell me."

Mamie nodded and began to relay the information, just as she had done with her instructors in nursing school. She told the details of speed, duration, rate. Hattie listened intently with her eyes closed. Jessica moved restlessly in the bed, struggling.

"Mrs. Pike," Hattie began after obtaining all the information Mamie could tell her. "Bring in some cool water and clean cloths. Make sure the container of water will hold a child."

Mamie thought that an odd request but did not question it.

Hattie continued, "And you, Nurse Mamie, must git yourself to the business end of this."

Mamie pointed to the end of the bed. "Remove the blankets and straighten the linens. Then feel the abdomen to time the contractions and their strength."

Mamie did as she was told, talking and explaining the situation over and over. "Mrs. Pike seems to be having some difficulty, but I cannot determine the cause. She has been in labor now for many hours."

Sweat was beading upon the forehead of Hattie. She was feeling lightheaded and dizzy. She continued to lean back in the chair, taking short, shallow breaths. Mamie saw the struggle Hattie was also enduring.

"If you can just instruct me, Miss Hattie, I can do the work. Just tell me what I must do."

Hattie nodded, never opening her eyes. "Take her wrist. Is her heart beating fast?'

Mamie followed her orders. "Yes, very fast, but it's regular."

Hattie nodded again. "They tell me you have a contraption that lets you hear inside the body."

"Yes," she answered and pulled her stethoscope from the bag. She listened to the pregnant woman's lungs and heart. "She's got good airflow, no wheezing or crackling, but she does have rapid respirations."

"And the child?"

Mamie placed the bell of the stethoscope onto the woman's protruding abdomen. She listened for a long time, through another contraction and beyond. The brow of the young nurse was furrowed with her eyes keenly focused on the muscles of contraction. She removed the tubes of the stethoscope from her ears and turned to Hattie.

"The child's heart rate is fast, but it declines during a contraction. Is that normal?"

Hattie shook her head slowly.

Mrs. Pike came through the door with her bowl of cool water and cloths.

"How's it goin'?" she asked as she began wiping her daughter-in-law's face with the cloth, removing sweat and tears and rinsing the cloth in the water.

Hattie opened her eyes and leaned forward in the chair. "It's about to get real interestin'. Jessica, Nurse Mamie's gonna git real friendly with ya, and I need ya to relax as much as possible. Mrs. Pike, give her some of that moonshine in my bag."

Mrs. Pike quickly did as she was told, but Mamie looked appalled at the idea.

"You might need some, too, Nurse Mamie, before this is all over."

Jessica took a big draught of the liquor as her mother-in-law dabbed her head with the cloth.

"Now, Jessica, you need to lay flat, so take out that pillow, and Mamie, you're gonna put your hand into the birth canal until you can feel the child's body."

Mamie looked with sheer terror at Hattie. "Why?" she asked with disbelief.

Hattie took a ragged breath. "You said the child's heart rate goes down with contractions, so there is something hindering it from moving further down the canal."

"The cord," Mamie said softly.

Hattie nodded. "You must free the child from its own cord. Keep one hand on the abdomen so you can feel the contractions, push down gently, then with the other hand, with fingers outstretched, gently slide them up the canal until you feel the child's body."

Mamie could feel sweat running down her back. It was terribly hot in this room. Her vision was slightly obscured by either tears or sweat dripping into her eyes. She stood beside the pregnant woman and placed her hands as Hattie had instructed. Mamie took a deep breath and began inserting her hand into the canal. It was not pleasant. Jessica arched her back, making moaning sounds and twisting her face to reveal the pain she was undergoing. Shortly, though, Mamie could feel something solid. Something that moved but would not yield.

Her voice was broken and soft. "I feel it."

Hattie leaned forward. "Good. Can you tell if it is hard like the skull or soft like the backside?"

Mamie moved her fingers slightly. "Hard," she said quickly. "Like the skull. I can feel bone."

Jessica had another contraction, and the child's body pressed against Mamie's hand. She felt of it quickly.

"Now," Hattie continued. "Gently move your hand down along the child's head and see if you can feel the cord. It will be supple and easily moved."

Mrs. Pike stood very still, nearly holding her breath as Mamie moved her fingers along the baby's head.

She whispered to Hattie, "Are you sure she's up to this?"

Hattie whispered in reply, "She must be. We ain't got no choice.

"I feel it," the young nurse said after a bit.

"Can you describe what you feel?" Hattie asked as she leaned back into the rocking chair, closing her eyes. She tried to imagine what was going on inside this young woman's body, how the child was laying, and how that cord was interfering."

"The face is down with its chin pressed hard against the child's chest, but I can feel the cord trapped between the chin and the chest.

"All right," came Hattie's response. "You must wriggle your fingers between the neck and the cord. Once you do so, the cord is delicate enough to slip out from between the two, but, Mamie, do so quickly. With each contraction, the cord will tighten, and the air to the child will be cut off."

Mamie nodded and moved her fingers as if she were playing a fine instrument. She began to manipulate the cord from its entrapped state. She was surprised, though, that once she started to move the cord from beneath the head, it slipped off quickly, and the head repositioned itself.

Jessica let out a sharp cry as a strong contraction occurred, but this time, the muscles did not give way. The contraction was full strength and full duration. Mamie wiped her hands on a cloth.

"Use the other rag there to wipe your face, too." Hattie said, pointing to the pile of clean cloths on the table.

Mamie wiped her face. She was unaware of the sweat and tears that accumulated there.

Jessica again groaned and moved about in the bed. Mrs. Pike wiped the young woman's face which was red and distorted with pain.

"Get back to work, Mamie. You are not done. Things should move quickly now. You need to be ready" Hattie leaned forward again. "The child looks to be crownin'. Get yourself prepared."

"I see it," Mamie responded with some excitement in her voice. She kept one hand on Jessica's abdomen, keeping the expectant mother in an appropriate position. "I see the head."

"Wonderful," Hattie responded softly. "Put the birthin' cloths underneath for when the babe drops. You will have only a few moments to gather it up, cut the cord, and clear the fluid for the child's mouth and nose."

"Yes, ma'am," the younger nurse responded in a more excited tone. She was unable to contain her happiness. She responded to Mamie as she had when she was in school responding to the instructor.

Mamie placed the cloths. Jessica gave one last long push, revealing the vessels in her own neck and brow. The woman's face was red and wet with sweat. She made a low, guttural sound, indicating she was using every muscle in her body to force this child from her body. Mamie watched as the rounded, wet child emerged from its journey.

"There," Hattie said with all the energy she could muster. "Turn the child slightly, gently and allow it to fall into your hands. Don't pull or force it. It will fall into this life at its own time."

Mamie could feel the weight of the child drop into the cloth in her hands. She turned the child sightly as told, wiping away the remnants of any fluids still clinging to its tiny body. She then took a piece of string and tied off the cord nearest the child's body and cut the cord on the mother's side. She started to hold the child up by its ankles and strike its bottom to induce breathing as she was taught in school, but Hattie stopped her.

"No, my dear. No child deserves to be punished upon its immediate arrival into this world. Mrs. Pike, the water, please."

Mrs. Pike pulled out the bowl of water that she had been using to wet the cloths used to wipe Jessica's face. It was a white alabaster bowl, long and low. The water within was cool but not cold. It held the sweat and tears from the baby's mother. Mrs. Pike took the baby from Mamie and laid the child in the water using a cloth to separate the child's skin from the surface of the bowl. Once in the water, the baby took a long breath in, followed by more breaths in and out, with no sign of struggle.

Hattie's voice was calm and quiet. "It is the child's first breath in the world, not brought about by violence, but by cool, clean water blessed with his mother's tears in his grandmother's potato bowl."

"The child is alive?" Jessica asked, breathing rapidly and perspiring profusely. "And it is a boy?"

"Yes," Mamie answered enthusiastically. Mrs. Pike took the child from the water and wrapped it in soft swaddling cloths. She handed the boy to his mother who began to cry with happiness. "It is a beautiful boy, my dear."

Mamie's eyes filled with tears, too. She did not know she was crying. The child was healthy, the mother was fine, but this was very emotional. New life was very emotional. She tried to compose herself.

"What are you going to name him?"

Jessica touched her new baby's face, memorizing every line and crease on the child.

"Armond," the new mother said softly. "He's named after his grandfather. Armond Pike."

The older Mrs. Pike wiped tears from her eyes, too. "I'll go get the child's father."

Hattie leaned back into her chair again. She was feeling dizzy and lightheaded again. This ordeal had taken its toll. She knew she would need to leave soon. She felt hot on the inside, but her skin was cold.

"Before Andrew comes into the room, there is one thing more you must do. Roll up one of the clean swaddlin' blankets and gently press down on the mother's belly."

Mamie looked at Hattie with questioning eyes but took a small blanket and rolled it up. She began rolling it on Jessica's stomach. The young woman groaned slightly. Mamie stopped the procedure.

Hattie shook her head. "No, cain't stop. It is a bit painful but necessary."

"This was never taught in nursing school, Mrs. Baker," Mamie said as she stood upright, looking suspiciously at the woman.

Hattie did not have the patience or energy to argue with the young nurse. She leaned forward and pulled herself up. Her legs were weak, and she was dizzy, but she held onto the bed frame and made her way next to Mamie.

"Like this," she said, taking the rolled blanket and pushing down onto Jessica's lower abdomen, rolling the blanket along the pelvic region and onto the legs. The young woman groaned and took a deep breath.

"Oh, Miss Hattie, don't do that no more. That is truly painful."

"Yes, it is, but it's needed to rid your body of any lingerin' birthin' products." Hattie rolled the blanket down Jessica's torso again. Jessica moaned and twisted in the bed.

Hattie began to feel very weak, and her legs buckled slightly. She held onto the bedpost, handing the rolled blanket to Mamie.

"Are you all right, Miss Hattie?" Mamie asked quietly.

Hattie nodded. "Keep rolling that blanket a couple more times."

Mamie took the blanket and looked at it, then looked at Hattie. "We never did anything like this in nursing school, Miss Hattie."

Hattie was leaning over the bed, trying desperately to compose herself. She gave the young nurse a sideways glance. "Did any of your new mothers have fevers after birthin'?"

Mamie nodded.

"Mine don't," Hattie whispered back. "Once you're done rolling that blanket a couple of times, help Jessica nurse the baby. Both these things will cause contractions and make sure she won't have no fever later."

Mamie did as she was told, carefully rolling the blanket and helping Jessica nurse her new child. Hattie walked slowly towards the door that led to the other room. She could again see those dark, black spots in front of her. She wanted to get out of the room before she started coughing. The urge was becoming overwhelming, and it was just a matter of time before the event occurred. Then there would be the blood, and the phlegm, and the weakness, and the dry heaving. She needed to leave now.

The door opened in front of her, and Andrew came in, beaming, smiling, so excited.

He grabbed Hattie by the shoulders. "Thank you, Miss Hattie. Thank you for comin' and helpin' my wife."

He released her and went quickly to his wife's side, kissing the new mother on the forehead and gently touching his son. Hattie could not see, but she knew he was shedding a few tears. She heard his voice crack and sniffle. It had all been worth it. To save one person was worth it, but now she had to get out of this room.

She started to cough and slipped through the doorway while the Pikes and Mamie were busy with the new baby. Hattie stood on the other side of the door, trying desperately to compose herself. She coughed again, but this time it was longer and deeper. She was fighting back the urge to cough, but she was losing. She took slow, measured breaths, but the increasing tightness in her chest was becoming too difficult to control. It felt as though she was being squeezed to death. She coughed again, deeper and deeper. She gasped for air and coughed again. She staggered over to a rocking chair and managed to get herself seated, but it was too late. The coughing would not subside, and her lungs were on fire. She covered her mouth with her hand. Red fluid dripped from between her fingers. From the side, someone handed her a clean cloth. She took it, not knowing who handed it to her. She coughed again, and more blood filled the cloth, but it seemed the worst was over. The squeezing sensation was releasing her. Only a few more minor spasms, and the spell was over. She was drained. There was blood on her hands and clothes. She looked up to see who handed her the cloth.

Mamie stood very still. She handed the diseased woman a cup. Hattie took the cup and drank from it. The cup's contents were strong and cut through the rancid phlegm and blood in her throat. It burned and hit hard in her stomach. Hattie knew this brew: moonshine. Not the moonshine Martin's brother made, but pure corn squeezins. She took another sip. It burned all the way down her throat, but it stopped the cough. She knew, though, that much more of this concoction, and she'd be under the table. She sat in a chair sitting nearby.

"So," Hattie said after a few moments. "How have you been?"

Mamie smiled slowly. "Good," she answered. "I want to thank you for helping in there. I don't think I could've delivered that baby without you."

Hattie nodded, weakly. Her voice was rough and hoarse from the coughing and the moonshine.

"I know I couldn't done it without you. I don't have the strength anymore."

She drank down the last of the moonshine. It was just as strong as the first swallow but helped remove the noxious taste of blood left behind in her mouth.

Mamie took the end of the cloth and leaned over Hattie. "Open your mouth, Miss Hattie. You got blood on your teeth."

Hattie did as she was told, and Mamie gently scraped the residue of blood from her mouth.

"Thank you," Hattie said as Mamie folded the bloody cloths together and wiped her own hands.

Hattie continued, "That contraption you had in there that can hear lungs and hearts is amazin'. I s'pose you and Dr. Tucker have some good ideas every now and again."

Mamie nodded. "Every now and again."

There was an awkward silence between the two women.

Mamie swallowed hard. "You know, Miss Hattie, I'm required to report your disease."

Hattie looked up at the young woman. All Mamie could see in her eyes was fatigue. She looked so weary, so beaten, so weak and frail. She had no one to fight for her. Hattie was certainly not able to speak for herself. She had no voice and no energy to speak up.

Mamie took a breath. "...but I haven't seen you in a long, long time, and when I come to your house, you're not there. So, I cannot make the report until there is a definite diagnosis.

Hattie smiled slightly. "Thank you, Mamie, but I know it is just a matter of time. If you will allow me a short amount of time to get my affairs in order, then you can make your report. As it is, I am becomin' such a burden to my family that maybe I should go away, at least for a while, until I get my strength back."

"Yes," Mamie answered, avoiding any further eye contact.

Both women knew that if Hattie were placed into the TB sanitorium, there was very little to no chance of leaving. Hattie's husband was correct when he said there were burial grounds on the property and nearly no live births. It was a death sentence to be placed in one of the facilities, but it was public health policy. In an effort to keep down the spread of the disease throughout the population, those diagnosed with the disease were sequestered from their families and homes, placed in a strange environment with a multitude of other diseased individuals and remain so until they died.

Mamie knew what she had to do, but she would delay it as long as possible. She thought it odd, though, that Hattie was the only case she'd run across in this territory. She wondered, if the disease was so contagious, why were there not more cases of it up here in these hills? This was puzzling to the young nurse. She could not imagine where Hattie was exposed. Hattie did not travel. She probably hadn't been out of this county in her entire life.

Andrew came out of the bedroom, all smiles and excitement. He held his son close to him, beaming with pride.

"Is he not the most wondrous child you ever did see?" he asked, pulling the blanket away slightly from the baby's face.

Hattie smiled, covering the bloody stains on her dress. Mamie walked towards the young man and took the baby.

"I believe Mrs. Baker needs to be taken home. I'm sure she is weary."

Andrew continued to look upon his newborn son, but he nodded and released him to the care of the young nurse.

"I'll bring the wagon 'round, Mrs. Baker, and help you out into it."

Hattie rose slowly. She nodded in understanding as the young boy left the room.

"Thank you for everything, Mrs. Baker," Mamie called after her as

Hattie made her way out the door. "I learned more from you in one night than I learned in years of nursing school."

Hattie smiled and waved as Andrew assisted her into the back of the wagon. She leaned back on the blankets. The night air felt good, cool, and clean. She was breathing a bit easier, but it was temporary. She knew the coughing would return, the blood would flow, and that nauseating taste of blood would sour her mouth again. She had to find the energy, though, to put her affairs in order. She knew she was running out of time. Unconsciously, she rubbed her belly. It was still so small and so quiet. She was too tired, though, to think on such things.

Mamie watched as the wagon pulled away and rambled down the dirt road. The moon was full and cast light onto the travelers.

"You and Dr. Tucker must think we're pretty stupid," came a hushed voice from behind her.

Mamie turned to see the older Mrs. Pike standing between herself and the bedroom door. The woman's voice was low, but full of disgust.

"No, ma'am," Mamie began as the woman took the baby from her.

"Backwoods, backwater hill people with no education, can't half of us read nor write, can't cipher higher than our fingers and toes can count. Well, I'm here to tell you that people who have survived starvation, illness, feuds, wars, births, burials, and a thousand other catastrophes have learned a lot, not from books or classes or school, but because there was no other way. At the end of the day, it's just you and Jesus. You might have a few good neighbors or friends who will help you 'cause it's the right thing to do, but it's really up to you. I'm sure your Dr. Tucker would not approve of what we done here tonight..."

The older woman looked sternly at Mamie.

"But where was he when my daughter-in-law was near death and might not have lived, or lost that baby, or both? Two lives saved by ignorant hill people."

Mamie had no answer. The older woman took all the soiled cloths and placed them in a large washtub. She poured cold water over them and began scrubbing them against a washboard, holding the baby in one arm and using the other to do the work. She was right. These were a determined people.

Mamie was mesmerized by this woman, by these people. The

near-death experience they just experienced was just another day in their lives. It was a turning point for Mamie, but to this woman, there was still more work to be done. Clothes to wash, food to cook, yards to sweep. These people were not simple. They were survivors. Their ways were different, almost foreign, but they were not simple. They pushed and clawed their way through, every day, every time. She could see it in the efforts of all these people. Do all you can, push, claw, push harder, claw more, but don't quit. For when you quit, it's over. Over for everyone. Life is precious. Mamie saw how that newborn baby fought to gain life, how Jessica fought to give life, and how Hattie fought to keep life. Dr. Tucker was not here, and his nurse was restrained by rules and protocol from doing anything outside her scope of practice, even to save a life. Rules and protocols were determined by people who did not live or work in these hills. The old woman was right. At the end of the day, it is just you, living with the decisions you make, and Jesus.

Martin heard the wagon coming up the road and went outside to help Hattie back into their cabin.

"I apologize, Mr. Baker," Andrew Pike began as he swung his legs down from his perch and walked to the back of the wagon. "I know your wife is ailin', but she saved my wife's life and, most likely, that of my new son."

Martin tried to feign a smile. He was still upset that Hattie left in the first place. He looked down upon her asleep in the back of the wagon.

"Congratulations, Mr. Pike. I'm glad all went well."

Martin reached into the back of the wagon, inserting his arms beneath his wife, who moved slightly but did not wake up entirely. She placed her arms about his neck and leaned into his chest.

"I'll help you, Mr. Baker," Andrew offered.

"Not necessary. Thank you, though. I can manage."

"I'll be on my way, then, Mr. Baker. Thank you, again."

The young man jumped back into his wagon and made a noise so that the horse moved, and the wagon lumbered back down the road. Martin carried his wife up the steps. She was so light, even with the added weight of pregnancy. She was too light, too frail, too pale. Martin could feel her bones beneath her clothing. He could feel her breathing. He felt crackles and wheezes and heard a strange rubbing sound with every breath she took. He took her into their bedroom and laid her gently onto the bed. She did not open her eyes. He began to remove her blood-stained clothes. She weakly participated but did not open her eyes or say anything as he slipped her nightgown over her head. He covered her with the blanket and took off his own clothes to lay next to her. She moved close to him.

"Martin," she whispered. "She's gonna turn me in."

Martin smoothed back her hair from her face. He was trying his best to remain stoic. He didn't want to think about this.

"Maybe," he said softly, holding her close. "Maybe not."

Hattie could hear his voice crack. She felt his hot tears drop onto her skin. He continued to hold her, his face next to hers. She knew he was fighting back his tears, choking on his emotions. He rubbed her hair.

"Martin," she whispered. "Sing to me."

In his broken voice, he began to sing. It was a slow, melancholy tune he rarely sang, but he could sing it so well. His voice was soft. Hattie imagined that was what Jesus' voice sounded like when he raised the little girl from the dead, so tender that your heart could almost break in two. Hattie could feel herself falling asleep, and what a divine way to go, listening to Jesus sing.

6

Mamie was not invited to spend the night at the Pikes. While Jessica and Andrew may have been more grateful, old Mrs. Pike was not. She had no faith in Mamie's abilities, but Mamie felt she had done her best. She needed help, and Mrs. Baker, thankfully, was there to give it. Mamie would know more next time – if there was a next time. If Dr. Tucker found out about Hattie's involve-ment, he would not be happy with either of them. He could fire Mamie and order the sheriff to take Hattie to the sanitorium. She rode her mule through the night air, enlightened by the brightness of the moon. It was not real-ly that terribly late, but the sun set behind these hills in mid-afternoon, making it a dark ride home. But the mule was cautious, stepping carefully along the pathway. Mamie kept her head down to watch for stumbling stones, tree roots, or anything live crossing their path. The journey was une-ventful, however, and she soon found herself back at Dr. Tucker's office. She was unloading the mule when she heard someone speak from the doorway of the barn.

"So," came a warm voice from the doorway. "How were your patients today?" Mamie turned and saw Dr. Tucker standing alone. The moon cast a soft light upon his white shirt. He moved closer and took the bridle from the mule's mouth.

"Good," she managed to answer.

Dr. Tucker hung the bridle and filled the feed bag. He nodded and smiled. "That's good news. An-ything interesting happen?"

Mamie pulled the mule into its stall, fastening the door behind the beast as she exited the enclosed area.

"Yes." She was hesitating. She knew she was required to tell him all that happened that day, but how to tell him was the question.

"And?" he queried, laughing slightly.

Mamie stood straight, looking him squarely in the eye. "Jessica Pike had her baby today."

"Wonderful," he answered, looking slightly surprised by this simple response.

"She had a boy. They named him Armond, after his grandfather."

The doctor nodded. "Everything went all right? Isn't she the woman with blood pressure issues?"

"Yes," Mamie responded quickly.

"Well," he continued. "Then congratulations are due for her and you. For her, as she has a new child, and you for delivering the child alone. Well done, Mamie."

He walked towards her and hugged her. Mamie was taken off-guard. She stood still, not respond-ing, her arms straight down at her side. He pulled away and smiled.

"Hattie Baker had to help me." Mamie was not sure why she said this. It was as if someone else spoke out. She could feel the sweat begin to break out on her skin despite the cool, evening breeze.

The doctor looked at her in amazement. "Why was she there?"

Mamie took a breath. "Jessica's husband went and got her."

"Because?" he continued.

"Jessica was struggling, and the cord was wrapped around the child's neck."

Mamie expected the doctor to explode. She knew she was fired. She knew her license would be revoked. She could envision her mother's disappointment, her father's anger, her own failure. But he said nothing. He just stood there, looking at her.

"So, you did not request her to be there? The family went and got her?"

Mamie nodded.

He continued, "And what happened when Mrs. Baker arrived?"

"She was able to determine that the cord was wrapped around the child's neck and instructed me on how to release it."

"I see," he answered quietly. "Both mother and child are well?"

"Yes, they are both well."

Mamie was biting her lip. Dr. Tucker stood very still. He remained very close to her. His facial ex-pressions gave no clue to his emotions. She could not determine if he was angry, disappointed, or unconcerned, but she knew this was not over.

After a few moments, Dr. Tucker took a deep breath. "Well, I'm glad she was able to help you. It appears all is well."

Mamie nodded, still waiting for the other shoe to fall.

He reached out and held her hand. She was not sure what any of this meant. She was confused but in a good way. She had expected him to be livid, but he was kind, almost understanding. He looked into her eyes. His face held a soft expression, one she could not understand but liked. They were alone in a dark building, sounds of crickets and tree frogs heard from outside. It was wonder-ful but unsettling at the same time.

"We should both probably be going home. It's getting late, and we have another day tomorrow. I will see you in the morning, Mamie. Sleep well."

He turned away, walking out of the barn and up the pathway that led to his house. Mamie stood quietly, not sure what to make of all this. She was unsure how the doctor perceived her actions this day. She doubted if anything she said gained his favor. She watched him walk alone into his house. A small, white light could be seen through one of the windows. Mamie could see his dark figure pass before it. It looked sad from this distance, alone and pacing. Maybe that was the real Dr. Tucker. The man she spoke with in the barn was the image he wanted people to see, but the real man was that dark figure moving in front of the light. Despite this, she felt something for him; perhaps it was pity. But she could not help but think that with the right incentive and someone who genuinely cared for him, the man in the barn could become the real man and that man walking in the darkness could just walk away.

Mamie went to the barn the next morning to pack up her things and head out for the day. She was still unsure about the fallout from yesterday, but she wasn't fired, not yet anyway.

"Hey there," came a man's voice from the doorway. Mamie turned and saw the sheriff standing there. He had on his black trousers and a white short-sleeved shirt with a glistening badge that read "Sheriff" across the front. He walked in, looking around.

"I'm Sheriff Barlow. Dr. Tucker ain't here yet?"

"I'm right here, Sheriff," the doctor said as he entered the barn. He smiled, shaking the sheriff's hand, making small talk about the weather and how they needed rain. Mamie stood silently, hold-ing the bridle for the mule.

"Nurse Mamie," the doctor began after laughing at some old joke the sheriff told. "Sheriff Barlow is going to go with you today."

Mamie was surprised and disappointed all at the same time. She knew what this was about but asked anyway.

"Why?"

The doctor hesitated slightly, and the sheriff interrupted.

"I understand there's a woman up in those hills that has TB, and she won't come down. So, I'm goin' with you today to git her. Dr. Tucker said her husband actually threatened to shoot you if you came back."

"He did no such thing!" Mamie shouted back.

The sheriff took a step closer to her and pointed his finger at her as if to accuse her of some crime. "Did that man say if you came back up there, you better bring your gun 'cause he would be bringin' his?"

Before she knew what she said, she spoke up. "Yes, but—"

The sheriff did not let her finish. "There ya have it, then. Threatenin' to shoot the public health nurse. That's a bad thing."

The doctor shook his head.

Mamie tried to correct her statement. "He didn't say he'd shoot me, he said he'd shoot you—"

The sheriff threw up his hands. "Even worse! Threatenin' to shoot an officer of the law. Well, now, I better make sure I got ammunition before we head up there." The sheriff turned and went to his car.

"Dr. Tucker," Mamie began with a whimpering sound to her voice. "That information was confi-dential, and you had no right to call the law."

Dr. Tucker walked close to her, putting his arm around her. It reminded her of how her father would put his arm around her when he was going to tell her something she would not like but about which she would have no choice. She knew she was not going to like this conversation.

"It was not confidential. I was concerned for your safety, Mamie." He looked directly at her, closer than he'd ever been to her. "This is getting out of hand, and I'm worried that something bad may happen to you. Besides, Mrs. Baker needs help. Maybe she would like to get help, but her husband won't let her. What if she's neglected by her husband? We need to get her to treatment as soon as we can, and I don't want you in the middle of this if it goes south."

Mamie didn't know what to think. The doctor did bring up angles to this problem that she had not considered. Hattie did not act as if she was neglected, but how could she? Her husband did seem to be volatile, threatening, and possibly dangerous. Maybe getting her away from him would be the best thing.

"Does she have to go the sanitorium? Is there not some other place she can go to convalesce?"

"Of course, Mamie. We can work on that together if you like. In fact, when you and the sheriff pick her up today, bring her here to the office, and we'll see if there is any place else she can go." He brushed her face with the back of his hand.

She nodded, confused but hopeful. She was not at all sure about any of this, but she wanted des-perately to believe him.

"C'mon, then, Nurse Mamie, let's git this over with!" the sheriff shouted, driving his car near the barn.

Mamie got into the passenger side and sat quietly. The sheriff, on the other hand, spoke incessant-ly. He spoke of how he came from humble beginnings and now was the sheriff of the county. On and on.

Mamie nodded occasionally, smiled, and said "yes" when appropriate, but otherwise, she did not hear anything the man said. Her mind was on the drama that was about to unfold. She had done nothing wrong but felt like Brutus betraying Caesar.

7

Martin got up early the next morning. He let Hattie sleep. Jack was moving around in the kitchen, using his crutch and one good leg, fixing breakfast for all of them. He'd become more agile with that walking stick and was able to hobble from place to place, though not long distances. Clemson and Eulalie sat at the table. "After we eat, I'm going to Mr. Godfrey's for a bit. I won't be gone long, but I'm leavin' Jack in charge. Let your momma sleep as long as she can." "What's at Mr. McCary's, Daddy?" Jack asked as he jumped from the stove to the table with fried eggs. "Oh, just a few things I gotta take care of." He ate the eggs and downed the coffee. "I milked and fed this morning, Jack, so if you'll just watch these two, I'll be back soon." Jack nodded. "Don't worry, Daddy. We'll go outside so they can play. Momma can sleep." Martin kissed them all on the heads and placed his hat on. What he had to do was the worst thing he could think of. After what Hattie told him last night, that the nurse would turn her in, he knew it would just be a matter of time before someone came to get her. He had to make arrangements for his children. He shook his head hard, trying not to let his emotions show. He had to be strong through this. Today, that was what was required.

"Mrs. McCrary," he said as he entered the front of the store. He removed his hat. "Is there some place we could talk?"

"Of course, Martin. Come on in. Let's go back here to the kitchen. Mr. McCrary's just finishin' up his tea. Would you like some?"

Martin shook his head. Mr. McCrary said good morning and motioned for his visitor to have a chair. Martin sat down. Both Mr. and Mrs. McCrary could tell that he was struggling with some-thing.

"I'm here to ask you both a favor," Martin began, his voice breaking. Somehow, this seemed easier in his mind, but when he actually was forced to say the words, he was unable to control his emo-tions.

"Take your time, Martin. Anything you need, you know you can count on us," Mrs. McCrary said as she patted his hand.

Martin tried to compose himself. "As you know, Hattie is ailin', and I'm not sure what that public health nurse is gonna do."

"Blasted government agencies. Why cain't they just leave us alone? Do they need to meddle in eve-rythin' a body does?" Mr. McCrary began shaking his head.

"Now, Mr. McCrary, let Martin finish."

"Well, I'm afraid it's just a matter of time before someone comes to git her. While she's away, would you be able to let Jack stay here with you?"

Mrs. McCrary folded her hands in front of her, her face full of joy. "Oh, Martin. That would be the answer to our prayers. Mr. McCrary and I love that boy. We love all your children, but Jack has a special place in our hearts.

Martin nodded. He was glad they were so agreeable, but a part of him felt like he was giving his son away. He felt cheap and dirty. "It's just 'til I can git things under control, not forever."

Mrs. McCrary composed herself. "Of course not, Martin, but we would be honored to help you take care of the boy."

"We would, Martin – glad indeed," Mr. McCrary answered.

Martin stood to leave, placing his hat on his head.

"Thank you," he said as he left the room.

He walked slower going home. His heart was so heavy. He felt as if he were being crushed by the weight of the world. He wanted to go off into the woods and break down. He had pushed this all to the side for so long, avoiding facing what was bound to happen. Now, though, he needed a quiet place. A place he could hang his head and weep – weep for the life they would never have, weep for the unborn child that would not see the light of day, weep for the uncertain life his other chil-dren would now face. He raised his face to the sun and took a deep breath. There was no quiet place just yet. He was needed back at his house. There was more work to be done.

From a distance, Martin could hear loud voices coming from his home. There was a man's voice and Jack's voice. Voices raised in anger. He started running up the hill. As he reached the top, he saw Jack standing on the porch with the shotgun leveled at a man. Clemson and 'Lalie were stand-ing behind him, crying and screaming. He could see tears running down Jack's face. The boy tried to wipe them quickly away without losing his aim with the gun.

"Jack!" Martin shouted as he ran up to the cabin.

"Daddy!" the boy shouted back, his voice nearly a scream.

Martin ran up the steps and grabbed the gun away as all three of his children held onto his legs, crying.

"What's goin' on here?" Martin asked as Jack wiped his eyes.

"That man..." Jack began with broken words. "...says he has orders to take Momma away. I said I'd shoot him before he came in here."

For the first time, Martin looked upon the man. He wore black pants and a white short-sleeved shirt. He had a badge that said "Sheriff." The man held his arms up. In his hands, though, was a shotgun. Upon seeing Martin now holding his gun, the sheriff pointed his gun at the family on the porch.

There were a few tense moments until Mamie opened the passenger side car door.

"Wait!" she shouted. "This is not what we came here to do. There does not need to be bloodshed."

Neither the sheriff nor Martin moved their guns.

"No," came a soft voice from inside the cabin. "There don't need to be any fussing 'bout this."

Hattie opened the screen door and stepped out onto the porch. Martin lowered his gun and put his arm around her.

"What are you doin'?" he asked, his eyes begging her not to leave.

She smiled faintly and knelt to face her children. "Momma's got to go away for a while. I'm ailin', and these folks are gonna take me to a place that'll make me better."

"D-d-don't g-g-go. M-m-momma," Clemson's little pitiful voice said as he hugged his mother's neck. "D-d-don't l-l-leave us, p-p-please."

She hugged him, fighting back her own tears. "I won't be gone long. I need you to practice your letters and singin' 'cause when I git back, I want you to read to me from the Bible and sing me a pretty song. Will you do that fer me?"

She wiped away his tears. He nodded.

"And 'Lalie, I need you to be a big girl while Momma's away. Say your prayers every night and mind your Daddy. Remember how we fed the chickies and sang songs on the porch?"

"You come back, Momma?" the little girl asked.

Hattie nodded. "I will always be with you, no matter where you are. Momma will be there."

Jack stood tall, trying to be a man, but he was overwhelmed by losing his mother. Hattie stood up and hugged him. The young man buried his face in her neck.

"Don't go, Momma. I won't let 'em take you." She could feel his shoulders shaking as his young heart broke.

Hattie kissed his head. "There ain't no choice, Jack. I gotta go with 'em. Don't you fret, though. As soon as I'm well, I'll be back. It's just gonna take some time is all." She hugged him again.

She held Martin's hand. She swallowed hard. Her voice was trembling.

"I know I don't have to ask you to take care of these babies 'cause I know you will. You are the best man I ever knowed, Martin Baker, and I'm proud to be your wife." She reached up and kissed him on the cheek.

"Oh, Hattie," he began with a soft voice.

She placed her finger across his lips and shook her head. "There ain't nothin' you can say that you ain't showed me already. I was blessed when I married you. Now go on and do what you have to do, and I'll do what I have to do, and it'll all be fine."

She hugged him and turned to go down the steps. Mamie came close to help her.

"No, thanks, Mamie. I believe I can manage without you."

Hattie walked to the sheriff's car and opened the back door. She sat down in the back seat, somber and stoic. Her children stood on the porch of that cabin crying, wiping away tears of sorrow. She did not look at their little faces. She did not want to remember them this way. She wanted to re-member them running, laughing, singing. She closed her eyes.

Mamie got into the front seat, and the sheriff got behind the wheel. He started the car and put it in gear. As he began to drive away, a cloud of dust followed them. He could see the two littlest chil-dren running after the car, trying desperately to catch their mother. They were crying and waving their hands, but they were soon left behind in the dust. Everyone inside the car was silent for a long while.

The car ride to the sanitorium was a long one. It was hot outside. The sheriff and Mamie rolled down their car windows, causing a loud breeze to blow throughout the car. Hattie could feel her hair blowing around about her head. The sound of the wind was deafening. She was becoming tired and lay down in the back seat. The humming of the tires on the road was lulling, and she went to sleep.

Mamie turned to see the passenger in the rear seat. She saw Hattie lying quietly. Her face was so pale, thin, almost a death mask. Mamie was not pleased with how this transfer took place today. It was cruel to Hattie and even more cruel to her family. When she saw Jack emerge from that cabin, a little boy pushed to the brink by other peoples' rules, she wanted to scream. She wanted to take Hattie and all her family away, some place safe, some place where no one would find them. But that is not the way things were done, at least from the view of the public health department.

"You passed our turnoff, Sheriff," Mamie said, pointing to the road now getting smaller in the rearview mirror.

"No, ma'am. I got orders to take this lady to the TB sanitorium."

"No, sir," she snapped back. "Dr. Tucker told me before we left this morning that we could bring Hattie to his office. That he and I would work together to find her a place to convalesce."

The sheriff looked at the woman in disbelief. "No, ma'am,' he said again, pulling some crumpled paperwork from his shirt pocket. "The orders are for the sanitorium."

Mamie unfolded the papers, reading and scanning quickly. The sheriff was correct. All the neces-sary signatures were there. There was no question and no contingency; the orders were for the san-itorium, and only the sanitorium.

She folded the papers again and handed them to the sheriff. He placed them back into his pocket.

"Sorry, ma'am, if there was some confusion, but you know the law. She needs to be put away so she don't infect others."

"And so they can heal her," Mamie said softly.

"If you say so, ma'am."

Mamie looked out the open window. The road was narrow, one lane, with a towering bluff on one side and a deep ravine on the other. There was no way to pull off except for the few gas stations along the way. They stopped to fill up, but Hattie remained asleep in the back. Mamie got out once to stretch her legs. This was so far away from where they were from. There would be no way Mar-tin and his children could come up here to see her. Their horse and wagon would not make this long trip in a day. They would have to catch a ride or hire a driver. She got back into the car and leaned her head back. This had all gone so terribly, terribly wrong.

"Pop, ma'am?"

Mamie opened her eyes and saw the sheriff holding a cold bottle of an orange soft drink.

"Thank you," she said as she took the bottle. It was cold, and it tasted good on this hot ride.

The sheriff got back into the car, started it, and took a long swig of his own bottle. "It's better this way, Miss Mamie," he said as he pulled out of the gas station and back onto the road.

"I'm sorry?" she asked.

He nodded towards the back seat. "I know that taking her to the sanitorium seems like a wicked thing to do from your viewpoint."

Mamie said nothing but drank her soft drink.

"Come now, ma'am. I can see the disappointment in your face. You think all of this is unneces-sary, that she should've been left to live at her home, with her children and husband. You think the doctor is a monster and I'm a paid assassin."

"I would not go that far," she answered.

"I would," he responded. "But I'll give you somethin' to think about. In my line of work, I see all sorts of people, and I cain't tell you how many folks I've pulled out of their houses, dead or dyin'. Nobody knows what goes on in there, how that person suffered, how their families suffered. I'd rather take a person like we are today where they still stand a chance. I grant ya their chances might be slim, but they have a chance. Truly, Miss Mamie, what chance did she have at her house? Were her children and husband to stand by and watch her slowly die in front of their eyes? Is that a memory you wish fer them to have?"

Mamie turned on him. "And what memory did we leave them with today? All those children will remember is that a man in a shiny car with a shiny badge took their mother, and they never saw her again. Does that make you feel better?"

The sheriff said nothing. He drove on through the mountains. Mamie could look down upon the valleys, trees, streams, and little hovels beneath. She and the sheriff were superior to them, above their menial lives and cares. Too high up to care about what happened down there. What a blessing it was to be one of the privileged, where TB and other diseases did not taint your house.

Hattie was awakened by strangers' hands pulling her out of the back of the car. She was hot. Sweat soaked through her clothes, and her hair stuck to her skin. She opened her eyes but was un-able to comprehend her surroundings. There were people there, mostly men dressed in white uni-forms. They said nothing to her, but she could hear them talking to Mamie. She could not under-stand what Mamie was saying. It didn't matter anyway. She closed her eyes again. She could feel her body being lifted from the car and onto a hard surface. She was raised, and then there was a sudden jolt. The sunlight hit her in the face then vanished. She opened her eyes once more to see the last place she would live or die. She saw the stone walls and felt a strange familiarity. She knew these stones. They came from the quarries near her home. The timbers that held up the tall, stark walls came from the woods near her house. The stones and lumber were like her – pulled up, torn away, and moved away from their home.

The men in the white uniforms lifted her over the steps leading into the main hall. It smelled of rubbing alcohol, camphor, and blood. Once inside, the men moved her from the hard surface to a small bed. They covered her with a light blanket and left the room without saying a word. She lay in a cold room. She figured it must be dimly lit for it seemed very dark behind her closed eyelids. She wondered if she was alone or if there were more diseased people here. She heard no one breathing or coughing, but maybe they were dead. Maybe this was the morgue.

"Miss Hattie," came a familiar voice. "Miss Hattie, it's Mamie. I just wanted to make sure you were comfortable."

Hattie did not open her eyes or respond.

Comfortable is an odd term, she thought.

"Good afternoon," came another voice, though lower and more masculine. "I'm one of the doctors here. And this is…"

There was a slight pause, and Hattie could hear the rustling of papers.

"Baker," she heard Mamie say. " Hattie Baker. I'm Nurse Mamie Starkweather with the Health Department."

"Oh, yes," she heard him reply. "Looks like the TB bug has a firm grip on this one."

Hattie wasn't sure what "firm grip" implied. It wasn't a term she used with people who she saw and treated. She wondered if all that medical school taught him what a "firm grip" looked like by just glancing at your patient lying in a bed.

"First," the doctor continued. "We need to get you cleaned up and in a hospital gown. Then, we'll do an x-ray of your lungs. Ever had an x-ray, Mrs. Baker?"

Hattie did not respond.

"Well, it's an amazing device. Created around 1895 by Wilhelm Roentgen, it actually uses cathode rays to take pictures of the inside of your body. It was first used mostly for broken bones but can also be used to see the lungs. Now, normal lungs show up mostly transparent, but diseased lungs, such as yours, will probably appear with a great deal of blackened areas. These are the areas that no longer function appropriately for the exchange of oxygen, but it may also appear as streaks throughout the lungs indicating…"

The doctor continued his lecture on x-rays, but Hattie heard very little of it and gradually heard none of it. She found if she lay very still in this cool room, she did not cough as much. She could conserve energy by not wasting time on medical lectures.

"Doctor," Mamie said after the lecture. "Her family was wondering if they could visit her while she is here. She has a husband and three small children." Mamie's voice became softer. "And another on the way."

Hattie felt the blanket that covered her being pulled away.

"Hmm," she could hear the doctor murmur. "Sad."

The blanket was replaced. "Sunday is the day families are allowed to visit, but they cannot come in. The patients must be well enough to go outside with them. If we let all the families into the facility, then what would be use of quarantining all the patients? They could all just go home."

Hattie heard him laugh, apparently greatly amused at himself.

"May I call the facility then and ask how she is doing before her family comes here? They live pret-ty far away, and it would be such a waste for them to come up here only to find she was unable to go outside." Hattie could hear Mamie's voice pressing the matter.

"Yes, yes of course," the doctor responded. "Now, Nurse Starkweather, I believe your job here is done. Our staff will take over from here." Hattie could hear their footsteps. "I'm sure you have a lot of people you need to see."

"I thought, perhaps, I could stay with her a bit until she's settled."

"Not necessary," the doctor continued. "Our staff does this admission work throughout the day. They have it down to an assembly-line method, and they'll have her buttoned up in no time. Be-sides, I think the sheriff is ready to leave."

There was silence. Hattie did not open her eyes. She could not see that Mamie looked out the win-dow to see the sheriff packing his mouth with tobacco, spitting on the ground, and pacing around the car. Mamie felt useless and neglectful. She hoped to ease Hattie into this transition, but once here, others took over, allowing no intervention and very little compassion.

Mamie walked to the side of Hattie's bed. "Miss Hattie," she said as she pulled up the blanket closer to the patient's neck. "I have to leave now, but I'll go by your house and check on your fam-ily. I'll call at your house every couple of days. I won't let them go alone. I'll try to get them here on Sundays when you are able to visit you."

"Oh, no," the doctor said. "She won't be ready for visitors for quite some time. She is quite ill."

Mamie looked at him in disbelief. Of course she was quite ill; that's why she was here. That was why everyone was here.

"But you will try to cure her," she said more as a fact than a question. Her voice was harsh, indicat-ing her frustration with this whole ordeal.

"We will do what we can do, but she's very ill and I doubt if there is much that can be done for her at this stage."

Mamie stood in disbelief. She wanted to cry. She wanted to pick up this poor creature who lay on the little bed and take her home with her.

"Six weeks," the doctor stated. "If she survives, she might be able to have visitors in six weeks."

Mamie was silent, allowing the weight of his words to envelop her like a great, wet blanket. The doctor motioned her towards the facility nurse who now stood at the door. Mamie remained ce-mented to the floor for a moment, looking down upon Hattie. It was the first time she realized that there was not much difference in their ages. Hattie looked much older. Her life had been much harder. Mamie pulled Hattie's hand out from beneath the blanket. She saw the wedding ring on her finger.

"Take that off, nurse," the doctor called across the room. "They can't have any jewelry or personal effects while here."

Mamie looked at it. The ring came off easily due to the loss of weight of the woman, but Mamie could still see the permanent indentation in Hattie's finger, like a tattoo. The imprint remained.

"I'll give your ring to Martin to hold for you, until you come home again," Mamie whispered in Hattie's ear.

She walked to the door. Hattie did not open her eyes or say anything.

It was as if she were already dead. She lay there so still. Mamie could tell that this memory of Hattie would haunt her for a very long time.

"Good Lord, Miss Mamie," the sheriff began as Mamie exited the building. "I thought you were never gonna come out of there. I would've come in to get you, but I don't know about them dis-eases. Why, them tricky disease pieces. What are they, germs? Bacteria? They might jump off one of them patients and get onto me. That's possible, ain't it, Miss Mamie? Pieces can jump from one person to 'nother?"

Mamie got into the car with no expression on her face.

The sheriff got into the driver's side and started the car, moving it quickly away from the sanitori-um.

"Droplets," Mamie said after a few moments.

"Pardon, ma'am?" the sheriff replied.

"Tuberculosis, also known as consumption, is carried by droplets. It takes prolonged exposure from an infected person. One must be exposed to the secretions of their body."

The sheriff made a sickening face. "Sounds revoltin'."

Mamie continued as if she had not heard him. "...such as sputum or nasal secretions. It takes re-peated exposure such as would occur when many people live together or when a caregiver is tend-ing a diseased person over and over."

Mamie returned to the question she asked herself from the beginning. Where could Hattie have come into contact with this disease? There must have been someone else who had it. Perhaps it was dormant in the other person where they were not showing symptoms. She thought the files in Dr. Tucker's office should have a list of anyone who was treated for TB or even had the symptoms. Mamie remembered learning in nursing school about patients who spread the disease quickly and exposed multiple people without their knowledge. The original victim, however, may live for years with the disease, having no clue that they killed countless people they met.

While the sheriff talked incessantly on the drive back home, Mamie was trying to think of any-where Hattie would have gone that she had not. They basically saw the same patients. None of them had any symptoms of the disease. Hattie never left her area, so there was no chance that she got it from traveling. It would have to have been someone traveling into their area.

"Sheriff," she said, interrupting his long-winded diatribe of politics. "Have you brought many peo-ple to this sanitorium recently?"

He thought a moment. "A few."

"Who were they?"

"I don't rightly recollect. They weren't none of them from here. Most of them were railway tramps. You know, passin' through and got sick while here. One in particular was a full-fledged rogue, deserved everythin' he had comin' to him."

"Do you know their names?"

"No, ma'am. I don't remember any of them. They were all men, though. Like I said, mostly found near the railroad, tramps, vagabonds."

Mamie nodded. It still didn't make sense. Hattie's home was not near the railroad. She would need prolonged exposure, too, to contract the disease. She would need to see Dr. Tucker's files. There was someone out there who caused this terrible situation in Hattie Baker's life, and Mamie wanted to find that person.

"I'll take you to the doctor's office, Miss Mamie," the sheriff said, interrupting Mamie's deep thoughts.

The ride back seemed to go much quicker than the ride to the sanitorium. She thought a moment.

"Sheriff, if you wouldn't mind, could you drop me off at the Bakers' house? I want to give her family an update on things."

The sheriff looked surprised. "Well, I don't mind, Miss Mamie, but this car is for official business only. If I take you up there, I'm not sure it's really sheriff business."

She smiled her most innocent smile. "Of course, Sheriff, I understand your need to always follow the rule of the law, but helping a poor family at a time like this would surely be an act of mercy, one the community would certainly learn about and think very highly of you for it."

He looked at her, not sure if he should believe her or not. He took a breath. "Very well, Miss Ma-mie, but make sure the story stresses my great concern and sympathy for the family."

"Of course," she answered as she smiled.

The sheriff made the turn onto the dirt road that wound back up into the hills, the one lane road with ruts and loose gravel. The mule handled the road without a problem, but the car had to be ma-neuvered through the terrain like a serpent. The sheriff struggled to turn left, then right, then left again in rapid succession to avoid bottoming out in the ditches or falling off into the ravines. By the time they arrived at the Bakers' house, the sheriff was drenched with sweat. He pulled out his ker-chief from his pocket and wiped his face.

"There you go, Miss Mamie. Will you be able to walk back alone?"

Mamie exited the car. "Yes, thank you," she said. "I've traveled these roads alone before. I will be fine."

She walked away as the sheriff turned the car around and began the descent down the hill. He was not looking forward to this. It was the same treacherous road going back as it was coming up.

Jack was sitting on the porch while Clemson and Eulalie played in the yard with a simple, wooden stick. Martin sat on the steps, whittling the stub of a pine branch. He looked up as Mamie came closer but went back to whittling his stick. None of them spoke to her.

"I am so sorry, Mr. Baker," she began as she came near.

Jack simply looked at her. The other two children stopped playing and stood very still, saying nothing. Martin continued whittling his stick.

She knelt before Martin as he whittled. "I am so sorry, Mr. Baker. I can't help but feel this is my fault, but I want you to know that I had no choice."

Martin looked up slightly. His eyes were dark, angry.

"What will you do, Mr. Baker? Who will help you?" she asked, feeling empty inside – helpless and guilty.

"What business is that a' yours?" Martin said in a low voice.

"I want to help you. I promised Hattie I would help you."

Martin put down his knife and stick. "I believe you have helped us enough, ma'am. Now, if you will please leave, I need to fix supper for my children."

"Perhaps I could help you." Mamie was desperate. Anything she could do might help heal her guilty conscience.

Martin stood and began to walk up the steps into the cabin. Jack used his crutch to maneuver him-self closer to the door, and the two smaller children ran up the steps to be close to their father.

"No, thank you. I do not need your help. We never did." He turned and went into the house with his children following him, leaving Mamie standing alone in the yard.

"The hospital is clean, and there are kind people there who will take good care of Hattie. I will look in on her every chance I get. I will make sure you are kept updated on her recovery. Here, I brought back her ring!" she shouted from her place on the dirt so they could hear her in the cabin through the screen door.

There was no reply.

"Do you hear me?" she shouted louder, feeling tears beginning to well in eyes. Her voice was breaking under the emotion and the strain. "She will recover. I will bring her back to you. So help me God, I will not let anything happen to your family."

She began to feel the tears creasing down her face. They were hot tears, full of anger and frustra-tion. And there was this terrible sadness, as if she lost someone dear to her. She took a breath and wiped the tears from her eyes. She wasn't sure if she said those words so Martin would hear her or so God would listen. She placed Hattie's little golden wedding band on the bottom step and turned around, making her way down the road, back to the doctor's office. It was dirty, dusty, hot, and dry. She felt she deserved no less.

By the time Mamie returned to town, it was late. She walked to the doctor's house. A small light remained on in the office. Mamie knocked softly at the front door. Dr. Tucker soon opened it and invited her in.

"I'm glad you made it back safely, Mamie. The sheriff came by and told me he dropped you off at the Bakers' house. How did it go today?"

Mamie knew her facial expressions would give her away. It had been hellish. She looked him in the eyes. "This has been the worse day of my life."

He nodded. "I understand."

She wanted to shout at him. Did he? Did he really understand? Had he seen the nameless faces ly-ing in those beds, sitting in those chairs? How many families were torn apart in the name of public safety? How many people did he send to that facility? How many people died there?

"We like to think we can help alleviate some of the pain and suffering in the world, but many times we are simply the bearers of terrible news.

Medicine cannot cure all, and we are left with only the knowledge that we did all we could, although it is never enough."

Mamie stood very still. He seemed genuinely affected by the events that transpired this day. She did not know what to think of him. Again, was he pretending to be this kind, gentle physician with the dark eyes and graying hair, or was he that man who walked in the darkness, concealing his true self?

"It's late, Mamie," he said at last. "You should be getting home."

"Yes," she responded quietly.

She turned to go, but he called after her. "Oh, Mamie, I would like to discuss something with you tomorrow before you leave."

Mamie was suddenly unnerved. If she had not been so tired, she may have been frightened, but, currently, she was too distraught to feel much of anything.

"Of course, Dr. Tucker. I'll stop by your office first thing."

He smiled at her. "I think what I want to ask you may be very promising."

The unnerved feeling gave way to many emotions: fear, hope, foreboding, excitement. She nodded and went on her way towards the boarding house.

For the first time today, Mamie realized it was Wednesday. Mrs. Stuckmeyer would have made roasted pork with mashed potatoes and gravy for supper, lots of gravy. The landlady said a good gravy can cover a multitude of sins. Mamie wasn't sure about the rest of the food, but the gravy was good, and she was correct – with enough gravy, a person could swallow anything.

"Well," the landlady said as Mamie dragged herself through the front door. "Another late night, I see. You know, it's not safe for a young lady to be out on her own. These are desperate times, and that can lead to desperate acts."

"Yes," Mamie quickly responded. "These are truly desperate times."

The older woman continued as Mamie made her way up the steps, "You must be starvin', dear."

"Not really, Mrs. Stuckmeyer."

Mamie truly had no appetite at all. In fact, she felt somewhat sick to her stomach and just wanted to lie down. She wanted to sleep, to forget everything that happened this day. She wanted to rise up in the morning, refreshed and clean, knowing that today never happened. It was all a bad dream.

"Well, at least let me fix you a cup of tea and a few crackers. You keep this up, and you'll be as thin as that doctor's sister. She didn't eat anything when she was here, either."

The woman turned to go into the kitchen. Mamie heard what she said but did not comprehend it until she was almost up the steps. She stopped and made her way back down the steps.

Mrs. Stuckmeyer came out of the kitchen with a tray, holding a cup of tea and few water crackers. "Oh, my dear, I was going to bring this up to you."

"Thank you, but I think maybe I'll sit down here with you."

"Oh, that would be wonderful. Let me get another cup of tea."

Mamie sat at the dining room table and pulled the cup in front of her. Mrs. Stuckmeyer had an amazing memory when it came to her renters. She could remember their names, their shirt sizes, and how much they ate. Mamie remembered the doctor saying he had dealings with the boarding house, but he did not elaborate.

Mrs. Stuckmeyer came back into the dining room bearing a second cup of tea and a few more wa-ter crackers. "I like to end my day with a nice cup of tea. It seems to settle me down for a good night's sleep. Don't you think so?"

Mamie nodded as she stirred her tea. "So, Mrs. Stuckmeyer, you said Dr. Tucker's sister rented a room from you?"

The woman nodded as she sipped her tea and munched her crackers. "Hmm," she said as she swal-lowed her mouth full of crackers. "Some time ago."

"You mean it was his sister, Flora, correct? He has no other sisters?"

"It was Flora. That girl never ate anythin', just tea and crackers. She became rake thin. Why, I thought there was something wrong with her, but the doctor never came to see her, so I guess she just didn't like my cookin', probably too rich for her blood."

The woman laughed and ate another cracker.

Mamie smiled and sipped her tea. "How long did she stay here?"

"Not long, 'bout a month or two." The woman leaned in towards

Mamie. "I heard gossip that there had been a disagreement between the doctor and her. I don't know anything 'bout that, though. The girl never said more 'an three words. She never confided in me at all."

"Did she have any friends with whom she may have confided?" Mamie prodded as she took an-other cracker.

"Not that I know of. That family kinda kept to themselves. Their father moved here years ago, mar-ried some woman from up north, and started his practice. I don't know where he was from. No-body 'round here ever heard of him. He said he was from Hot Springs, but nobody ever said they knew him. Why the sudden interest, Miss Mamie?"

Mamie took a deep breath. "No particular reason, Mrs. Stuckmeyer. Dr. Tucker just told me that he had some dealings with your boarding house, but he didn't say it was in reference to his sister."

"Probably ashamed that his sister was renting a room from an old widder woman when she had a beautiful room of her own in their house."

Mamie smiled and nodded. "That could be true, especially if they had a falling out. I wonder what they were at odds over."

Mrs. Stuckmeyer shrugged her shoulders. "Rich folks are odd and keep many secrets."

Mamie chuckled. "Yes, they do."

8

Mrs. Baker," came a lady's voice. "We need to get you cleaned up." Hattie did not move. She hadn't moved since the sheriff and Mamie left her alone in this cold room. She did not open her eyes. She was not coughing as long as she lay very still. She could feel the woman removing her clothing. Normally, Hattie would be too shy and prudish to allow another person to undress her. She didn't even undress in front of her husband. Usually, the idea of nakedness in public view would have caused her to recoil, to attempt at least to cover herself. Now, though, she was beyond caring. Everything she loved had been taken from her: her children, her husband, her home. She found it difficult to believe that there could be any more degradation she could suffer. She was empty inside. "I'll keep you covered as best I can while I wash you," the lady continued. "Once you are clean, then we will wash your hair." Hattie felt the warm cloth on her skin. Her arms were lifted. She was rolled gently from side to side as the lady spoke softly, trying to comfort the patient. Hattie still did not open her eyes.

She was dead in her spirit. She remembered when someone she took care of died, she would wash the corpse just like this. It seemed fitting since she viewed herself no more than a corpse at this point. After the lady placed a loose-fitting gown on Hattie, she stood back.

"There now, Mrs. Baker," the lady stated when she finished her task. "We're going to take you to the x-ray room. Have you ever had an x-ray?"

Hattie still made no response.

The woman continued, "No matter. It is not painful at all, not invasive. You just stand there, and the x-ray takes a picture of your lungs and bones." The woman's voice was soft. "I know this is very difficult for you, and please believe me when I say we only want to help you. We want to make you as comfortable as possible."

The woman tucked the blanket in around Hattie's body. She smoothed it across the top so there were no wrinkles.

"This blanket will keep you warm." She patted the small, protruding abdomen of her patient. "And this little one, too."

The woman stood beside the bed for a moment. "I understand you were a self-trained midwife where you came from. You can understand, then, that we can only do so much. Ninety percent of a patient's outcome depends on the will of the patient. Without the patient's fight for survival, our work is useless."

Hattie did not open her eyes. Her voice was barely above a whisper. "Then what do you do with those who lost their will?"

The woman smoothed back Hattie's wet hair. "Give us a chance, Mrs. Baker. If anyone can help you get better, it is us. Please let us try."

Hattie nodded slightly as two men came into the room. Each grabbed the corners of the sheet Hattie lie upon and, with one quick move, transferred her from the cot onto a gurney. It was a bit jolting but painless, and Hattie could feel herself being wheeled away. She heard the sound of large, metal doors opening and closing. She heard people talking. She smelled rubbing alcohol, camphor, and bleach. There were noxious odors she could not identify, but she could identify the unmistakable odor of blood.

She was moved from one cold room to another cold room. This room was darker, though. From behind closed eyelids, she could tell there was no window in this room. She heard a man clear his voice.

"Mrs. Baker, we're going to x-ray your lungs and the bones in your chest. It's not painful, but we do need to move you from this gurney into the x-ray booth. You must stand with your torso exposed, but this doesn't take long, so you will only be there for a short time." The man's voice paused. "Gentlemen," she heard him say.

With that, she felt the jolt of the sheet again as she was maneuvered to the edge of the gurney, her gown lowered from her shoulders, leaving her upper body naked. Two arms lifted her and pushed her into a small closet. She was feeling faint and unsure if she could stand.

"Take a deep breath, Mrs. Baker," she heard the doctor say. She did her best, but the coughing began, and she could feel herself sliding down inside this space.

Someone came to her and lifted her back up into the closet. "You must stand for a moment, Mrs. Baker," the voice said.

Hattie could not see who was talking to her. There were large, black dots in her field of vision, but a leather belt was fastened around her waist with the other end attached to the wall behind her in an effort to help her stand.

"Take a breath," the voice said again.

She tried, leaning forward and holding onto the far wall of this booth. This position was uncomfortable, and she knew she could not hold it. Her breathing was compromised in this position, and she would begin to cough in a few moments. She took the breath, as deep as she could, but it was painful. There was that burning sensation deep inside, tearing, ripping, and she knew she would begin to cough.

"Done," the man said.

She exhaled and released the beast within her. The coughing began – slowly at first, but after a few token hacks, the real beast came out. She took a breath, and it felt like all the air in her entire body was forced out, bringing with it any blood, tissue, phlegm, or anything else from her lungs. She could hardly breathe again before the next spasm of coughing took over, just as violent as the first.

The men in the white uniforms released the belt and pulled the arms of the gown up over her shoulders. They removed her from the x-ray machine and laid her back onto the gurney. She turned to her side, coughing up blood onto the blankets and floor. There was a feeling of a thousand razors released within her chest, slicing away lungs and tissue at will. The nurse held a cloth to her mouth as the blood began to collect. She struggled to draw in a breath against the pressure of her chest forcing out the air and the blood.

"Calm yourself, Mrs. Baker," the nurse said in a soft voice. "Try to relax. Your lungs are in spasm. You need to slow down your breathing. Purse your lips like this..."

Hattie could barely see the nurse through the black dots in front of her, but she tried to emulate what she thought the nurse was doing. She could not tell if it was helping for the short, shallow gasps of air were all she could do.

"Mrs. Baker, we're going to give you something to relieve the pain and calm you."

The doctor pulled out a silver metal contraption and a glass bottle from a cabinet nearby. She could make out letters on the side of the bottle: "MS04." The doctor turned the bottle upside down and inserted what looked like a long, metal needle into the bottle. He drew back the plunger section of the mechanism, and she could make out the liquid in the bottle oozing into the cannister. He then withdrew the needle from the bottle, and, in one quick motion, moved the blanket from Hattie's side and sunk the needle deep into her hip. Hattie felt the pain and flinched, but soon the pain subsided, and the burning in her lungs began to ease. The urge to cough gradually lessened, like the tide of the ocean retreating from the beach. Her body became calm, almost numb. The muscles of her arms would not respond, and they seemed to have a will of their own. She was sure her legs were gone for there was no feeling in them at all. While it was a disquieting sensation, it was also wonderful: no pain, no coughing, no fear, no memories. She imagined this was what death felt like.

9

D r. Tucker straightened his vest as he donned his white lab coat. He was an educated man. Alt-hough his parents led a rather rough life at times, he and his sister were taught to be gentle people. While he loved medicine, he had been given no choice in the matter. His father was a doctor, so he would be a doctor. He would inherit the house and the family business and carry on the family's good name. He did sympathize with his patients, probably more than anyone knew. They had such terrible dis-eases. It was hard for him to fathom how in this day of science and knowledge, people were still suffering from Rickets, TB, trench foot, or leprosy. In these times when economics and politics were so uncertain and poverty was causing riots, homeless camps, and starvation, the scourge of disease was unforgiving. Science was making such great advances with sulfa, penicillin, and insu-lin – all medications to cure and prolong life, but there were still so many ailments that needed in-terventions. He had seen firsthand how the ravages of disease could take a healthy, young body and turn it into a walking skeleton, too weak to walk or care for itself. Other diseases would force many people to decide if they should eat or breathe. Cruel and heartless, no respecter of persons, rich and poor, old and young. It did not matter. They were all susceptible, and, with some of the diseases, the diseased would be taken away, forcefully if necessary, to a place far away. They would die among strangers. They would never recover. They would never come home. But it was the law, and he had to follow the law, if he could.

"Pardon me, sir," Celeste knocked gently on the doctor's office door, opening it slightly.

"Yes," he responded, jolted back from his morbid thoughts. "Come in."

"Miss Flora is again not well, sir. She asked if you would come upstairs when you have a mo-ment."

The doctor finished buttoning his coat. "Tell her I'll be up shortly."

Celeste nodded and closed the door behind her. He listened to the woman's footsteps as she climbed the stairs. He remembered a time when he and his sister would run up those stairs, chasing each other with playful exuberance. She loved to play tag. He was always "it," and she would run away screaming in delight. That was a long time ago. Her screaming now was of a different kind.

The doctor left his office and went to his sister's room. He knocked softly on the door. He knew she was ill. She'd been ill since she returned from her escapade over a year ago, but he was doing all he could for her. He was putting his license and reputation on the line for her, a reputation he'd worked his whole life to uphold.

"Yes," came a hoarse, raspy voice from the other side of the door.

The doctor opened the door and entered the room. His sister lay flat in her bed, covered to her chin with a thick blanket. Her skin was pale and tissue-thin. The doctor could see the vessels on her forehead and neck. It was an uncomfortable appearance. He'd seen it a lot, but not on his sister.

"Flora," he said as he approached her. "You look terribly unwell this morning. What is the prob-lem?"

Flora opened her eyes slightly, her raspy voice betraying her. "I'm not well today, brother. I'm sor-ry. I don't think I can help you in your office."

He smoothed her hair away from her eyes. "You feel feverish."

"But I am so cold," she answered, shivering beneath her layers of blankets.

He nodded. "I will get your medicine, and I'll ask Nurse Mamie if she can help out in the office until you are well."

"Of course you will," Flora responded with a snide look. "I'm sure she will be most eager to assist you."

Dr. Tucker stood up straight, looking down upon his sister. She closed her eyes. He could hear her breathing, rough and irregular. He wanted to say something cruel back to her. That had been his way since she returned. He knew he had been unkind to her, but he was so angry. Everything he and their parents built was put at risk with her antics.

That man, he thought to himself. That terrible, stupid man. Why did I hire him? The repairs on the house could wait, but he was a drifter and needed a job, so I saw the opportunity. But I got my revenge. That man will never bother us again, and Flora need never know.

Although he knew the disappearance of her young lover broke her heart, it was better this way. After what the man had done to her, she would be better off here, especially now. The doctor knew he'd bent some rules, but it was for his sister, so the rules would have to be bent, just a little.

"I'll get you some water to take with your medicine. Then you can rest."

His sister did not respond. She turned her head to the side.

"Celeste," the doctor shouted as he came down the stairs. The woman appeared quickly at the foot of the stairs. "Please let me know when Nurse Mamie arrives. I would like to speak to her in my office."

"Yes, sir," Celeste responded as the doctor walked past her and into his office.

He closed the door behind him and walked across the room to a glass medicine cabinet from which he pulled an amber bottle and a small clear bottle with golden-colored powder. He withdrew a shiny silver hypodermic from the drawer, drew up the clear liquid, and inserted it into the powder. He shook it vigorously, then refilled the syringe with the new, liquified powder. Removing a sec-ond syringe from the drawer, he drew up a thick liquid from the amber bottle. He'd performed this routine so many times in the past few months, it was becoming routine. He'd given his sister other bottles of medicine. Some were for curing; others, for killing. Placing both loaded syringes in his hand, he proceeded up the steps to his sister's room.

"Flora," he said as he knocked again on his sister's bedroom door. "I have your medicine."

"Please," came the raspy voice again from the other side.

He entered as she removed one cachectic, white arm from beneath the blankets. He held her fore-arm and inserted one syringe after the other. Her body relaxed.

"Thank you," she whispered as she floated off to oblivion.

Dr. Tucker stood there for a few moments, watching her. He devoted his life to medicine, and this is where it led him. He placed her arm beneath the blanket.

His voice was quiet, remorseful. "Sleep now," he said, and then left the room.

"Excuse me, Dr. Tucker," came a voice from down the stairs. "Nurse Mamie is here."

He was pulled away from his thoughts. "Thank you, Celeste. I'll be right down."

He heard Celeste's voice saying something, but he could not understand anything she said. He then heard another woman's voice and assumed it was Mamie's. He took a deep breath. Everything was beginning to come unraveled. He wasn't sure what to do, but he would keep this up for as long as he could. Maybe it would work out. Maybe something would happen that meant everything could be managed. He put on his smile, smoothed down his jacket, and pretended all was well.

"Nurse Mamie," he said, smiling and doing his best to hide the syringes in his hand. "I'm glad you are here. I have something I need to ask you."

Mamie nodded, said her greeting, and following the doctor into his office. The doctor motioned for her to take a seat in front of his large, wooden desk. He sat on the edge of the monstrous piece of furniture and folded his arms in front of him.

"I have a favor to ask of you, Miss Mamie. I find myself in need of an office nurse. As you know, my sister Flora has been assisting me for some time, but she has fallen ill…" His voice trailed off, and his eyes looked out the window at some distant object unseen to Mamie.

"I am sorry to hear that, Dr. Tucker. I hope she will be well soon." Mamie was not sure where this was going but was not surprised that Flora was ill. In fact, Mamie wondered how she was able to help in Dr. Tucker's office prior to this. The woman looked so gaunt and pale, unhealthy at the least.

The doctor regained his composure and focused again on the conversation at hand. "Yes," he be-gan. "I'm sure she will be well in a few weeks, but, in the meantime, I was wondering if you would be able to assist me in the office?"

Mamie remained silent for a few moments. This was a surprise. Her first thought was for the pa-tients she tended in their homes. She was concerned about who would tend them, especially now with Hattie Baker so ill in the TB sanitorium.

But, she thought to herself, this is an excellent opportunity.

To work next to Dr. Tucker where she could learn so much. This was especially important to a new nurse such as herself. She would have access to the newest and latest medical innovations. She could ask the doctor questions. She could learn so much from him.

"What would happen to the patients I'm presently visiting in their homes?" she asked for a few moments.

"You could still visit them, just not as often. You could help me the mornings, as that is when I am the busiest. I try to schedule my appointments during that time and reserve the afternoons for emergencies and town meetings."

She could feel her heart lighten. This was such an amazing opportunity, as if a great gift had been dropped into her lap. She could barely believe her good fortune, especially after having such a mis-erable week so far. Perhaps Dr. Tucker was not the scoundrel others thought. This could be her chance to bridge the gap between Dr. Tucker's modern medicine and the archaic methods many patients were still practicing. Everyone could win if she could accept this opportunity. She might even be able to discover if anyone nearby had TB and find out where Hattie was exposed. That person should surely be taken to the sanitorium.

She was embarrassed to admit it to herself, but the thought of spending every morning with Dr. Tucker was very appealing to her. She wanted to do the right thing, but she also wanted to spend time with him. She was both excited and fearful, but she smiled and nodded.

"Wonderful," the doctor answered as he arose from his perch on the side of the desk. He was smil-ing broadly as he grabbed her by both shoulders and tightened his grip. "I am so grateful to you, Mamie. I just don't know how I can thank you enough. This means so much to me."

He stood there for a few moments. Mamie looking intently into his eyes as he held her with his hands.

"When shall I begin?" she said softly, breaking the awkward silence.

"Today, if that is all right. My patients will begin to arrive around nine, and I will need assistance. Could you help me this morning?"

She smiled and nodded.

He released her. "You are truly a wonder, Mamie." He turned and picked up some papers from his desk. "Here is a list of the patients that have made appointments, but, of course, there are always others who just walk in. We will try to squeeze them in between the appointments. Can you man-age that?"

"Yes," she answered, really not quite sure if she could or not, but she would give it her best effort.

"I knew I picked the right girl the first time I saw you. I said to myself, 'there is the nurse for me,' and I believe I was right."

Mamie could feel herself begin to blush. She was not prepared for the emotional effect his words had on her. She fumbled with the papers, pretending to read the names and times.

"Now," he continued, turning away and apparently paying no attention to Mamie's disposition. "If you will assist the patients into my office. You can do the blood pressure, temperature readings, and heart rate. Then document that on the patient's chart, and then I'll come in as soon as I can to examine the patient. Flora usually stays with me while I examine the patient. In that way, she can follow up, making sure the patient gets their medications and has an appointment for a return visit if needed."

"Yes, Doctor," Mamie answered as she left the office and went into the foyer.

There was a small desk in the anteroom where she sat. Hard, wooden chairs lined the wall where the patients sat, waiting their turn. Everyone sat very close together, coughing, sneezing, moaning. They were a sorry sight. Pale, unhealthy, in need of (what appeared to be) extensive medical care. Mamie found herself taking care of the same sort of people she tended in the mountains. One thing was sure: Illness was a great equalizer. Even with more money and more resources, disease would take the victim to the edge of the river. Some would survive, but in the end, all would cross that river.

"Where's Miss Flora?" an elderly gentleman asked as Mamie tried to roll up his long-sleeved flan-nel shirt to affix the rubberized blood pressure cuff on his arm.

"I'm afraid she's under the weather today, sir. My name is Mamie Starkweather."

The man continued, smelling of pipe tobacco. "And are you a real nurse?"

Mamie stood up straight, frustrated by her lack of ability to get this cuff beneath the flannel shirt.

"Yes, sir, I am a real nurse. I graduated top in my nursing class. Dr. Tucker hired me to work as a field nurse for the Health Department. I usually visit the patients he has in the hills."

"And do you take their blood pressure, Miss Mamie?"

Mamie looked disgusted, holding the blood pressure cuff in her hands.

"Then let me show you how to do it." The man took the cuff from Mamie, wrapped it around his arm over the shirt, and began to compress the bulb that filled the cuff with air.

"Now, if you'll git that hearin' thing over there on our desk, I think we're ready."

Mamie did as she was told and listened to the man's heartbeat on the inside of his elbow, listening carefully for the first beat and the last.

When all the air had been released slowly from the cuff, the man asked, "So, what is it?"

"130/70."

"Is that good?"

Mamie tried to force a smile. "Yes, it is excellent for a man..." Her voice trailed off.

"...of my age," the man finished.

"No disrespect, sir, but yes."

The man laughed. "How old do you think I am?"

"Well, without looking at your records, I really couldn't say."

"Oh, c'mon, young lady, You know you have an idea. Tell me, how old do you think I am?"

"Sir, I really have no idea."

The man leaned towards her. "I'll tell Dr. Tucker you didn't know how to take a blood pressure if'n you don't guess my age."

Mamie knew this was not a good scenario. There was no way to win, so she would have to make the best of it.

"57," she said at last.

The man threw his head back and laughed out loud, showing darkened teeth and a tobacco-stained tongue.

"Lilly," he said to another woman sitting in the foyer. "This here lady thinks I'm 57. Why, honey, I got underwear older 'an that."

The waiting rom burst into laughter. Mamie smiled, trying not to be embarrassed or angry. The man had played her, and he knew it.

"I'm sorry, Miss Mamie. I'm an old man, much older 'an 57, and I gotta laugh when I can. Most of my people are dead, and if I cain't have a little fun now an' again, then I might as well be dead, too. I hope there's no hard feelins."

The other patients in the foyer nodded and mumbled their agreement. Mamie looked upon him with more sympathy. He was right. No harm done, and she knew how difficult it could be to gain a pa-tient's trust. She smiled and nodded.

"No hard feelings, sir, and now that you've helped me with your blood pressure, I think Dr. Tuck-er is ready to see you." She assisted the man out of the chair and helped him into the doctor's of-fice.

"Mr. Skaggs," the doctor said, arising from behind his desk and shaking the patient's hand.

"Please, come in and sit down. How may I help you today, sir?"

Mamie gave the doctor the patient's updated information. She stood very still behind the patient as the doctor listened to the man's heart and lungs, tapped his knee, and looked at his hands, eyes, and mouth, and into his ears.

"You look pretty good for an 80-year-old man," the doctor said.

The patient turned and grinned at Mamie. She smiled in return.

"Is there something funny in that statement, Mr. Skaggs? You are 80 years old, are you not?"

The man nodded, "Sometimes, though, I still feel about 57."

"Well, good," the doctor continued. "Then what brings you in today?"

"It's my heart, Doctor." The man became very serious. "Sometimes, it feels like a great stone is lying upon my chest. I get real short-winded and dizzy. I have to stop whatever I'm doin' and sit down, and, after that, I'm so weak and feel like I might vomit." The man looked at the doctor with questioning eyes. "What's the matter with me, Doc? Is there anythin' you can do to fix this?"

Dr. Tucker listened again at the man's chest. He listened for a long time, moving the diaphragm of the stethoscope over multiple areas of the man's chest. He flipped the stethoscope over and, using the bell portion of the instrument, listened carefully to the man's carotid vessels in his neck. After a bit, Dr. Tucker stood up straight and shook his head.

"Mr. Skaggs, you have a definite murmur in your heart."

The old man looked confused. "And is that a bad thing?"

The doctor went behind his desk and sat down in the chair. "I'm afraid at your age, there is not much that can be done. Your pressure is good, and the heart rate is regular, but that murmur could indicate some trouble with the valves in your heart as well as some blocked arteries. That could lead to some chest pressure and shortness of breath, especially when you exert yourself."

The man looked discouraged. "Is there anythin' you can do to fix it?"

The doctor shook his head. "No, I'm afraid not. I can give you a prescription for some medicine that might help with the pain. Take one of the pills every time you feel an attack oncoming. You probably need to carry these pills with you at all times. Don't take more than one an hour, though, because they could cause your heart to stop altogether and lower your blood pressure to unsustain-able levels. Take these pills for a couple of months and come to see if they don't help."

The man sat very still. The shock of this unexpected news could be seen on his face. "What do you mean, 'unsustainable levels'?"

The doctor was writing the prescription. He did not look up at the patient. "Inconsistent with life." The doctor looked up when he handed the man the prescription, "They can kill you."

Mamie placed her arm around the man. "These pills work very quickly, Mr. Skaggs, and many people live for years using them. Using them as the doctor prescribed will keep you safe and man-age that fast heart rate. I'll put you on my list of patients to visit when I make my home visits. So, I'll be up to see you this week. Does that sound all right?"

The man held the prescription in his hand. He looked pitifully across his shoulder into Mamie's eyes and patted her hand on his shoulder. She felt such empathy for him. Only a few minutes be-fore, he had been laughing and teasing her about his age, and within just a few minutes, his life was stripped from him. He left the office, his head low, walking slowly. Mamie watched him leave, feeling helpless.

"Don't loiter, Miss Mamie. Bring in the next patient."

The doctor did not look up from his paperwork.

"Yes, sir," she answered quietly and went to retrieve the next person.

Dr. Tucker's practice was hectic in the morning. There were a few walk-in patients, mostly cough-ing and sore throats. A few prescriptions, but mostly, chronic illnesses. Mamie noticed, though, that not one person had any symptoms suggesting lung disease, specifically TB.

"So, Miss Mamie," the doctor said as he came out of his office and into the foyer. "The morning session is over. There are no further appointments until later today, so we may have lunch now, if you would like."

"Lunch?" she asked, a very new concept for her.

"Yes, Flora and I usually take our lunch together in the dining room. Celeste prepares a light meal for us, and afterward, I must attend a meeting at the bank. I am on the board of directors, and their meeting is this afternoon. So, after we eat, I will go to the meeting." He buttoned his cuffs and re-moved the white lab coat he wore in his office.

"Of course," Mamie answered, still a bit bewildered. "Will your sister be joining you?"

"No, she is too ill, but I would ask you to join me, if you can?"

"Oh, thank you, but I am not properly dressed…"

"Nonsense."

The doctor put his arm around her and ushered her into the dining room, where two place settings were arranged on the large dining table.

"See? Celeste has prepared everything."

He pulled a chair out for Mamie. She sat down, still feeling a bit uncomfortable but wanting des-perately to participate. No man had ever shown her such attention. Although she was an attractive young woman, there were always other things that hindered her from seeking companionship, edu-cation, money, and opportunity. Somehow, this seemed liked destiny. All the pieces were falling into place, and all she had to do was walk through.

"Tea, ma'am?" Celeste asked as she held a small, white porcelain teapot at Mamie's side.

"Yes, please," she responded, moving slightly so the woman could pour the hot tea.

"Sugar or cream, ma'am?"

"Neither; I'm not British."

"Ma'am?" Celeste asked, puzzled by this odd comment.

Mamie smiled and pulled her teacup in front of her. "Nothing, Celeste. I was just remembering a conversation I had with one of my patients."

"In the hills, ma'am?" Celeste continued as she positioned a plate in front of Mamie.

The plate held small sandwiches with the crust removed from the bread. Pickles and celery cut into fancy shapes lined the edges of the plate.

"Yes, a storekeeper and his wife. Lovely people, from Ireland. They still have the accent."

Her mind wandered slightly, remembering the conversation she had with Mrs. McCrary not so long ago. But it had been a long time ago, like dog years, a lifetime since she'd met Hattie Baker and her son when the razorback attacked him and tore up his leg. She remembered the little boy's face when he told her his dog was killed and his face when she took his mother away. She saw how he tried to fight back the tears, his heart breaking, but with such defiance in his eyes. He would not break. He would fight until there was nothing left of him.

"Miss Mamie, shall I say grace?" The doctor's voice startled Mamie slightly.

"Yes, please."

He reached out his hand, smiling at her. She placed her hand on top of his. This was unusual for her. Usually, people just folded their hands during the prayer offered at mealtime, but he held her hand. His voice was low and soothing.

"Dear Lord," he began. "Thank you for this bounty. May it nourish our bodies to do Thy will. We pray humbly that you would help those in need, heal the sick, comfort the dying. Thank you, dear Lord, for allowing this fellowship with Mamie and me. May you bless us and help us in our work, as well as our time together. In Jesus' name. Amen."

He squeezed Mamie's hand. "Amen," she repeated quietly.

"So," Dr. Tucker began as he placed the white, cloth napkin on his lap. He picked up one of the small, delicate sandwiches. "How did you like your first day with me?"

Mamie found herself repeatedly confused by Dr. Tucker. She was not sure if his words were in-sinuating more than their simple definitions or if she was reading more into the words than he meant. In fact, she was so unfamiliar with a man and woman's conversation, she was not sure where she stood with the man.

"Busy," she replied after a few, awkward moments. "I was unaware how many patients you saw in the morning.

"Yes," he replied, continuing to eat his lunch and drink his tea. "There are many sick people in this area. I could use an assistant. Flora is helpful, but she is not a trained nurse, such as yourself."

Again, Mamie was not sure what Dr. Tucker meant. Did he mean he wanted her to be his assistant, and just in his office, or was he just talking out loud? He said no more, but finished his meal and wiped his mouth with his napkin.

"When you are finished, Mamie, would you want to accompany me to the board meeting at the bank?"

Mamie swallowed her last bite and looked at the doctor in amazement.

"Me, sir? You want me to accompany you to the bank's board meeting?"

He smiled and nodded, offering his hand to help her out of the chair. "Yes, I thought you might like to meet some of the heads of the community. A bright, young lady as yourself has a promising future in this town. It is time the community met you."

She smiled and stood beside him. "But, Dr. Tucker, I am not dressed appropriately."

"Nonsense; you look wonderful. You shall show the other men in this town that a professional woman can not only do a good day's work – she can manage affairs appropriately, also."

"Yes, sir," she replied. "I'll get my cape."

The doctor waited at the door while she buttoned her long, black cape at her chin and followed him out the door. She stopped momentarily to adjust her nurse's hat and turned to see the house behind them. In the upper window, she could see a thin, ragged frame. Flora was watching them from her room.

10

Hattie lay quietly in her bed. There were other women in this room. They were coughing at various stages of their illnesses. Nurses dressed in white dresses with aprons and crisp, starched hats cared for the patients. The nurses' voices were low but commanding. Pills, liquids, tinctures, powders, creams, salves, and all sorts of medicines were used to lessen the suffering, but none of them cured the disease. "Mrs. Baker," her nurse said gently. "We need to get you up. Normally, we prescribe strict bedrest, but the doctor said your chest x-ray shows a great deal of infiltration, so it is necessary for you to sit upright several hours a day. Besides, I believe movement is good for the body, the mind, and the soul." Hattie did not respond and did not open her eyes. She wasn't sure how long she had been here. The last thing she remembered was that hypodermic injection. Wonderful thing. Oblivion in a syringe. Wonderful thing. "...and so another nurse will assist me in helping you get into this wheelchair." Hattie could feel her body being rolled to the side. Her torso was lifted so as she was placed into a sitting position. Her head hung down. She felt limp all over as the two nurses stood her up onto her feet. She did not bear any weight at all. She was dead weight, staggering between the two women, but the wheelchair was positioned nearby, and she felt her body placed into the chair.

"Mrs. Baker," the nurse continued. "We can only do so much." Her voice became very close, and Hattie knew the nurse's face must be very near her own. "You must take an active part in your care, or your time here will be useless. We cannot cure you unless you want to be cured."

Hattie made no response. Her eyes remained closed as she felt herself moving in this chair. She felt the air brushing past her face and her hair blowing slightly. She heard other voices and the sounds of the wheels of the chair rolling over the tile floors. She had no idea to where she was being taken, and it really didn't matter. She heard the big steel doors open, a slight bump, and then cool air on her face. Even though her eyes were closed, she could see the brightness of the sun through her closed eyelids.

The nurse secured the breaks on the wheelchair.

"I'm going to let you sit out here in the sunshine and fresh air for a while. We will do this every day. I'll go get you some soup and bread. After you eat, I have some medicine for you."

Hattie made no indication she heard the nurse's comments. She sat motionless in her chair, her head leaning to one side. It was as if her head were too heavy for the rest of her body to manage. Her chest was tight, constricting her breathing as if she were being hugged by a bear. But her mind was loose, as if there were no limits to where it could end. Clouded in fog, swimming in memories and dreams, it was difficult to distinguish between what was real and unreal, and she wasn't sure she even wanted to.

"Mrs. Baker," she heard the nurse continue. "You have more to think about than yourself. You have that child within you."

Hattie, for the first time in how many days, opened her eyes. She looked out upon a garden, large hardwood trees, and blue hazy mountains in the background. It reminded her of her home. When she would lay in Martin's arms and look out the window of her bedroom, she could see hills and vegetation while he stroked her hair and spoke gently of his dreams and ambitions, the new crops he would plant, the cattle he would raise, the repairs on the barn and the house, and the fine dresses he would buy her.

Hattie opened her mouth to speak, but the nurse was gone.

"They will win if you let them," she a heard a man's voice say. She closed her eyes again.

"They mean well," the voice continued. "But they are really ineffective. There is currently no cure for what we have, so we've been sequestered here out of the way and out of sight."

She heard him cough. It was deep and wet. The same sound as hers and the other people who were dying in this solarium.

"...but they mean well. If you cooperate, they will feed you well. Not that you can eat it because you must breathe, but what you can consume is good, and there is plenty of it."

She heard him try to breathe. It was harsh with audible crackles.

He cleared his voice. The sound of freshly churned-up phlegm could be heard rumbling in the back of his throat.

"It is better if you try, though. Without your participation, they may try other means, and, in your condition, those other means could be detrimental to your little visitor."

Unconsciously, Hattie smiled a very small smile. It had been a very long time since anyone used the term "little visitor." She found it amusing.

"See there," the voice continued. "I made you smile, so there is hope for you."

Hattie opened her eyes and turned her head to see a young man lying on a cot several feet from her. He was turned onto his side, leaning on his arm. He had long, black, curly hair that hung in his face. He made no effort to move it.

She shrugged her shoulders.

The man continued as he tried to straighten himself on the cot. "They use new drugs not yet approved, all experimental, some sort of chemicals and radiation, like the x-rays. It burns your skin after a while." He moved the blanket that covered him, revealing the skin on his chest. It was dark, leather-like, damaged to the point that it no longer looked like skin.

Hattie did not turn away. "They should put something on that to keep it from festerin'."

The man covered himself again. "So, you can speak."

"Yes," she replied, turning her gaze back towards the hills.

"When is it due?" the man asked.

"I'm not sure," she responded.

She heard the man moving in his cot, but she continued to look straight ahead as he spoke. "You don't look like you're at term. Is it a small child?"

Hattie took a breath. "It is a dead child."

If she had any more tears to shed, she would have shed them now, but she was empty inside. She could feel the sun and wind go through her as if she was no longer present, like a vapor or floating haze of smoke.

"Are you sure?" the man asked.

Hattie nodded slowly, closing her eyes unconsciously. She realized that so much of her time was spent in the dark, either outside her body or inside.

He continued, "How do you know?"

In that voice she had acquired that came somewhere between sadness and hopelessness, she managed to say, "It hasn't moved for a while."

"Is that a definite sign of fetal demise?"

She heard him cough. There was a time she would have had sympathy on the man. He looked terribly ill, and his cough sounded like hers: a death rattle.

She opened her eyes again and turned to face him. His eyes were a brilliant blue but soft. They seemed kind but mischievous. She believed that before he was ravaged by this disease, he must have been a fine-looking man.

"I'm not sure what 'fetal demise" means..." she began. "...but if it means the child is dead, then, yes, although it is not a certainty, it is not a good sign."

Her looked her in the eyes. "And does that not upset you?"

"It did at first," she began. "But I came to terms with it when I was dragged from my home and family and forced to stay here."

"You have other children?"

"Yes."

"How many?"

"Three. I have two boys and a girl."

"That sounds nice." He repositioned himself on his little cot. "Aren't you going to ask me about my family?"

Hattie was becoming very tired. "I don't care," she said softly.

"Good," he continued. "Then my sad story of heartache and woe won't affect you. I loathe sentimental women who cry and get so emotional at pitiful stories."

Hattie made no response, but sat quietly in her chair, allowing the sun to warm her paper-thin skin.

"I have no one," he began. "My parents died when I was very young. I would like to say they died from some tragic ending like motorcars or bootlegging or something romantic, but it was not. My father suffered a heart stroke, and my mother died from complications of diabetes mellitus." He paused. "Sugar diabetes, you know, where the pancreas cannot keep up with the demand for insulin?"

Hattie made no response.

"And that left me an orphan at a very young age. So, my maiden aunt took me in and raised me."

"That was kind of her," Hattie finally responded.

"Yes, I suppose so. I'm sure it didn't hurt, though, that my parents left me money. She was set for life as long as I was around. Of course, there was nothing left for me." He began coughing, softly at first and then more violently. He wiped his mouth and chin with the kerchief he carried.

"Damn blood," his voice was raspy and wet. "Don't we eventually just run out of the stuff?" He looked up to see her watching him. "Does this offend you?"

"No," she answered. "Why would it?"

"Most women don't tolerate this disease very well. They recoil at the sight of others gagging on and regurgitating their own secretions."

"I've seen worse." Hattie turned her head away and closed her eyes again.

He continued wiping his mouth, chin, and hands. "This is the worst part of this awful disease, all this blood. It stains everything it touches: your clothes, your skin, your teeth. And it leaves a stain that can never be removed."

"It is your body's way of purging itself," she answered calmly.

He looked up at her and smiled. "Then I suppose that accounts for the large amount of blood I expel because I surely am in need of much purging."

"Mrs. Baker," came the familiar voice of the nurse as she rounded the corner of the doorway and made her way down the aisle of patients, who all sat silently, save for the coughing and wheezing.

The nurse pushed a wheeled cart that made a rumbling noise on the wooden floor. It reminded Hattie of the sound the gurney made when they brought her here. It was not a welcomed sound.

"I brought you some soup and tea," the nurse continued as she brought the cart next to Hattie.

She took Hattie's hand and attempted to place the teacup into it, but Hattie's hand was limp and nearly dropped the cup. The nurse quickly recovered the tea and placed the cup back onto the cart.

Hattie did not open her eyes. "I want nothin'."

The nurse's voice was harsher now. "Most patients must eat in the dining room with the other ladies, but since you are so frail, I thought it best if you ate out here in the sunshine. So, will you eat it yourself or must I feed you?"

Hattie opened her eyes to see the nurse picking up the bowl of soup and the spoon. The nurse offered the bowl to her. Hattie looked at it for a moment, then, for the first time since she was brought to this place, she looked up at the nurse. The nurse was a tall woman with striking red hair, cut short to frame her face. She had pale blue eyes and freckles. Hattie took the bowl with her remaining hand.

"My little boy has red hair," she said softly.

She raised both of her hands to hold onto the bowl. She lowered it to her lap and grasped the spoon.

"People with red hair are called gingers in the old country. They are supposed to be fiery and hard-headed but very smart."

Hattie nodded, her head lowered as she tried to get the spoon of soup into her mouth. She sipped from the spoon slowly. It was warm and did seem to soothe her throat. She could feel the warmth travel down her throat and into stomach, just as she had when Mrs. McCrary fed the broth to her back home. She felt that overwhelming loss and sadness covering her again. If she had any strength, she would cry, but her body had forsaken her. It was now almost a foreign object with a mind of its own. It coughed when it needed, it ached when it wanted, and it left her stranded alone at its leisure.

"There is bread and warm tea here for you, also, Mrs. Baker. The tea is an herbal mixture. It should help with the cough."

The nurse placed the teacup on a small table that sat next to Hattie's wheelchair. "I'll be back soon with your medicine. Please, try to eat as much of the soup as you can, and drink the tea. Nutrition is vital to you at this point."

The nurse looked across to the man. "And you, sir, keep a good distance from the ladies. As soon as a bed becomes available for you, we will be transferring you over to the men's building."

"Do you see me, ma'am?" the man asked as he pulled away his blanket, revealing a skeleton-like body with scars and leather-like skin. "Do you truly believe I could do any damage in the shape I'm in?"

The nurse shook her head. Hattie could hear her ugly, white nurse's shoes stomping away.

"Hayden," the man on the cot said after the nurse had rounded the corner.

Hattie looked at him, still swallowing her soup.

"My name," he continued. "My name is Hayden Smith."

Hattie nodded. He continued to watch her as she placed the soup bowl onto the table and picked up the teacup. She took a small sip, swallowing slowly so the herbal mixture could ease the rawness of her throat.

"Hattie Baker," she replied after a few moments.

"Little ruler of the home," he replied.

"I'm sorry?"

"Your name, Hattie, is short for Harriett, which is the feminine term of Henry. Your name means 'little ruler of the home'."

"Really?" she responded, somewhat surprised at his knowledge and the fact that her name meant something so close to her heart.

The man nodded and sat up on the edge of his cot, facing her. She was able to get a better look at him like this. He was a tall man, whose hair hung carelessly around his face. In another world, he would have looked like Martin, all tousled and in disarray, but handsome in a rough manner. Their eyes, however, were different colors. Martin's eyes were brown, like a warm, winter coat. This man's eyes were clear and blue, like a great, endless sea. A sea that, if a person dove into it, they could drown or swim away. What both men had in common, though, was they had a way of looking at you and looking through you at the same time.

"Yes," he answered. "That is what it means. I have a lot of time on my hands, and I read a lot. One of the things I like to research is the origin of words. Mostly Latin."

Hattie finished sipping her tea. "And your name, Hayden. What does that mean?"

"Hedged valley," he answered, smiling. "Old English, it means hedged valley."

For the first time in uncountable days, Hattie felt herself laugh slightly.

He smiled back at her and continued with his liturgy. "Your last name probably originated with occupations. Names, last names, can be a form of the family's occupation. Take your name, for instance. Your ancestors must have been bakers – or your husband's ancestors. I took it for granted that you are married…" His voice trailed off.

Hattie said nothing for a few moments, leaving him in an awkward position. Finally, she answered. "I am married."

Hayden grinned, revealing a boyish charm from beneath that unruly hair. Hattie liked to hear him speak. He had that soft, slow voice of this region where he elongated his vowels and neglected ending consonants. It reminded her of her own father's voice, slow and deliberate. She found herself listening to him but not really hearing him as he spoke about words, their origins, and his love of Latin.

"It's ironic that I like to study Latin. It is, after all, a dead language. Perhaps that's why I do like it. Who else can appreciate a dead thing more than another dead thing?"

Hattie smiled and nodded. "I agree."

"Well," the nurse said as she approached the two. "It is good to see you smile, Mrs. Baker. Your attitude is the most important component in your health. A positive attitude will do much more for you than any medication we can offer."

The nurse placed several bottles and a silver hypodermic down on the side table. Hattie's smile disappeared when she saw all the medication. The sight of all of it brought her violently back to this moment. She looked down into the empty teacup she still held in her hands. She did not feel guilty. She truly felt nothing. The nurse had simply caught her finding that very small part of her that was not yet gone, the memories of a people who loved her and whom she loved in return. But these memories were simply that – memories, long since past and probably never to be relived.

The nurse handed her the pills and a spoon of some liquid. Hattie didn't ask what the medications were. It didn't really matter, anyway. The nurse then moved the blanket that was wrapped around Hattie's upper body to reveal her arm. The nurse then found a suitable region and inserted that long, delicious needle into the muscle. Hattie could feel its effect almost immediately: relaxation and comfort. Her lungs became quiet, and she could feel herself melting into the chair.

She could hear the nurse's voice but not comprehend the meaning of her words. There was something about going back to her room, but she could not make it out. She could barely feel herself moving, but perhaps not. Perhaps it was just her spirit that was moving away. At any rate, it didn't matter. Oblivion awaited her, and the young man in the cot disappeared.

11

Martin's sister, Sarah, lived just a few miles from his farm, although her cabin was higher up into the hills. No roads existed between Martin's house and Sarah's. One had to walk or ride a mule to get up that hill. In fact, many horses weren't able to make it up that steep embankment to the cabin. The cabin sat back in the woods. She and her family lived barely above the margin of survival. Hattie had always been so good to them. She took food up there, sewed their clothes, offered medical care when they needed it, and never asked for anything in return. She thought of them as family, and family took care of family in Hattie's view. While Sarah may have shared Hattie's view, she married a man that did not. He preferred to sit under a shade tree and drink moonshine from a jug. Although, Martin had to admit, his brother-in-law did make good moonshine. He said he learned it from a man from Tennessee, and Martin thought that man should open up his own still, which he did. Martin never knew what happened to that whiskey-making man from Tennessee, but he was sure he'd done well. With all the favors he and Hattie had done for his sister and her family, Martin now found he was the one in need of favor.

He'd found it nearly impossible to watch his children and farm, especially when some of his ground was so far away from the house. Those fields lay in the valley, prone to flooding but dark, black dirt once the water receded. He tried taking his children with him, but they were too young to stay in one place all day, and he found himself checking on them so often that he could hardly get any field work done. When he didn't check on them, they were scratched up, bitten, and sunburned. So, in an effort to keep everyone safe and so he could make some money, Martin took Jack to Mr. and Mrs. McCrary's and Clemons and Eulalie to his sister's house. Clemson and Eulalie were excited to stay with Aunt Sarah and her children, but Martin was concerned about Ben, Sarah's husband. He could be awful mean-tempered, and the presence of two more young mouths to feed could send him into a fire-eating rage. Martin offered to pay Ben and Sarah if they would keep the two young children just on a temporary basis, until Martin could think of something else to do, or until Hattie was well enough to come home. Sarah refused, but Ben held out his hand. Martin placed five dollars into his brother-in-law's hand.

"And I want all that corn you're growing down in the bottom land," Ben said as he turned and walked away. Martin usually liked Ben and got along with him, but Ben turned surly after prohibition was stopped. His golden goose had been legalized. Martin didn't want to see his sister die in poverty, so he arranged the dance parties where he played to purchase Ben's moonshine. If it hadn't been for Martin's help, he didn't know where Ben would get his money.

"Daddy, daddy!" came the two little voices of his children as he reached the top of the hill.

A crowd of children with ages ranging from young adult to newly walking came running towards him, shouting and laughing. He knelt down close to the ground and held out his arms. His children ran to him, hugging him with every bit of strength they had. They kissed him and tried to talk over him, telling him how much they missed him and asking if Momma was home yet. The other children hugged him, too, making it almost impossible for him to move. Their voices were loud, and they shouted about how good it was to see him. Martin buried his head into his own children's soft hair and kissed them both, picking them both up into his arms as he stood. They were both so light. Eulalie's cheeks were not as pudgy as they were when he left them here weeks ago. Clemson's eyes had dark circles, and Martin noticed his stuttering was worse than before. He carried them both up to his sister's house and entered.

The cabin leaned to the right. The only thing that kept the whole house from falling over was the hill to which it had been built into. The floors slanted, and the doors would not close all the way as the frames were bent from the weight of the crooked house.

"Well, brother," his sister said as he pushed open the screen door. "How good to see you. We was wonderin' if you was ever gonna come back?"

She then turned her attention to the group of children that had entered the house with her brother.

"The rest of you git on out a'here before I put a knot in your tails."

The many children ran out of the cabin, jumping off the porch and scattering into the woods like wild animals.

He cringed under the guilt of her words. It had been several weeks, and although he had good intentions, the time slipped by. His loneliness had made him lose track of time and events. He found he was working himself to death during the day and crying himself to sleep at night. It was a miserable way to live.

"I know, I am sorry. These few weeks have been hard on me, too, but I'll make things up now."

His sister continued, wiping her hands on the dingy white cloth she used to dry dishes. "A few weeks for you, maybe, but an eternity for these youngins and me, who has to tend to everything for everybody day in and day out without a moment's rest. If it ain't one thing, 'tis another. How do you 'spect me to tend to your youngins when I got youngins of my own to tend to?"

Martin knew this was a burden to her. With extra mouths to feed and laundry, it was a lot for his sister, but he bristled under her words, anyway.

"Where's Ben?" Martin asked as he sat down placing his hat on the table.

He sat one child on each knee. Martin knew the answer; it was just a diversion to change the subject. He'd brow-beaten himself enough lately without letting someone else have a turn.

"Huntin'," his sister replied as she brought over a hot cup of coffee.

Martin took a sip, trying to hide his smile. Ben was a terrible shot. He couldn't kill a squirrel or hog if it ran up his shotgun barrel. Martin knew then that Ben must be out at the still. Unfortunately, Ben drank more of his product than he sold.

"We g-g-goin' home now, D-d-d-daddy?" the little boy asked his father as he laid his head down on his father's shoulder.

Sarah brought her coffee to the table where Martin and his children were sitting. She placed her cup of coffee on the table and took a seat directly opposite her brother. "Yes, Martin. Is Hattie better?"

Martin sipped his coffee and shook his head. He rubbed his son's head and kissed him. The child said nothing more. His dark, sad eyes looking up at his father, then laid his head back down upon that shoulder.

Sarah sighed. "Martin, you know I love you and Hattie, and your chil'ren, but times are tough, and I don't know how much longer Ben's gonna let your two stay here with free room and board."

Martin placed his cup of coffee onto the table and looked at his children. "Why don't you two go outside for a minute? I gotta talk to Aunt Sarah."

The children obeyed, slowly and sadly. Eulalie turned to her father just before leaving the house.

"Daddy, you leavin' ag'in?"

Martin smiled slightly. "No, Eulalie, Daddy's not gonna leave you again."

The children went outside to join their multitude of cousins. Martin turned to his sister. "I asked you to take care of my children for a short time while my wife is in the hospital, sick and with child. She might die, Sarah, and the child, too."

Sarah leaned forwards, towards her brother, "She ain't in no hospital, brother. She's in a TB sanitorium, and you know as good as me that chances ain't good she's gonna git better. So those two little 'uns out there are as good as mine and Ben's, and we cain't hardly make it now.

So, what are you gonna do?"

"I gave you five dollars a couple of weeks ago, and Ben made me promise to give him all the corn in the bottom land. That's worth a couple hundred dollars right there."

His sister was unrelenting. "That corn in the bottom ain't puttin' food on the table tonight, so 'less you brought some bags of flour and coffee, you better have some hard cash money on you. Besides, there's rumors goin' 'round that all that land in the bottoms is bein' bought up. So, Ben might not git that corn in the fall."

"Who's buyin' the land?"

"I dunno. Ben's been saying somethin' 'bout the gov'ment's buying a lot of land, but he ain't got no names."

Martin sat very still for a moment. His dear, sweet sister, Sarah, once so kindhearted and caring was turning into a shrew. He knew she was frightened and desperate, but that was still no excuse to turn out two small children when their mother was so ill. He also knew that what she said was true. Hattie's chances were not good. He remembered his wife's face as they took her away. She was so ill. He wondered if she was even still alive now. He'd received no word from her or the sanitorium. The public health nurse, Mamie, hadn't been back to see him since the day she took Hattie away. Her words were just as empty as his sister's. Denial would not solve these problems by avoiding facing their reality, and he wasn't sure he believed his sister regarding the buying up of the land. He drank his coffee.

"I can see your point in all this, sister, but I truly thought you would be more sympathetic to your own family, knowin' us as you do. Hattie helped you so much, and I got sales for Ben's moonshine. I didn't think it was too much to ask for you to watch my children for a few weeks. That would give me time to see how Hattie was doin' and get some plans made, but I can see now that I was wrong."

He placed his coffee cup on to the table with a hard sound. His sister leaned back into her chair, her face a bit pale.

"I went too far, brother. I apologize. I'm just so fearful. Ben's takin' to bein' gone night after night. Sometimes days go by, and he ain't come home. I'm afraid he's either gonna leave me or I'll find him in jail or worse."

Martin had no room in his soul for another person's problems. He was consumed with his own. He wanted to help her, but he had no resources. He also had no energy.

"We all got our problems, ain't we, Sarah?"

She nodded.

"I'll be takin' my children with me."

"What'll ya do?"

He placed his hat on his head. "Whatever I have to."

12

In the TB sanitorium, hours turned into days, and days turned into weeks. Hattie wasn't sure what day it was. She'd received a couple of letters from Martin. They were short and said the children were well. They missed her and knew she would get well, but she knew it was just pretty words written down to ease her mind and not distress her. She did hope her children were cared for. Nurse Mamie said she would check in on Hattie, but she had not returned to the sanitorium since the day the sheriff left her here. How long had it been? Hattie thought she should be disappointed with the nurse, but she wasn't. She was too tired to really care about that. Her coughing seemed to exhaust her, every day more and more. The nurses here told her to lie quietly as they brought in her food and tea. She took her medications without question. She would open her eyes, and it was daytime. She would open them again, and it was night. One day just bled into another. She was having cramping pains in her lower back that circled around to her lower abdomen. These were familiar pains. Currently, the pains would come and go, but eventually, they would become more and more common with harder and harder pressure until the pain would be all-consuming. But, right now, they remained random and weak, but they were enough to keep the nurses from taking her out of her room.

Hattie wasn't anxious to have this child. As long as it was near her, she didn't have to face reality. She could still hope it would be born alive and healthy, but once it was born, she would have to face the facts. As long as it was so close, she could hold it near, rub her hands across the bump, and tell this child how much she loved it, how much she cared, and how sorry she was that it would never see the sunshine, or smell a rose, or see the smile of its father's face, but that wasn't something she wanted to face. As long as the child was within her, she could live in this life of denial.

"Mrs. Baker," came a familiar voice. It was the day-shift nurse. She had tea and toast, the usual meal for Hattie each morning. "I've got your breakfast here, ma'am. Let me help prop you up a bit so you can eat."

The nurse lifted Hattie's torso – light as she'd become, one person could move her about with ease. Pillows were placed beneath the patient's shoulders, neck, and head, so now she lay in a semi-reclining fashion. The tray on the table was placed near her so she could reach it easily.

"Please try to eat and drink this, Mrs. Baker. You need every bit of nourishment you can get."

Hattie opened her eyes slightly. They were tiny slits in her face. Her vision was cloudy and obscured, but she could make out the nurse's frame. Hattie's mouth was dry. Her lips stuck together, and she tried to dampen them, but her tongue was so dry, it could barely moisten her lips.

"I don't think I can eat or drink anythin' this morning. These pains in my back are coming faster and fiercer. I don't think they're gonna let up this time."

The nurse moved the table and placed her hands on Hattie's abdomen. She moved her hands around a bit, just long enough to see Hattie close her eyes and breathe slightly more rapidly. The increased breathing and strain caused a sharp cough, followed by a series of deeper, more productive coughing. The nurse removed some the pillows behind

Hattie so she would be in a more recumbent position. She wiped the blood from Hattie's mouth.

"Yes," the nurse said after a bit. "That was certainly a contraction. I'll get the doctor."

Hattie lay quietly, not knowing which was going to be worse: the pains of childbirth or this wretched coughing. She was unsure how long she lay there. The contractions continued, becoming stronger and faster.

"Well," a man's gruff voice said. "I see you are at your time. Let's take a look."

Hattie opened her eyes enough to see his white jacket with "MD" on the lapel. He felt of her abdomen, which again became tense, and Hattie could feel that vise-like pain start in the lower back and reach around to the front like closing fists squeezing so tight that she could hardly breathe, and when she did breathe, the coughing started. So now she had the unrelenting contraction as well as the burning, tearing coughing.

The doctor saw her anguish. Even though the contractions were close, they were short-lived. Each contraction was only long enough to trigger the cough reflex.

"Let's get you more comfortable, and then I'll examine you." He spoke quietly to the nurse, off to the side, where Hattie could not hear. The nurse nodded her understanding and left the room.

"How fast are the contractions coming, Mrs. Baker?" the doctor asked as he removed the other materials beneath her so now she lay flat.

Her voice was soft and sounded so far away to her, as if it were someone else's voice. "I don't know. They seem to be changin'."

"How so?"

"They've moved from back to front and deep inside with a lot more pressure now." Hattie strained to say the last words as another contraction occurred with the same results, pain and coughing.

The nurse came back into the room, pushing a wheeled cart that had supplies and medications on board. She picked up a syringe and a bottle.

"What dosage, Doctor?" she asked as she inserted the needle into the rubber top of the bottle. She then inverted the bottled and withdrew some of the liquid.

"Let's start out with two milligrams. She has a small body, and I don't want to sedate her, just make this less traumatic."

Hattie could hear the nurse moving the bottles on the cart and shuffling across the floor.

The doctor held Hattie's arm. "Mrs. Baker, I'm going to give you something to help ease the pain. It will make you a little sleepy, but you will still be conscious."

Hattie nodded as another contraction began. It was strange that as these contractions grew closer and closer together, they did not seem as hard as she recalled with her other children, but it didn't matter. The drug was in her body now, and she could feel that unbelievably relaxing feeling, where she lost total control of her limbs. She was totally at the drug's mercy now. She could hear people talking, but she could do nothing. The sensation to cough was minimal. It seemed the muscles that wretched so violently to rid her body of the phlegm and mucus in her lungs were pacified and lay sleeping until the medication would wear off.

She heard the doctor say he was going to examine her. The nurse's voice was heard, but Hattie could not understand her words. Hattie felt the nurse's hands move the hair from her face and eyes. The nurse spoke calming and reassuring words as the doctor moved the blankets and lifted Hattie's gown to expose the "arena of activity," as he called it. Hattie had never had a man examine her. She'd never been to a doctor. No man had ever seen her totally naked, not even her husband, and they had children together. Normally she would have screamed and slapped his face before running out of the room, but all she could do now was lie quietly. She was helpless.

"Mrs. Baker, we are going to take you to the operating room. Not that you need an operation, but you are dilated to an eight, and I think it best if you deliver in a controlled environment."

Hattie was not sure if the doctor was asking her permission or telling her of the plan. Not that it made any difference. She wasn't sure of the definition of a "controlled environment." All her other children were born in her house. Her house with the dirt floors and the wooden cabinets containing her mother's dishes. The picture of her and Martin on their wedding day, which was placed on the dresser in the bedroom. Her children playing in the yard. The sound of their laughter and sweet, little voices heard from outside as coffee brewed on the stove, and Martin's voice calling out to everyone that the fiddle was off the wall, and it was time to sing.

"Sing to me," she whispered.

She could hear people talking around her, but she was unable to understand them. Through her closed eyes, she could still see a bright light above her. In her drug-induced state, she imagined it was the sun shining on her at home, outside, where Martin played his fiddle, and they sang. They were laughing, liked they once did. Eulalie clapping her hands and dancing a funny little dance while Clemson and Jack sang the words of some silly song, but every few minutes, there was pain. A pain that caused her to temporarily come back to reality, but she didn't want to come back. She wanted to stay in this sweet, safe dream.

"Push," she could hear a voice saying. She didn't want to, but her body was out of her control. She could feel hands upon her, pulling and tugging at her.

"Push," she heard again, and again her body responded with a long, arduous contraction.

She could hear someone moaning and gasping for air. When they placed a rubberized contraption over her mouth and nose that blew air into her face, she figured out that the moaning and gasping must be coming from her.

And then suddenly, a long contraction was over. A great feeling of relief came over her body, like one where a person is drowning and then suddenly can breathe. She could hear the muffled voices but no sounds of a baby crying. She tried to speak, to cry out, "What is it? Is it alive?", but the mask on her face muffled her voice, and the medication made her voice soft and mumbled.

The voices became more understandable. She heard the doctor say, " Go ahead and put her under. We'll finish the episiotomy and address the remains."

These were the last words she heard. She knew the answer to her question. The gender of the child didn't matter. It was "remains" now, and the next medication made her fall into a deep sleep with no dreams and no memories. Everything now was black.

13

Mamie was settling into her new position now at Dr. Tucker's office since Flora remained too ill to assist. Mamie didn't seem to have time to do her public health nursing now. Each morning she would arrive, open the back door to the office, and begin preparing for the day. She also still had her old duties, however, of feeding and tending to the mule. He seemed to like her new position, too. No more hot, dusty trips up the side of those mountains. Now, it was leisurely days spent in the barn or small pasture, grazing on grass and daisies. Mamie enjoyed her new life, too. She was learning more and more from Dr. Tucker. He shared his medical knowledge with her and encouraged her to learn as much as she could. In fact, he had given her free reign to his library to remove any book she liked, take it home, and read it. Dr. Tucker also was fond of taking her to lunch with him, especially when he was meeting with the mayor or Reverend Abbot of the First Baptist Church. These outings allowed Mamie to meet the society of the town. In fact, she was invited to the Ladies' Garden Party next week. Quite a compliment, per Celeste, who encouraged Mamie to buy a new dress with matching hat and gloves. It had been a long time since Mamie purchased such finery for herself. She found herself living more and more in her nurse's uniform, but this would be a chance to be herself again.

Celeste entered the office where Mamie was preparing for the day's appointments. She carried a small tray with a teapot and teacup. It was customary for Celeste to bring Hattie hot tea in the mornings since Mamie arrived so early. Celeste thought it only proper since Mamie still took care of the mule. The least she could do was offer her a cup of hot tea. This morning, however, Celeste seemed in a rush. Her face was flushed and her hair askew, not at all like her regular appearance.

"Good morning, Celeste," Mamie began as she took the tray from the woman.

Celeste brushed back her hair, realizing how she must look. "Good morning, ma'am. Although, I dare say, it is not such a good morning at that."

Mamie poured herself a cup of the hot brew and asked, "Why? What's the matter?"

Celeste sighed and placed her hands on her hips. She had a frustrated look about her. "Well, nothin' I can really speak about. Safe to say, Miss Flora and Dr. Tucker are quarrelling again, and that always means trouble."

"What are they quarreling about?"

Celeste shook her head. "Stupid stuff. Stuff that cannot be changed, and there's no need to bring up the past when it's done."

Mamie remained silent, sipping her tea, while Celeste continued her tirade. "If they didn't try to keep stuff from the other and just came clean with everything, I think they could find some common ground, but this way, this sneakin', and lyin', and backbitin' – it all leads to heartache, and nobody's happy."

She shook her finger. "And a little forgiveness wouldn't hurt them, neither."

Mamie was taken slightly aback by Celeste's comments. She wondered about the lies and sneaking. She was unsure what the woman was speaking about. Mamie hadn't seen Flora for some time. She knew the woman was upstairs and rarely ventured out. She thought she perhaps heard Flora coughing occasionally, but with all the coughing, wheezing, and carrying on of the patients in the waiting area, it was hard to discern where the noise was even coming from. Celeste was seen taking trays of food and a teapot up the stairs throughout the day, but by spending much of her time with Dr. Tucker, Mamie hadn't even really thought much about Flora, and the doctor didn't mention her much, either. It was as if his sister were no longer in the house.

"I best be going now, Miss Mamie. Miss Flora will be ready for her breakfast, and I don't want to make her any more angry than she already is. Be apprised, ma'am , that Dr Tucker will likely be in a foul mood himself."

"How is Flora doing, Celeste? Is there any improvement at all?"

Celeste stopped before she opened the door. She did not turn to face Mamie. "She is very ill. More ill than I ever saw her. I think it's not only an illness of the body, though; I think it is a sickness of the soul." The woman turned, facing Mamie with a deep sadness in her eyes. "And that is a sickness we mortals cannot cure. Some broken hearts never mend – at least, not without leaving a terrible scar."

She opened the door and left the office, leaving Mamie with her teapot and questions. But there was no time to dwell on these things. Patients were beginning to arrive, and there was work to be done. Besides, all of that was Dr. Tucker's private business, and she had no right meddling.

"Good morning, Doctor," Mamie said as Dr. Tucker entered his office.

Celeste was correct. The doctor was in a foul mood. He nodded in Mamie's general direction, muttered something under his breath, and put on his white lab coat. Mamie thought it best to close the door between his office and the waiting area, just in case any of the patients saw how disconcerting the doctor was this morning.

"Good morning, Mr. Davis," she said as the first patient entered the waiting room. "How are you doing this morning?"

The man hobbled into the waiting area, removing his worn-out hat. "Oh, I been better. I think it is my heart. It seems to be tryin' to burst outta my chest."

"Well, that does not sound good, Mr. Davis. Please, have a seat over here, and I will take your blood pressure along with some other vital signs before you see Dr. Tucker."

The man did as he was directed. He was pale, and his breathing was elevated. His blood pressure was a bit on the high side, but his pulse was definitely faster than normal. Mamie smiled at the man to reassure him.

"You are correct, Mr. Davis. Your heart does truly believe it can run the whole show, so I'll tell Dr. Tucker you are here and ready to see him. Please, just stay seated here, and I'll be right back."

Mamie left the patient and knocked softly on the doctor's office door.

"Dr. Tucker?" she said softly as she opened the door.

She found him seated behind his desk, his head in his hands. She was not sure he heard her knock, so she knocked again, but he still did not respond. She discreetly closed the door behind her and entered his office.

"Dr. Tucker," she said softy. "Mr. Davis, your first patient is out in the waiting area. His heart rate is elevated. Would you be able to see him now?"

The doctor finally acknowledged her presence. He leaned back in his chair, laying his hands flat upon the desk. "I know, Mamie. Duty calls, and I must keep a stiff upper lip."

Mamie did not respond. She wasn't exactly sure what to say or do. She remembered Celeste's comments earlier about the doctor and his sister quarrelling, but he would have to get past this if he was going to treat patients today.

"Very well," he said at last. "Show him in, please."

Mamie nodded and went to retrieve Mr. Davis.

"Good morning, Mr. Davis," the doctor began as the patient entered the office. He spoke as if nothing were wrong, and as if the scene Mamie witnessed prior were just in her imagination. The doctor was smiling, cheerful, and asked her for the chart on this patient. He reviewed it quickly, then listened to the man's lungs and heart.

"Yes, Mr. Davis," the doctor said after listening, feeling pulses, and checking the swelling on the patient's legs. "You certainly do have a contrary heart, but I think we can keep it from acting out so much by some simple pills."

The doctor went to his glass cabinet and pulled out a small bottle of little white pills. He handed them to Mr. Davis. "I'm going to give these to you temporarily. Whether they work or not, I want you to come back to see me in one week. If these pills help, I'll give you more. If they don't work, we will have to look elsewhere."

"Thank you, Dr. Tucker," the patient said as he was escorted from the office by Mamie. She made him a follow-up appointment, and the man placed his old, worn hat back onto his head.

He turned to her just as he was leaving, "That Dr. Tucker is a real good man, ain't he?"

Mamie smiled. "I think so."

The doctor opened his office door and stuck his head out the opening. "Next patient, please, Nurse."

"Yes, Doctor," she replied obediently as she assisted an elderly lady into the office.

And so the day proceeded: Mamie preparing the patients, the doctor examining them, and them leaving the office. Over and over, one after the other, a never-ending stream of illness and disease. Through all of this, the doctor remained pleasant to them, but Mamie could tell there was an underlying current of anger within him. After a countless number of patients, it was finally time for the day to be completed. They had worked through lunch without a break all day. Mamie assumed that since the doctor was so angry, he wanted to work off his anger by staying focused on the patients. While it may have sounded good for him, she was exhausted.

"Dr. Tucker," she said as she knocked on his office door for the last time today.

"Yes," came an exhausted response.

Mamie opened the door and walked inside. "I'm getting ready to leave for the day. Is there anything I can do for you before I leave?"

For the first time today, he looked at her. "Yes, please come in and close the door behind you."

She went inside, closing the door. He motioned for her to sit in the chair in front of his desk. He sat behind the desk and leaned forward, his arms outstretched.

"I wanted to talk to you," he began.

"Yes, sir."

"As you know, my sister is very ill. Unfortunately, I don't know when she will return to a state of health where she will be able to assist me again. I wanted to ask you if you would be willing to stay on as my nurse for an indefinite period of time?"

Mamie wasn't sure what this meant. On the one hand, she was elated to think that she would be working with him for a longer period of time, but she was not sure where this was going. She did not answer immediately but simply looked down to her lap, thinking of all the scenarios that this could lead to.

"I know..." he continued. "...this is not what you signed up for, but this is a thing that cannot be helped. I have come to rely on you a great deal. Although Flora was good at what she did, you are better. By having a nurse here in the office, I can see how much smoother and easier the day goes. Take today, for instance. There is no way Flora and I could have seen that many patients in one day, but thanks to your knowledge and skill, I can do my job more efficiently because you have done the menial tasks for me."

Mamie was highly encouraged by all that he said, except the last part: "menial tasks." Part of her was insulted. The "menial tasks," as he so aptly put it, were the foundation for medicine. That was why they were called "vital signs." They were vital to the patient's life.

"I'm not sure, Dr. Tucker, what all of that would entail."

He looked at her in surprise, apparently taken off-guard by her hesitancy to work with him.

"What are your concerns?"

She took a breath, "Well, firstly, I haven't been able to leave the office to visit the patients at home. Our original agreement was that I could leave in the afternoon to visit them, but, so far, that has not been possible."

He looked at her with his eyebrows cast down, "You could leave any time you desire. You only need let me know. I do not believe that issue is my fault, but yours."

She lowered her head. He was right. She had neglected her home patients, and it was her fault. She had put others ahead of them. She had put Dr. Tucker ahead of them.

"Then there is the money," she said softly.

"What about the money?"

She raised her head and looked directly at him. "I am paid by the Public Health Department. If I work for you personally, they will not pay me any longer. Would you be willing to pay the same as they?"

He thought for a moment. "Perhaps we could work something out. I am on the board of public health and have a say in their actions. Possibly a deal could be worked out where they pay you some and I pay you some."

That was not really an answer. She was nervous at his hesitancy to offer to pay her what she was making now. She did not want to get herself into a financial bind. Her father would never forgive her nor help her.

"Maybe we could also offer you other things in lieu of actual cash," the doctor continued. "Such as free housing. You could stay here in our house free of charge. You could dine with us, without having to pay for food, as Celeste does."

Mamie could feel her excitement dwindling. His first comment referring to her "menial tasks" and now comparing her pay to that of a house servant. Not that she had anything against house servants, but Mamie had gone to school, invested in education and equipment, and now she was to be paid "in kind."

"I'm not sure, Dr. Tucker. I will need to think about it. My mother and father might not approve."

The doctor smiled. "Your father will have no objections to the arrangement."

She looked at him with surprise. She did not know he knew her father. Her father never mentioned Dr. Tucker, but, then, her father never mentioned anyone he knew.

He stood up abruptly. "I must leave now, Mamie. I have a meeting I must attend. May I ask you to please close up the office for us? I will see you in the morning, and we can discuss this further."

Mamie nodded, remaining seated in the chair, as the doctor removed his white lab coat and grabbed his suit jacket. He smiled kindly as he left her sitting alone in the office. She was confused and concerned. The doctor had been in a vile mood all day, but she thought he had worked it out of his system only to find this abrupt proposal at the end of the day. Her pride was still suffering from his comments, but her concern was for the way he asked her about the changes. It was as if he assumed she would jump at the chance to work with him on a daily basis. Her pride was insulted even more.

She was still seated in the office chair when the office door opened suddenly behind her. Celeste came rushing through the door, hair straggling and skin moist with perspiration.

"Where is the doctor, Miss?" she asked breathlessly.

"He's gone for the day. He said he had a meeting he needed to attend. Why? What's the matter?"

Celeste tried to catch her breath. There was a distant sound of a raised voice and coughing.

"Did he say when he'd return?"

Mamie shook her head. "Can I help, Celeste?"

Celeste hesitated. Mamie could tell she was stalling, trying desperately to make a difficult decision. There was a loud thud heard from upstairs. Celeste's eyes grew large. "Yes, please, Miss Mamie. It's Miss Flora. She's half-mad, and I don't know what to do."

"Of course," Mamie answered, rising from her chair and following the servant out of the office and up the stairs.

"Miss Flora," Celeste said softly as she knocked on the woman's bedroom door. "Miss Flora, I have the nurse here, and she's gonna help me. We are coming in."

Celeste opened the door slowly, cautiously. Mamie could feel her heart beating in her ears. Celeste was nearly bent in half as she opened the door and stepped inside. Mamie was afraid of what they might find. After hearing the noises, Mamie wasn't sure what was on the other side of that large, wooden door.

Both women stepped into the room. It was dark. The curtains were drawn so that no sunlight entered the room. It was hot and stuffy. A rancid smell permeated the room. Celeste opened one set of the drawn curtains, allowing some natural light into the room. Mamie looked around, searching for the body of Flora. She did not need to search long.

Sprawled out across the lower half of the bed was the cachectic body of the doctor's sister. Her head was hidden on the far side of the bed with her arms strewn out at her sides. Celeste tried to assist her mistress to a more comfortable position.

"Please, Miss Flora, let me help you back into the bed."

She was able to roll Flora over onto her back with very little assistance from the patient. Mamie walked closer and helped Celeste pull Flora up into the bed. The covers were tossed about, and the servant began straightening them and covering the near-naked body of Flora.

"Stop it!" Flora shouted, slapping her hand down onto the bed but nowhere near Celeste. Celeste stood up, her eyes large with concern.

"Please, Miss Flora, let me help you."

Flora leaned her head back and laughed a pitiful laugh. It was not a joyful sound but a release of disgrace and despair. "Help me," the woman said, her voice raspy and quiet. "There is no help for me."

"Please, Miss Flora," Celeste continued, still fussing with the blankets and pillows in an attempt to make the bed more comfortable for the patient.

Mamie stood at arm's length away from Flora. Now, Flora opened her eyes and glared at the young nurse. Flora smiled a devilish smile, as if she were possessed by something not of this world. Mamie was somewhat afraid. She had taken care of many patients, but none looked at her the way this woman was looking at her.

"So," Flora began. "You brought up the miracle woman. The wonderful Nurse Mamie who can heal the lame and cause the blind to see?"

Celeste completed her task of tidying the blankets. She brought over a tray of tea and toast from the dresser and placed it on the side table next to Flora's bed.

"Now, Miss Flora, there is no need to be hateful. I did ask Nurse Mamie to help me only because I was so concerned for you. You seem to be having a really bad day today. I thought, perhaps, she could help."

Flora smiled that wicked smile again, revealing stained teeth. Mamie drew nearer to the patient.

"How can I help you, Miss Flora. Are you in pain?"

Flora's smile faded. She nodded very slowly.

"Where is your pain?"

Flora tried to take a deep breath, but she could not. Mamie watched as a violent coughing fit grasp her, causing the woman to bend over and gasp for air, her head almost flush with the neatly folded blankets on her lap. Flora raised her head, trying to suck in enough air to stay conscious. Her face was blood red. Dark blue vessels protruded from the neck and forehead. Mamie thought that Flora's heart would burst if this continued. Flora lowered her head again, allowing a long, red ribbon of blood to drain from her mouth onto her dressing gown. Mamie's eyes grew large. She stood very still, taking in all that lay before her.

"Please, Miss Mamie," Celeste said, pleading, "Do something."

Mamie was at a loss. She could not believe the events that were unfolding before her. She herself was having trouble breathing. The noxious odors of this room were suffocating her, making her dizzy and somewhat nauseated. The woman who lay before her was struggling to bring in every breath, every breath punctuated by severe coughing ending with bloody sputum, only to be followed immediately by another coughing spell.

"Let's get her sitting in a more upright position," Mamie finally managed to say, trying to bring herself back to reality.

Both women pulled Flora higher up in the bed, placing pillows behind her so she was in an upright position. It helped a little; at least the woman was able to pull in enough air to quell the next attack. The redness of her face drained and faded into a pale gray color, her teeth and lips stained with blood. She leaned her head back onto the pillows and tried to slow down the breathing.

"Is there any medication the doctor is giving you?" Mamie asked, her voice low and barely a whisper. She was not sure why she spoke like this, but it seemed inappropriate to speak in a regular voice.

Flora's voice was barely audible, ragged and crackling as she spoke. "My brother always gives me something to help with the cough. He keeps some of it in the bureau."

She pointed a long, anorexic finger at the furniture across the room.

Mamie walked quickly across the room to the cabinet where Flora pointed. When she opened the doors, she saw several small bottles of chemicals held within. Mamie handled one bottle after the other, reading and trying to determine which medication would be useful and the dosage of each.

Flora's voice was distant as she closed her eyes.

"I thought you knew medications. I thought you knew everything."

Her voice trailed off, and she hugged a pillow laying nearby.

"Do you know why I am here? Did my brother tell you what I did?"

She stroked the pillow as if it were a person. "I made the mistake of falling in love, falling in love with a man beneath us, a beautiful man, a wonderful man."

Mamie did not respond but watched the pitiful woman lean back into the pillows and close her eyes.

"Hush now, Miss Flora. Miss Mamie is just trying to help. She's doing the best she can. She's not familiar with these drugs, and she don't want to give you something that might hurt you."

Flora cast an angry sideways glance at her servant. "Yes, Celeste, we wouldn't want to hurt me. I mean, I am the picture of health, and I have so much to live for."

She began to cry softly, caressing the pillow as if it were a child.

"Shh," she whispered to the pillow. "Momma will join you soon."

She began to cough again.

"Miss Flora..." Mamie began reading one of the bottles. "I don't have the authority to give you this medicine. This bottle contains morphine, and Celeste is correct – too much of this could kill you."

Flora looked up at Mamie with an evil stare. Mamie's blood ran cold. The look Flora gave her was unearthly, like one possessed.

"I must have that medicine."

She threw off the blankets that Celeste had painstakingly tucked in just moments before. Her movements were almost out of her control, jerky and disjointed. She attempted to climb out of the bed.

Celeste grabbed her in an attempt to keep Flora from falling off the bed. Flora screamed and turned on the woman like an animal, grabbing and slapping her, knocking the unfortunate woman to the floor.

"Flora!" came a loud, angry voice from the door.

All three women turned to see Dr. Tucker standing in the doorway. His anger was apparent as he quickly crossed the room and grabbed the bottle out of Mamie's trembling hand. He helped Celeste up off of the floor.

"Are you hurt?" he asked her as he aided her into a chair.

Celeste shook her head, appearing to be somewhat embarrassed about the whole incident.

The doctor withdrew a syringe barrel with needle from the bureau. He withdrew several milliliters of the liquid in a bottle with "MS04" written on the side. He walked to his sister, who continued to thrash about in the bed, coughing. He repositioned her arm so any muscle she had would be exposed. He sunk the needle deep into her arm and depressed the syringe, pushing the intoxicating medication into her body. Mamie watched as Flora responded almost immediately as the elixir floated through her. In a few minutes, the wild spirit that possessed her was exterminated, and the woman lay limp in the bed, her breathing shallow but uninterrupted by coughing.

"Please help me reposition her in this bed," Dr. Tucker asked, motioning to Mamie.

She walked to the other side of the bed, and they moved the emaciated body of his sister up in the bed, covering her with the blankets. Dr. Tucker smoothed the hair back from her face. She lay quietly with almost the look of the dead – pale and gaunt. Mamie noticed multiple small, black marks on her arms and legs, not bruising, but deep, circular blotches resembling holes in the skin.

The doctor stood up straight and sighed.

"I'm sorry you got drug into this, Mamie," the doctor said, making sure he did not make eye contact. "My sister is very ill, and the morphine helps her sleep. She relaxes enough so her breathing is easier."

Mamie said nothing. She looked at him across the bed. There was too much here for him to think Mamie would be satisfied with this.

To Dr. Tucker, this silence was like a hot light exposing all the dirty little secrets he had. He wanted to just walk out of the room – not explain, not listen, not care – but his sister had gone too far for that. She'd exposed her own dirty little secret and pulled all of these people into that dark corner in which she dwelt. Now, a light exposed her, and everyone in the room could see the ugliness. It left a bloodstain on the bedclothes, the nightgown, and on his sister's mouth.

He took the little brown bottle of magic back to the bureau. He withdrew several other bottles and syringes. Injecting saline into the bottle of powder, he shook it well and filled the syringe.

He looked at Mamie.

"I know this is probably much more than you anticipated, but Flora has been ill for some time, and, I fear, her chronic bronchitis is becoming much worse. So extreme, in fact, that I don't know if I can help her much more."

He returned to his sister's bedside and injected the powder and saline solution into her arm. Mamie watched carefully. Soon, the area he injected began to discolor, darker and darker until that circular black spot remained.

Mamie walked over to the bureau where Dr. Tucker placed the medicine bottles. She picked up the bottle containing the powder that he just used. She held it up and turned back to the doctor.

"She has chronic bronchitis, and you are treating her with gold salts?"

Her tone was cold and condemning.

The doctor stood firm, showing no emotion on his face.

"Yes," he began. "New studies are showing that it can be effective for pulmonary disease."

Mamie continued looking at him, her disappointment apparent. "Pulmonary disease, like tuberculosis?"

He glared at her. "This is not TB. She has suffered from chronic bronchitis for years. The symptoms are similar, but this is bronchitis. I can see where you could get them confused."

Mamie placed the bottle down onto the bureau. She walked over to the bed and lifted one section of the blanket. It was covered with blood.

"And does chronic bronchitis cause pulmonary hemorrhage, uncontrolled coughing, muscle wasting?"

Her voice was becoming loud. She was unable to hide her anger. "How long has she had this?"

The doctor was unremorseful. "I don't owe you any explanation. I am the doctor here, and she is under my care."

He walked around the bed to leave the room, but before he left, he turned and said one more thing to Mamie: "I urge you, Nurse Mamie, to speak to no one about this. I have the authority to revoke your nursing license, and I will do so."

He left the room, leaving Mamie steaming in her own anger. Celeste remained silent in her chair across the room.

"Ohhh," Mamie grumbled beneath her breath. "He is impossible. How can he be like this? He sends everyone else, regardless of their family or finance, to the TB sanitorium, but his own sister languishes here in her bedroom addicted to morphine and slowly dying a pitiful death."

She looked down upon Flora, who lay silently in the bed. The woman was nearly unconscious with stained teeth and lips, dehydration, and no quality of life. Mamie's revulsion was apparent.

"And, to make matters worse..." she continued in her tirade. "...she has been exposing all the patients to her disease. Lord only knows how many people she's infected. How long has she been ill, Celeste?"

Celeste looked down at the floor, "Well over a year now, ma'am. She came back home with it."

"She came back with it? Where did she go?"

Celeste looked uncomfortable. "She went away with a man."

Mamie sat down on the edge of the bed. "What man?"

Celeste shrugged her shoulders. "I don't know his name. He was a man that came through town lookin' for work. Dr. Tucker hired him to do some work on the house, you know, fixin' the roof and windows."

Mamie nodded, intrigued by this story.

"Well, Miss Flora, took a liking to him, and when her brother found out, he told the man to leave. Except, when the man left, Miss Flora went with him. I can't blame her, though. As you can see, Miss Flora isn't what we would call a beauty, but he was a nice-looking man. He had dark hair and such beautiful eyes. He had the prettiest voice."

Celeste looked pitifully at the woman on the bed.

"Where did they go?" Mamie inquired.

Celeste shrugged again. "I don't know. I heard it was somewhere up the hills."

"And then what happened?"

Celeste gave a sympathetic look at the sleeping, drugged woman. "Miss Flora came back by herself, but she was not well. She lost a lot of weight. She stayed at that boarding house across town. I saw her and went to check on her. She looked so bad, so pale. I took her food, and the landlady had food for her, but Miss Flora just ate crackers and drank hot tea. Finally, she got good enough to come back home. Dr. Tucker was real mad at her, but soon she started coughing, and then he wasn't so cross. She just kept getting worse and worse, though, 'til she just couldn't hardly do anything without coughing. That's when the doctor started with that little brown bottle, and now she's coughing up blood and acting like a wild animal."

Mamie was trying to process all of this information. She turned her gaze away from Celeste and the drugged woman lying in the bed. Her eyes wandered across the room and out the only window in the room with the curtains open. Movement outside drew her attention. She walked over to the window and opened it.

"You, sir," she shouted to a man walking out of the barn below. "Where are you going with that mule?"

The man was bringing the mule out of the barn with a rope tied around its neck. The mule obeyed, as it was used to Mamie walking it out in the morning. The animal did not rebel but walked obediently after the man.

The man looked up to see Mamie in the upstairs window. He tipped his hat. "I'm taking this mule with me. Dr. Tucker sold it to me."

"He sold it? Why? Where are you taking it?" Mamie's voice was louder and more emotional than she anticipated, but there were a lot of feelings twisting inside of her, and it was difficult for her to separate them.

"Yes, ma'am," the man replied, continuing his walk. "Money changed hands, so this here mule is mine now. Dr. Tucker said he had no further use for this nag and needed to git rid of him."

An overwhelming sadness covered her. She did not understand this. She could not imagine why the sale of that stubborn mule affected her so. Perhaps it was the method that the animal was sold – quietly and with no mention of it at any time. Or perhaps it was the comment the buyer said at the last.

What was it exactly?

"Dr. Tucker said he had no further use for this nag."

Well, maybe Mamie could see the real doctor now, not the kind man she wanted him to be, but the dark figure lurking through the shadows, hiding his real motives and real self from the outside world. The realization that the doctor was not who he pretended to be was seeping into her skin. It was a cold feeling. A cruel realization that he was manipulating her. He had been manipulating her from the start, and what was worse, she fell for it. She was just like that mule with blinders on, led to the pasture, allowed to graze at will, feeling safe and comfortable, but the moment the doctor was done with it, he would release it, and he would release her. It was just a matter of time.

14

Let's go out to the solarium, Mrs. Baker," the red-haired nurse said as she uncovered Hattie. Hattie opened her eyes slightly. It was light outside, so it must be daytime. She had no idea what time it was or what day, and she didn't care. One day looked just like the next – no more, no less. The nurse helped Hattie dress. She placed her slippers on her feet, clothed her with a clean gown, and placed a robe around her shoulders. The nurse then stood to the side of Hattie and placed her arm under Hattie's. "I'm going to help you stand and get into this wheelchair. You don't have to stand long, but I do need you to try." Hattie felt her body being lifted, but she had no strength with which to help. Her legs were like water, fluid and uncontrollable. They buckled to the side, then back to the front, and would certainly give way if not for the nurse's steadiness. Hattie's body was swiveled to one side and placed into the chair. Just the mere motion of rising and standing started Hattie's coughing, short and catching at first, but soon long, breathless heaves that drained her of the little strength she had.

It was difficult to bring in enough air to support consciousness and those big, black dots obscured her vision, and she tasted the blood in her mouth.

The nurse pulled one arm, and Hattie felt the pain of the needle. Then there was that familiar warmth, that relaxing feeling swimming through her body like salvation to a sinner, saving her from the hell her body was experiencing. The nurse wiped the blood from the corners of Hattie's mouth, and then began to brush her hair while the medicine continued to work its effect. In a few minutes, that overwhelming, uncontrollable urge to cough was calmed. It was still there, although not as chaotic as the wild beast it had been before, but it was not gone, just waiting.

The nurse pushed Hattie's chair out of the room and down the hall. She chattered along about the fine weather and birds now appearing on the birdfeeders outside. She continued by commenting on how good all of this was for the patients and how Hattie could convalesce better in the fresh air. Hattie heard none of this. She was melting away in her chair. Between her sadness and the morphine, she had become a mist of air, thin and frail. She could be blown about by the prevailing wind for she had become opaque, unnoticed.

She was gone.

"Here you go, Mrs. Baker."

The nurse stopped on the sunporch, locking Hattie's chair in place. Hattie faced the gardens, lawn, and woods. The sun was shining. It was a lovely day, but Hattie could not see it. She was blinded from within. She heard the nurse continuing to say something about food and medication but only noted that the woman walked away.

"So, Hattie Baker, you couldn't keep away from me," came a soft voice from her side.

It was a lovely voice, calming with that drawl that refined men of the south used in years past. Hattie wasn't sure how long it had been – days, weeks, months – since she'd been out here on the veranda. There was no time here. It was like living in a black hole: no entrance, no exit, no up, no down, no here, no there, no matter.

"Where have you been?" that soft voice asked.

Hattie did not turn towards the man. She continued to stare blankly out onto the grounds. A black cap chickadee popped from one limb to another on a sycamore tree not far away. It was so light, so fast, that Hattie's vision could not keep up with it in her drug induced state. She moved her eyes slowly to follow it, but she could never quite keep up with its movement.

The young man was lying on his cot. He pulled himself up into a sitting position. "What have you been doing?"

"I had a baby," she answered with no emotion in her voice or on her face.

"What was it?"

"I was told it was a girl." Her voice was as calm and uncaring as if she were discussing the weather. She felt nothing.

"What did you name her?"

"I did not name her," she responded in the same flat, unaffected voice.

Hayden was sitting up now on the side of his cot. He leaned forward. His voice was low and gentle.

"She needs a name, Hattie. Everyone needs a name; otherwise, who will remember them? Who will tell their story? Who will weep for them, Hattie?"

Hattie turned her head to face him. There was no emotion in her eyes. "She has no story, and I no longer weep…"

She could see the sympathy in Hayden's eyes. He felt more of a loss than she did. Perhaps he had not had the amount of morphine she was given.

"Where is she?" he asked after a few moments.

Hattie's gaze turned again to the grounds. "They told me they buried her in the sanitorium cemetery. Apparently, a lot of people die here."

Hayden tried to pull his cot a little closer. "A lot of people do die here, Hattie, but not all. Many are caught somewhere in between, dead on the inside but languishing in the body, existing somewhere in a dark, lonely space. They think they are alone and give up. They are the most pitiful of all God's creatures."

He began to cough, deep and crackling with the blood expelled onto his ever-present handkerchief.

He struggled to catch his breath but continued his argument.

"She needs a name, Hattie. Something to remember her by. A name that means she was here, she mattered, that someone loved her."

Hayden looked down on the floor. Hattie did not respond. She sat motionless with no emotion on her face, silent as the grave that held her baby girl.

"What were you going to name her?" he asked after a few minutes.

"Bonnie," Hattie replied softly. "Bonnie Izell."

Hayden smiled very slowly. "That is a beautiful name. It is perfect."

She turned to face him. Hayden thought he saw a hint of an emotion from her for the first time. That dead person she had on the inside was not totally embalmed.

"Perfect?" she asked quietly.

"Yes," he answered. "Bonnie means beautiful, and Izell means unique. So, this child who never saw the light of day, who was never held in her mother's arms, and never had a chance to change the world was loved by someone. She was truly beautiful and unique."

Hattie looked at Hayden for a long time. Somewhere, piercing through the numbness, she felt a melting of the ice. There was a burning in her chest, not affiliated with her lungs. It stung like a nest of hornets, but it was so deep – deeper inside than even her heart was. It was a burning in the soul. So much of her was wasting away: her body, her mind, and her soul. But this man, with those wicked blue eyes, could see right through her. Hattie could not let her own self-pity wipe out the existence of her own child. The beast that consumed her lungs was consuming her heart and soul, but it was not the child's fault. She was concerned when days would become brighter, when the air was sweet, and life held so many promises. If those days ever came, she would regret her decision now. She could not let this beast consume her baby, too.

Hayden was staring at her with those blue eyes. Although gaunt and pale, he was still handsome beneath his disease. She could see how someone could become close to him. He was a broken man. She could tell, as one broken human to another, that there was something inside his heart, too, just as in hers, that kept him from letting go. Something that pushed him on but could not defeat the disease. And at last, he was near the end, probably nearer than she.

He reached out his hand across the space between them. He placed his hand on hers. She looked down upon it. It was the first time since she left home that someone other than staff touched her. It was the first time in a long time she'd been touched by someone who cared about her and not just for her.

"And what did your husband say?" he asked after a few moments.

"Nothing. I haven't told him yet." She had a pitiful sound to her voice, a realization that her self-pity was punishing others.

Hayden shook his head. "Hattie, the man needs to know about his child. Take it from someone who knows – to think you have a child and abandon it. It has a profound effect on the father, too. We may not show the loss as keenly as the mother, but it is a great loss to us. A loss from which we may never recover. It will drop us to our knees. You will pray to God Almighty to forgive you for your cowardice, your weakness, and your ignorance."

His voice cracked under the strain of his words. He was pouring out his heart, and Hattie was surprised by the emotion in his words. She was surprised that he spoke as one who had firsthand knowledge of such heartbreak as losing a child. His face was downcast. He no longer had that soft, gentle look. He now looked as a man in pain – not pain of the body, but pain of soul. She moved her hands to embrace his.

She spoke quietly, leaning towards him. "I will write to my husband soon."

Hayden shook his head, blinking, trying to push away memories and tears. He pulled his hand from Hattie's embrace and wiped his eyes. "That would be a good idea."

Hayden leaned on one arm and leaned back onto his cot.

"Did you lose a child?" she asked after a few moments.

"Lost it, ran away from it, abandoned it. I'm not sure what you would call what I did. Sinful is probably the best word that describes it."

He lay supine in his cot, eyes closed. Hattie could see tears rolling down his temples.

"Did you love her?" she asked.

He took a ragged breath. "I thought I did, but I was frightened. There was a time she and I would sit on the porch of our little cabin, and she would hold my hand while I smoked my pipe, but the fear of having someone depend on me was too much, and I ran. By the time I realized I made a terrible mistake, it was too late. The child was gone, the woman was gone, and I had TB. The doctor had the sheriff bring me up here, and now I'll die here."

He laughed on uneasy laugh. "Poetic justice, I suppose, or maybe the sins of the father…"

His voice trailed off.

"And the woman?" Hattie continued.

"I heard she went back home. I'm not sure what happened to her. When she left with me, she lived with her brother. He was a doctor."

Hattie leaned over the armrest of her wheelchair. She wiped the tears from his face.

"We are such fools." His voice was broken. "We strive for what we think is important, but what is important is how we think." He opened his eyes and looked at Hattie. His eyes were clouded with tears and pain, a reflection of her own.

He continued, "…because how we think determines our actions, and my actions were those of a fool. Self-pity and sadness caused me to waste my life. The only life I will ever have. The only chance I will ever get, and I squandered it on myself. So, you see, Hattie Baker, we all have our crosses to bear. Some of us accept the help and love of others, while we fools allow ourselves to be crushed by the weight of our mistakes."

He turned away and closed his eyes.

Hattie smoothed his hair back away from his face. Suddenly, she felt very sorry for him. She also felt sorry for herself and the little baby girl that lay buried in that cemetery, which was in her line of sight.

"Hayden," she said, stroking his face. "Do you sing?"

Hayden opened his eyes and cast a sly sideways glance at her. She could see the tears unformed, but pooling, in his eyes. He smiled slightly. "Not very well, Hattie. I only really know one song. An old Irish song our housekeeper sang. How odd it is. I can't remember one church song or one song I heard my whole life except that sad, old Irish song from so long ago."

Hattie sat back in her chair. "Hayden, sing to me."

He repositioned himself in his cot, turning onto his side and trying to clear his throat. He started to sing. His voice was crackling, but he knew every word. There were a few other people on the porch. They, too, knew this song, and began to sing along quietly with him. For a few moments, the coughing stopped. Only the sound of near-death voices could be heard. They knew the words and sang as if they were feeling each syllable of the song, breathing in the air that was so precious to them, and releasing the words as if they were the last things they would ever say while on this earth.

Hattie sat back in her chair, closing her eyes. She was unsure if she was hallucinating from the morphine or if her spirit truly left her as she walked in the woods back home. She was barefoot and could feel the warm, red clay against her skin. She was surrounded by trees. The air was clean and fresh. The trees blew gently alongside her, brushing her skin with a soft breeze. She could breathe easily for the first time. She could hear her children playing in the yard. She saw Martin coming out of the barn, his hat tipped back on his long, dark hair. He was smiling. She wanted to run to him, hold him in her arms again. She wanted to kiss her children and tell them how much she loved them and missed them, but then she could hear footsteps. Hard steps on tile floors like those of the nurse in the sanitorium, but she did not want to leave this place, and she tried desperately to remain. She opened her eyes to see the red-haired nurse, the light reflecting off the silver hypodermic. She felt a slight pinch and then that soft feeling of disappearing.

15

Johnson grass and morning glories grew up the corn stalks quickly and voraciously in the hot, southern sun. Martin used a sharpened corn knife to hack the weeds away from the stalks, pulling and yanking them away from the precious ears of corn. These uninvited guests did not give way easily. The Johnson grass had deep, infiltrating roots that choked the corn from beneath while the morning glories encased the upper stalk and starved the corn of sunlight. Either invader would be enough to ruin a corn crop, but both, together, meant no harvest at all. It was back-breaking work with long, hot hours that turned into long, hot days. Sweat dripped from his face like tears from heaven, but Martin welcomed the exertion. He needed to stay busy, so busy that he could not think. He did not want to think. He just wanted to chop and hack at these weeds, viciously and without any mercy. His heart was sore, nearly to the point of breaking. He had received a letter from Hattie.

"Good morning, Mr. Baker," came a husky voice from behind him.

Martin stopped the horse and wiped the sweat from his own face with the sleeve of his shirt. He turned to see the sheriff standing at the end of the row. Martin wiped the sweat with the back of his sleeve and walked towards the man.

"Good mornin', Sheriff. What brings you out this way?"

The sheriff spat snuff onto the ground. It left a wet, clotted spot in the soil. He looked up, tipping his hat back onto his head. He moved his head from side to side. Martin could tell the man was procrastinating, which meant this was not good news he brought. By the time Martin reached the end of the row, the sheriff began to speak.

"Well, I gotta proposition for ya." The sheriff pulled several rolled up papers out of his hip pocket. He handed them to Martin.

"What's this about?" Martin asked as he unfurled the papers and began to read them.

It was hot in this field with that unrelenting Arkansas sun causing sweat to form on the faces of the two men. The sheriff took his white handkerchief from his pocket and wiped his face.

"Good Lord, it gets hot down here in these bottom lands." The sheriff swatted at several buzzing insects now lighting on his shirt and neck. "And these blood suckers are thick as fleas down here."

Martin did not notice. He was reading the papers and trying to understand them. His brow furrowed, and his lips were pinched.

"Who sent you down here?" Martin asked after gleaning over the documents.

"Roosevelt," the sheriff replied flatly, pointing to the paper. "Them's orders from the president of the United States of America."

Martin shuffled through the papers trying to make sense of this.

"So..."

He hesitated.

"These papers say I gotta sell you my land?"

The sheriff nodded. "Yes, sir. The federal government is buying up all this low land 'cause it floods so bad. Their idea is to flood it good and turn it into a lake."

The sheriff placed his hand on Martin's shoulder and began to laugh.

Martin didn't smile. He pulled away from the sheriff, rolling the papers back into a cylinder.

"And what happens if I don't want to sell?" he asked as he handed the papers back to the sheriff.

The sheriff stopped laughing and removed his hand from Martin's shoulder. He wiped more of the sweat from his face, but Martin could see the friendly demeanor of the man was gone. He had gone from the sheriff of the people to a man with a job to get done, and, apparently, the job today was to take Martin's land.

"Mr. Baker, these papers aren't an invitation to a party. Them's an order from the gov'ment. According to them papers, you can either sell your farm to the president, or he'll take it from you. Them's your choices."

Martin looked defiantly at the sheriff. His squared his shoulders, his face intent.

"My family..." he began, his voice low and threatening. "...has lived and worked on this land for more generations than I can count. Some of them died tryin' to defend it with arrows, black powder, and guns, and now you think with the stroke of a pen from a man a thousand miles away, who I never even met, that you can take it from me? You tell me I can either sell to this man for whatever money he decides to pay me or he'll throw me off, homeless, penniless, with youngins dependin' on me and this land to survive? What country is this, Sheriff? When did it turn into such a cruel and unfair place?"

The sheriff did not move. His jaw was set. He had the same low, threatening voice as Martin.

"It's the law, Mr. Baker. So, you gonna sign these papers so I can go cut you a check, or am I gonna have to come back here with my deputies and my guns?"

16

Mamie did not give the doctor an answer to his request for her to work with him in his office. How could she when she knew his sister lay dying upstairs from TB, the very disease with which Hattie was afflicted? Only Flora was allowed to die at home surrounded by her family, what little there was of it, while Hattie was carted off hundreds of miles away from her home and left to die among strangers. Mamie shook her head. She was ashamed of herself for falling for the gentle words and sly winks of the doctor. She was a fool, and it was a schoolgirl error that cost all these people dearly. She'd hardly spoken to the doctor since that day with Flora. He acted as though the incident never occurred, that his sister would be fine. But she would not be fine, Mamie knew. The pale, thin woman would languish in that dark room, an addict to morphine, until the ropes of blood strangled the life out of her. It was a bitter end to any life. Mamie was forced to drive the motor vehicle the doctor purchased after he sold the mule. He said the thing was for her use, but she was wiser now. She had a feeling that the vehicle was actually for his use, but he used public health money to purchase it. She missed the mule, his stubbornness, the unbelievable maneuvers she went through to get from point A to point B, but she'd grown fond of him. She looked forward to early mornings in the barn, with the sun filtering through the loose boards of the barn, where dust specks floated in the air and moved silently along that stairway to the sun. But the animal was gone, like so many things determined useless or unproductive. She thought it odd that she missed all the things that, at one time, made her angry and frustrated, but it was those things that made her life special, made for good stories, and brought color to her otherwise colorless life.

She quickly found that the motor vehicle was next to useless up these hills. The roads, what roads there actually were, were too rough and narrow, so she'd parked the thing at the McCrarys' store. Jack was there. He looked well, although still walking with a bit of limp. He told her that he was going to go back to school in the spring. Mr. McCrary had a brother in Chicago, and Jack would go there to further his education. Mrs. McCrary arranged a tutor for him so he could catch up. The McCrarys set great store in that boy. He said he missed his mother greatly, but the McCrarys kept him busy helping out at the store and working with his tutor. Mamie was glad for the boy. He'd a hard way to go, and Mamie had done nothing to ease his burden, but the McCrarys had. They'd given him a chance, and that's all this boy needed.

Mamie's guilt drove her to visit some of the hill people she'd neglected. Jessica Pike was doing well, and the baby was healthy. He was growing fast, already crawling around and making babbling noises, but Jessica made it clear she would not be having any more children until Miss Hattie returned. Old Mrs. Pike patted the younger woman's shoulder and looked away. The older woman knew the score. She knew the days of Hattie Baker coming to the house were over. Mamie remembered forcing a smile and nodding.

Mrs. Lowery, though, had not fared as well. Without anyone to check on her and help with her dropsy, her heart failed, and she passed away a couple of months ago. The house was falling into disrepair, and the weeds overgrew the garden. The foxgloves were nowhere to be seen. A neighbor man said he'd found the woman sitting in her rocking chair on the front porch, her one hand on a bowl of apples in her lap, the other hand on the arm of the empty rocking chair. Mr. Lowery had finally come home to fetch her.

The greatest guilt Mamie had, though, was towards Hattie. Mamie had not seen her nor written to her in all this time. She wasn't even sure if the woman was still alive, and as far as that unborn baby...

Mamie walked to the Bakers' cabin. There was no one around, but the warm odors of coffee and biscuits told her that they were not gone for long. She could hear the sound of the river flowing nearby, only interrupted by red hawks calling above her. Sitting down on the porch step, she watched them effortlessly riding the warm air currents that took them above the clouds. She closed her eyes, letting the sun warm her face. At this moment, she wished she was one of those hawks. Then, she could fly away from here, higher up into the sky until she disappeared behind the clouds, but then she knew she would never be able to fly so high because she was weighed down with her guilt. Guilt because she felt she abandoned these people who needed her. She took away the only person who cared for them, Hattie Baker. She took her to that place so far away where no one could reach her. It may as well have been Golgotha for no one ever returned.

She opened her eyes, shielding them from the sun to watch the hawks circling. She did not see Martin walk up in front of her. When she returned her gaze to the ground, he startled her. He was sweaty and hot, eyes dark with anger. He looked like someone possessed by an evil demon, and she was sorry she came alone.

He walked past her, up the steps and into the house, letting the screen door slam behind him. Mamie was not sure what to do, but shortly he came out of the house holding a dark, brown jug in one hand and a tin cup in the other. He sat down on the step beside her and filled his cup with the pungent liquid that came from the jug. He drank it down quickly, throwing his head back. He didn't bat an eye as the burning liquid made its way down his throat. He poured another cup of the liquor.

"Mr. Baker," she began, her voice soft. "What has happened?"

Martin threw back his second cup of moonshine. With a voice slightly out of breath, he answered, "I sold my land today."

Mamie looked at him with disbelief, her eyes wide and mouth gaping.

"Who bought it?"

"Roosevelt," he answered as he poured his third cup of liquor and drank it down.

Mamie couldn't believe what she heard. She shook her head and repositioned herself on the step. She now faced Martin as he continued to swill his liquor.

"You mean the president, Franklin Roosevelt?"

Martin nodded, taking a short break from his drinking.

"Why?" Mamie asked in disbelief.

"He wants to put a lake on it."

Mamie shook her head. None of this made any sense. "How much have you had to drink today, Martin?"

He lowered his head. "Not enough."

"You must have misunderstood. Why would the president want to buy your farm and put a lake on it? Surely, there's a reasonable answer to all this. What was said? Who did you talk to?"

She was rambling, and she knew it, but she could not make sense of this conversation. Martin finally sat down the jug of moonshine and the tin cup. He rubbed his hands through his black, curly hair before he pulled the rolled papers from his pocket. Mamie unfurled them and began to read. She scanned quickly, understanding very little. The wording was difficult, mangled with legal jargon, but she was able to discern that the government was using a law Mamie had never heard of before, the law of Imminent Domain.

"This law gives the government the right to buy your land and use it for the good of the country," she said softly as she continued to read. "How can this be? I thought if you bought the land, it was yours, until you sold it of your own freewill."

Martin stared blankly out onto the front yard. His eyes were red with anger and tears. He looked like a man that could do something desperate. Mamie could see the pain in his face. She knew there was more. She placed her hand on his shoulder, trying to keep a professional distance, but feeling, somehow, drawn to a more human response. Martin reached back into his pocket and handed her the letter from

Mamie. She opened it and began to read. She was unable to read much, though, as her own tears began to blur the wording.

"So," she said after a bit. "The child was stillborn."

Martin made no response but continued looking out over the land.

"Would you like to go see her? I have a vehicle. I can drive you there."

He shook his head, blinking, fighting back the emotions that were overwhelming him.

"She asks me not to come. She says she wants us to remember her as she was, not how she is now, so close to death." He wiped his eyes with his hand.

Mamie could feel the hot tears forming in her own eyes. She did not want to cry. She wanted to be strong, to have some answers. She wanted to help this man.

He forced a half-smile and looked at the young nurse. "It's funny, too, though," he began, trying to make some sense of this. "I do remember her that way. She was so lively and fun. We used to go skinny dippin' in the river off the sandbars. She always told her momma we were picking berries." He laughed slightly. "I don't think we ever picked one berry." He lowered his head. "I cannot watch her die."

Mamie could see he was being crushed by his grief, his shoulders trembling as he fell into the darkness. She placed her arm around him as a few tears rolled down her own face. He turned and buried his face into her neck. She felt him sob. It melted her heart to see this tall, strong man brought to this by the actions of others. The cruelty of all this was overwhelming. Those people who were supposed to help others were now only the means to drive others down into the dust. These people were powerless against the stronger, the wealthier, the so-called "educated." She wished all those people who made these decisions could sit here now, in her place, and hold onto this sad, broken man knowing they were the cause of this great pain.

Martin slowly regained his composure and pulled away, embarrassed by his action. He wiped his eyes and swallowed hard.

"Forgive me, Mamie. I am not myself."

Mamie nodded. "Nothing to forgive, Martin."

They sat on the porch for a few moments, breathing in the clean air, trying to free their minds from the dark fog that had overtaken them.

Mamie patted Martin's knee. "You sit here for a bit. I'll go in and make some coffee for us. I saw Jack at the McCrarys' store. Where are your other children?"

Martin sighed, bringing himself back to this reality. "At my sister's. I need to go git 'em. She'll only watch 'em for a few hours a day, and I have to pay her."

"Let's drink some coffee, and then you can go get them. I'll fix their supper while you're gone."

Martin did not argue. He had no strength or will to do anything. He nodded and rolled the papers back into their cylindrical form. He placed the letter back into his pocket.

Mamie went into the house and lit the stove to heat the coffee. He could hear her moving pots and pans to find the skillet and the potato drawer. He sat on the porch step, silently, watching the red hawks fly away.

Mamie rode the train back to Helena. It seemed like it took longer to get home than it took to get to Russellville. She could not remember how long ago it had been since she left home. It seemed like years and years. So much had happened, and not all of it good. She knew her father would be furious with her. She quit her job as the public health nurse and gave her resignation to Dr. Tucker. He said nothing, just nodded. She was disappointed in him, again. She thought he would at least ask her why she was leaving, but maybe he knew. But she was also disappointed in herself. She was not sure how much longer this self-deprecating blanket would envelop her. She didn't like it, but somehow thought it appropriate. She'd been the cause of many heartaches. Lashing herself seemed a just punishment.

When she got off the train, there was no one at the station to meet her. She picked up her one travel bag and walked towards the large, white house at the end of the street. It had been her home all of her life. It would be good to get back home and be with the people who cared for her. She needed a break from the chaos left behind.

She walked into the front door. Her mother came from the kitchen, wearing that same flowered apron she'd worn for years, and smiled. Mamie put down her bag and reached out her arms, just the way she had done when she was a little girl and had a bad day at school. Her mother embraced her, patting her back and whispering how glad she was to have her back home. Mamie could not control her tears. She sobbed into her mother's neck.

"My dear," her mother began. "Whatever is the matter? Are you hurt?"

Mamie pulled away, wiping the tears from her face. "Not outwardly, Momma, but I am definitely wounded on the inside."

Her mother hugged her again – a long, crushing hug.

"Well, come in and eat some supper with your father and me, maybe you'll feel better after you eat."

Her mother's arm remained around Mamie's shoulders as they walked into the kitchen. Her mother fussed around in the kitchen with bowls and plates as the two prepared the evening meal. Mamie sensed there was some nervousness about her mother. She had always been "high strung," as her father said, but her mother seemed even more so tonight. Perhaps it was the sudden appearance of her daughter, or the way in which Mamie explained the events leading up to her return home. Whatever the cause, Mamie felt more comfortable here than she had in her rented room at Mrs. Stuckmeyer's house and certainly more comfortable than at Dr. Tucker's house with his dying sister upstairs.

"So, Mamie, what brings you home?" her father asked as they sat down to supper.

He was a large man, a bit brisk at times. He was known to have a bad temper, but he had always been kind to her. She had seen him lose his temper, but that was usually only when he was working. She respected him but wasn't afraid of him. He was, after all, her father.

He passed her the mashed potatoes. "I had some situations with Dr. Tucker, Daddy."

She passed the creamed corn to him. "Really? What happened?"

Mamie took a deep breath. "Oh, a lot of things, Daddy. I think we just didn't get along."

Her father took a bite of his food. He nodded, seemingly less concerned than Mamie anticipated.

"Bread?" her mother asked, handing her daughter a basket.

"Thank you."

209

Mamie's father took a few more bites, sighing often and wiping his mouth. Her mother remained silent, except to ask if anyone wanted more bread in a nervous, jittery voice.

"…and what happened?" her father asked, pushing away his plate.

Mamie was slightly taken aback. "I'm sorry?"

"You and Dr. Tucker. What sort of a quarrel did you have?"

"He wanted me to be his office nurse, but I wanted to continue to do public health nursing."

Her voice was much more stern than she anticipated. Remembering the lies Dr. Tucker told her put her in a bad mood, and she was releasing the anger through her words.

Her father nodded. "I don't understand why agreeing to be his office nurse is such a problem. You still have a job, you still get paid, and you can still pay your bills."

"Well, I felt he betrayed me, so I quit."

Her father looked up at her. His eyes were not sympathetic. In fact, they were angry. His face became red, and the veins on his neck protruded.

"You quit?" he asked in a deep, unsavory tone.

For the first time in her life, she could see her father's anger directed at her. She could not remember a time when he reacted so angrily to anything she'd done. Although, she had done very few things wrong in her life. She went to church. She got good grades. She was never in trouble, but his reaction seemed extreme.

"Yes, Daddy, I quit. He was not the man I thought him to be, and I don't think I can work for someone who says one thing and does another."

Her father leaned back, balancing himself on the back two legs of the chair. He crossed his arms and smiled a very frightening smile. His eyes were dark and brows furrowed. "What are your plans, then?"

"Well," she began, feeling perspiration breaking out on her forehead. "I thought I could stay here until—"

She was cut off by her father's laughter. "Oh, you did? You thought you could quit your job and just move back in here?"

She nodded, slowly, avoiding his gaze.

He dropped his chair hard onto the floor, leaning forward. He placed his elbows on the table.

"Well, you will have to think again."

Mamie raised her eyes. Her father's face was so close to hers that she could feel his breath.

"Daddy..."

He slammed his fist down onto the table. Mamie jumped at the sound her father made. Her mother rose quickly from the table, nervously picking up some dishes and taking them into the kitchen.

"After all I did for you to get you into that school, and then I called in some favors to get you that cushy job with the public health, you think you can just quit when things don't go your way? You think during these times you can just quit a job because your boss 'misled' you? You are a fool."

Mamie was trying hard to understand all the things her father said. "What are you talking about? I got into that school because of my good grades. I got that job with public health because I am a good nurse."

He laughed, pulling out a cigarette and lighting it. Her mother came back into the room but said nothing. She continued picking up the dishes.

"Let me tell you something, little sister," her father said in a hateful tone. "You got into that school because I paid some people to let you in. You got that job with the public health because Dr. Tucker's family owed me a favor, a big favor."

Mamie gave her father a disconcerted look. "What kind of favor?"

The man took the final drag from his cigarette and snuffed it out in his plate. Mamie's mother came back into the dining room. He looked at her. She said nothing but gathered a few more dirty plates.

"When I was a young man, things were bad. My family was poor. Really, really poor. I was fortunate enough to get a job as a security guard on a train. A train that was owned by a man out of Chicago. The train hauled bottles labeled "spring water" out of Hot Springs. We went through St Louis to avoid too many people wanting to investigate our load. Then, we went on to Chicago. There were a couple of us assigned to each shipment. One night, when we were taking a load up north, some special police in St Louis decided they wanted to check our cargo. They forced the train to stop and insisted on boarding that train. Our job was to keep them off the train. Somehow, in our discussion to convince them that we were just hauling spring water, one of the officers got shot, and that man died."

He lifted his eyes to Mamie's. She sat very still, numb to the words she was hearing.

"Well, the man that did the shooting liked one of the train owner's cousins. So, the man that owned the train cut a deal with me. He said if I'd confess to shooting that guy and go to prison for the other man, that train owner would pay me off. Like I said, I was really, really poor. So, I agreed."

Mamie could feel her heart melt inside her. "So, you went to prison for murder?"

He nodded. "Yep. Fortunately, that man that owned the train was able to bargain a deal so I only served ten years for a thirty-year stent, and when I came out, he paid me. That's when I met your momma. She was in a bad way and needed some help. I thought it best if we got out of Hot Springs and moved away, start new. We had the money, so we changed our names, she had you, and here we are."

Mamie looked down at the table. A thick fog was lifting from her memories. There was a reason they had no pictures of family, no family gatherings, no talk about grandma or grandpa.

"What was your name?" she asked after a few minutes.

"It doesn't matter. It wouldn't be your name, anyway."

Mamie looked at the man with disbelief. Her mother came back into the room. She and the man looked at the woman. She stood very still, eyes cast down to the floor.

"Do you know who my father is?" Mamie asked her mother, her voice broken and quiet.

Her mother shook her head.

The man who had been her father only a few moments before took a deep breath. He appeared now as if a heavy weight was lifted from him.

"So, there you have it, little sister. I'll write to Dr. Tucker and tell him it was just a misunderstanding and get your job back."

"I don't think he'll give me my job back."

The man stood up. "He has no choice. The man that shot the officer was his father. It would ruin his family and their practice if anyone knew his father was a murderer, a coward, and where that family got all their money. So, you see, it is not what you know, it's what you know about them."

The man left the room. Mamie looked across the table.

"Here" she said, handing her mother the last bowl on the table. It was the gravy bowl, almost completely consumed. "I don't think I'll be needing any more of this."

17

Hattie sat in the solarium along with the other twenty or so people who came and went as the nurses moved them. Some left and were never seen again. Others were there nearly every day. It was difficult to determine if anyone ever got well or died. Sometimes, when a patient was nearing death, Hattie could hear the nurses close all the patient room doors. They would start at one end of the hall and, one by one, close each door so the patients couldn't hear the gasping of the dying patient. Then the sound of the gurney could be heard, its wobbly wheels rolling along the tile floor. After a while, the gurney could be heard on its return journey, although this time it sounded different. The wheels were no longer wobbly. The weight of the dead body held them in place, and the sound was smooth and steady. It had become a macabre game she played, to see if she could count the door closures and figure out which patient died. She was usually correct unless she'd had morphine. She'd learned tuberculosis was a slow, reflective disease. It gave its victims ample time to reflect upon their lives. There were the dreams that would never come true, the children they would never see again, or never see at all, and the mistakes that were made when they were young and thought they would never die. Lost lives that would end too soon.

The regular coughing and raspy breathing sounds were broken by a familiar voice. Hattie turned to see Hayden's cot rolled in by the red headed nurse. Hattie was a bit embarrassed, but she was secretly glad to see him. He was the only bright spot in this death house. He was like a light in the darkness, a buoy in the river of despair.

"I brought you a visitor, Mrs. Baker. Mr. Smith requested a visitation with you. I thought it might do you both some good."

"Thank you," Hattie replied as the nurse adjusted Hayden's blankets. She brushed his long curls from his face. Hattie thought him paler than she remembered, and his face displayed pain when he tried to inhale.

"Good morning, Miss Hattie," Hayden said, his voice so soft it could hardly be heard.

"Good morning, Hayden."

The nurse left the solarium, tucking a clipboard beneath her arm.

Hayden swallowed hard and tried to breath. Hattie could tell this was a definite change in his condition.

"Is this a bad day for you, Hayden?"

He tried to reposition slightly, grimacing and jerking when the stabbing pain was sent through him.

He nodded. "My disease is progressing. So, they tried to collapse the most diseased lung. They removed a couple of my ribs so my collarbone drops, stuck a needle in my side and filled the area around my lung with fluid." He stopped for a moment and took a painful breath, closing his eyes. "Then, because none of that was painful enough, they cut the phrenic nerve, so my chest is paralyzed on one side."

He moved the blanket that covered him, revealing discolored skin, macerated areas, multiple cuts, stitches and swollen, red wounds. There were white gauze bandages on some of them, but clear, thick fluid leaked out from around them. His body looked like something that was in a haunted house, broken, pale and unreal. Hattie watched him, repulsed by the idea of what they'd done to this man. He was now closer to death than ever.

".,.and they call me a witch," she said softly.

He grinned, discomfort painted his face.

"Did they give you anything for pain?" she asked as she leaned towards him. His hand was outside the blanket. Unconsciously, she placed her hand on top of his and squeezed it.

"Not during the inquisition. They asked me questions, and I had to be lucid enough to answer, but they gave me something before I came over here."

"Why would they do such a thing?"

Her voice was full of sadness, but she did not want to be so emotional in front of him. At this time, he needed reassurance and support, not a weepy co-hort.

"It's all experimental. They do a lot of experimental things here."

He pointed to a building down the road. "See that building? They have scientists and doctors in there who work on surgeries, medications, radiation, anything they can think of to cure this disease or treat it."

"How successful are they?"

He grinned that sly way again. "I'm hoping they are very successful."

He took a few short breaths, trying to outrun the pain. He closed his eyes again. She knew he felt that fire in his lung and tasted that familiar metallic taste in the back of his throat. He was emaciated, even thinner than she. Gray-black circles surrounded those blue eyes, like a great storm coming upon the sea.

"So," he said after a while, opening his eyes. "What've you been up to?"

Hattie could not help herself. She laughed.

"It is possible," Hayden replied, wiping his mouth with that kerchief he always carried.

"What is possible?"

"You can laugh. No one here has ever heard you laugh." He took a labored breath. "Some said it was not possible, but I said the woman can laugh."

She smiled, "It has been a long time. There's not much here that makes me laugh."

Hattie started to move back in her chair, but Hayden grabbed her hand with a surprising amount of strength and agility. She was sure this was pure fear and desperation that gave him this energy. He placed her hand on his heart. She could feel his heartbeat, fast and thready, like a dying fawn.

"They got some new, experimental medications they're working on in that building. If this surgery doesn't work, they said I can try that." His breath was quick and strained. "Should I try it? Should I try that medication, Hattie?"

She could feel her own heart begin to beat faster. "I don't know, Hayden. I don't know anything about this."

He held her hand on his heart so tightly, as if to remove it would tear away the last vital organ he possessed.

"They say the medicine could kill me, but if I don't try, I'm dead already. I don't know what to do. I don't want to die."

She stared into his eyes. She thought how odd this was that they were complete strangers a little over a year ago, and now, it was as if they were the same person. His eyes, his voice, his very heartbeat seemed so familiar. She didn't think she could bear to lose him. She'd already lost so much. She knew she was selfish, but she leaned forward and placed her forehead on his. She did not see the hollow eyes, the frail man. She didn't feel the thin skin or smell the blood.

"Please," she whispered on his skin. "Take the drugs."

She felt him nod his head and squeeze her hand. She pulled herself away. Somehow, he did not seem quite so fragile.

"I will," he answered quietly.

Hattie leaned back into her chair. She saw Hayden relax on his cot. His breathing was still difficult to watch, but there didn't seem to be as much pain. Hattie was unsure if the change was from his mental attitude or the morphine taking effect. In any case, it was good to see him more comfortable.

The solarium door opened, and the red-haired nurse returned. She held envelopes. The sanitorium had its own post office. Patients received little tokens from home, letters, post cards, and sometimes money from their families back home. Hayden and Hattie didn't pay her much attention. Hayden never received anything, and Hattie only occasionally received a letter from Martin. Although Hattie looked forward to hearing from her husband, she had mixed feelings when reading his letters. The heartache they left when she read them left her dark on the inside, even darker than she was prior to receiving the letter.

"Mrs. Baker," the nurse said in a happy voice, holding out the last envelope to Hattie. "Looks like a letter from home."

18

I'm here to see Hattie Baker." Mamie was burdened with guilt. She promised Hattie so many things and failed miserably at all of them. Now, she had to perform penance. She must atone for her sins. She judged her mother and the man she thought was her father harshly, but she was no better. Perhaps the apple did not fall far from the tree, but she could try to do the right thing. This visit would be the hardest thing she'd ever done. The things she needed to tell Hattie were painful. She wondered how many ways there were to say you were sorry, that you made a mistake, and that you would try to make it up to her. Mamie's main concern, though, was the reason she'd taken that train all the way back here to talk to this woman. Was it because she thought she owed Hattie the truth, or was it because Mamie was trying to unburden her own soul of the sins it owned? A nurse came from behind the desk and motioned the young woman to follow her. Mamie fol-lowed, a little unnerved by the sights and sounds of this place. Many people were lying in the beds in various stages of diseases. Some were talking to friends and family members as if they were completely disease free.

Others were leaning off one side of their beds with cloths held to their mouths to catch the blood that exuded from the bodies, but they were unsuccessful. Drops of the blood formed little pools on the speckled tile. The smell of blood and disease were everywhere, mixed with the vain attempt to clean and deodorize with bleach and antiseptic. It was a sickening odor that stayed in your nostrils even after you let the building, permeating your clothes and hair. It was a fragrance that haunted your senses like the ghosts of the diseased, decaying and putrefied.

The nurse stopped and pointed to a closed door, and they walked away without saying a word. Mamie stood in front of the door for a moment. She had good intentions, but she believed herself a coward. Her hands trembled as she knocked on the door, but she hesitated. Her heart was beating so loudly, she could hear it beating in her ears. The noise was so loud, in fact, she did not hear Hattie's nurse walking down the hall.

"Is she not in there?" the nurse asked as she came closer to Hattie's door.

Mamie did not have time to answer. The nurse knocked hard on the door.

"Mrs. Baker," she said, pushing the large, wooden door open. "Oh, yes," she continued, turning to Mamie. "She's in here. She just didn't hear you knocking."

The nurse turned her attention to the woman lying in the bed. She was alone in the room. The other patients had visitors or were sitting in the solarium.

"Mrs. Baker, you have a visitor."

Mamie smiled at the nurse as the latter left the room. Mamie scanned the room. It was dark, except for one, lone window on the far end. Lying in the bed next to the window lay a cachectic, pale woman. She lay facing the window, back to the door. Upon entering, the woman did not turn her attention to Mamie, but continued looking out the window.

Mamie walked across the room, her shoes making tapping noises. She had never noticed how loud her shoes were until this moment. It made her uncomfortable and embarrassed.

When Mamie stood beside Hattie's bed, she noticed how much older Hattie looked. It had only been a little over a year since she and the sheriff brought this woman here to the sanitorium. Hattie's hair was cut short with more gray, and her skin was wrinkled and thin. It looked like crepe paper stretched over a skeleton.

Hattie's eyes were open, but she said nothing. She lay very still with her gaze fixed on the view outside the window.

"Hello," Mamie finally managed to say.

Her voice was shaky. Hattie did not respond.

Mamie spied a chair across the room and walked over to pull it nearer to Hattie's bed. Mamie thought these were the loudest shoes in the world. Dragging the chair across the floor made a grat-ing sound on the tile. Every noise seemed to be exceptionally loud, echoing in this empty chamber.

"How are you doing?" she asked as she sat down in the chair.

As soon as the words left her mouth, she regretted them. She wondered what kind of a question that would be to a person in Hattie's condition forced to live in the sanitorium.

Hattie turned her face towards her visitor and blinked slowly. What Mamie saw in Hattie's eyes was not anger or even hatred. It was something she did not expect. It was indifference. Mamie real-ized she was nothing to this woman. Hattie's former life seemed so long ago, as if it happened to someone else. There was no blame.

"I'm fine," Hattie finally answered. There was an awkward silence.

Mamie tried desperately to summon some courage. "Hattie," she began, her hands trembling. "I wanted to let you know I checked on Jack. Mr. and Mrs. McCray are so fond of him. His leg is healing well. You did an excellent job of tending to him. He doesn't even need to use a cane any-more."

Hattie nodded.

"In fact," Mamie continued. "I think he's become the son the McCrarys never had. He helps them with the store. He even started delivering for them. I think that's a good idea. That way, the elderly and infirmed can get their food and supplies without having to leave their homes. They got him a tutor to help him with his studies. Did I tell you they're going to send him back to school?"

Her voice broke a bit, and she shook her head.

"Of course, I didn't tell you that, but they're going to pay for him to go back to school in Chicago. He's smart, Hattie. He'll go far with their help."

Mamie realized she was rambling and probably not saying appropriate things to the mother of this boy who may never see him again.

Hattie could read the young woman's thoughts. She smiled, slightly. "I'm glad he's doing so well."

Mamie nodded.

"...and Clemson and Eulalie are fine. I saw them just before I came up here, and Martin.."

She stopped short.

"I mean, Mr Baker, is doing well and is taking real good care of them."

Hattie reached a thin, bony hand into a small shelf beside her bed.

"Martin sent me a letter." She handed the folded paper to Mamie.

Mamie began reading. The letter was short, one page. She read it within a few minutes and then returned it to Hattie. Mamie's head was lowered, her eyes focused on the floor.

"I'm so sorry, Hattie," she said softly.

Hattie again turned her gaze to the window. "It's probably better this way. Jack's doing so well with the McCrarys, and now Martin's been forced to sell the farm. At least, with the money, he can take the two babies to Oregon. His letter says there's lumber mills out there, and he get a job."

Hattie continued, swallowing hard. "He said he couldn't bear to watch me die."

Hattie folded the letter and placed back into the little shelf.

"It is difficult," she continued. "Watching someone you love die right before you, knowing there's nothin' you can do. You feel so helpless and useless. All the love in the world can't cure them, can't keep them, can't save them, and then they are gone."

"Mrs. Baker," came a voice from the door. "Oh, excuse me," said the red-haired nurse as she en-tered the room. "I didn't mean to interrupt, but I thought Mrs. Baker would want to know."

Hattie turned her face towards the nurse. "Know what?"

The nurse came closer. "Well, we don't normally do this, but Mr. Smith has taken a turn for the worse. He's in the men's building and all alone. He's asking for you, Mrs. Baker."

Hattie tossed the blanket that covered her. "Yes, please take me over there."

The nurse went into the hall and pulled a wheelchair close to the bed. She assisted Hattie into the chair and tucked a blanket across her lap.

"Who is this Mr. Smith?" Mamie asked as she moved her chair out of the way.

The nurse wrapped a shawl around Hattie's shoulders. "He is another patient here. Nice man. Such a sad story. He ended up a transient, doing odd jobs for people, handyman work."

Mamie's blood suddenly became very cold. "Did he?" Her voice was lost in the rumbling of the wheelchair as the nurse pushed Hattie from the room.

"Wait," Hattie said suddenly before they left the room. She gave Mamie a determined look. "Take care of them. I hear Oregon is beautiful, and I want to ask you a favor."

Mamie could feel the tears forming in her eyes. She had wronged this woman, and now felt she was hurting her again. This would be her burden, to carry this great guilt for the rest of her life. Purgatory was on the horizon, but it was the least she could do for this woman.

"Anything," Mamie responded.

Hayden lay flat in his bed. He was gray in color, his lips a sick shade of blue. The bones of his body protruded through the skin like a skeleton. Hattie could see his heartbeat through the skin of his chest. His facial features, surely once so beautiful, were now hollow and sunken with exagger-ated cheekbones. The sockets around his eyes were sullen, deep with dark circles, but the eyes were still that sapphire blue. His body was in ruin, but the window to the soul, his eyes, showed the soul was still alive. Perhaps weak and lonely, he was still inside despite what condition the mortal remains portrayed.

"Mr. Smith," the nurse said softly as she rolled Hattie's chair next to Hayden's bed. "I brought Mrs. Baker. She is here to see you."

He turned his head slightly towards Hattie.

Hattie reached out to him with delicate fingers, tracing his face. "Before you leave," Hattie began talking to the nurse. "Will you hand me a cool cloth?"

The nurse placed a clean cloth beneath the water, wet the cloth, and handed it to Hattie.

"Please call me if you need me," the nurse said as she left the room.

Hayden lay quietly, breathing slowly and deliberately. Hattie wiped his face with the damp cloth. His lips were parched, and she ran the cloth across his mouth. There were traces of blood left on the soft, white cloth. After a few minutes, Hattie began to speak. She was not sure what she want-ed or needed to say. She'd sat vigil with so many people, but this time it was different. It was as if she were losing a part of herself, the part that was kind and beautiful, slipping away from her.

"What can I do for you, Hayden? What do you need?" she asked in that calm, soothing voice she used at times like these.

"I want you to make me a promise." His voice was almost imperceptible. It was harsh, quiet, and gritty.

"What do you want me to promise?"

He swallowed, still showing that uncomfortable pain he had shown right after his surgery. His wounds had never healed. His skin was rebelling against the sutures and cuts that assaulted it.

"I never got the drugs. I was too sick to even try."

Mamie nodded. "What now?"

"I die."

He said it with such calmness that she thought she misunderstood. It took her a minute to process this simple reply.

"Hattie," he continued. "I want you to take those experimental medicines." He opened his eyes as wide as he could so he could see her plainly. "You are stronger than I am. I told the doctors about you. They said you sound like a good candidate."

He was exhausting himself. He stopped talking and closed his eyes, trying to take shorter, faster breaths rather than deep breaths, but Hattie could see that heart beating rapidly indicating his body was struggling to stay alive.

She leaned towards him and placed her forehead onto his. She could feel large, hot tears begin to form. There was no use in trying to hold them back. She let them drop onto his face.

"Why would I want to? My husband and children are gone, my home is gone, and you…"

She felt a terrible sadness crushing her.

"I need you to."

His words came quickly as if he knew his time was running out. "I need you to remember me. There is no one else. When I die, I will be forgotten. Hell may be fire and brimstone, but I think hell is darkness where you are alone and forgotten, and there is not one soul that loved you. When I die, no one will weep for me, or miss me, or even know I was ever here. I spent my life unhappy, pitying myself because I thought no one loved me, but I was wrong. Love does not mean happi-ness, but you can achieve both when you give them to another."

Hattie sat up, wiping the tears from her face. Hayden began to cough, turning his skin an unhealthy shade of crimson and the vessels bulged from the pressure exerted from the violent coughing. Hattie wiped his face and mouth again with that cloth. The blood now came not only from his mouth, but his nose. It had a putrid odor, not the metallic odor it had before. It was thick and tena-cious. Threads of the fluid clinging to the corners of his mouth like long fingers of decay.

"Please," he began again after a few short breaths. "Please promise me you will try, if not for your sake then will you do it for me?"

Hattie thought how pitiful he looked. She knew she could not refuse him. She didn't know if these medications would work, but it really didn't make any difference. If she died from complications of experimental medications or tuberculosis, dead is dead. The reason is really inconsequential. She'd come to terms with this the first time she saw the blood on the dishcloth in her home. She knew the dreams she had would be lost and if agreeing to take this medication would give this sad man peace at his time of death, then she could do this small thing for him.

She nodded.

She watched his body relax. His last request accomplished, he could rest. He seemed to struggle less. His breathing was shallow, and that heartbeat she could see had slowed, and she could tell the pressure behind it has lessened. She leaned towards him and kissed him softly.

He whispered to her as her face was near him, "Hattie amatum."

She didn't understand what it meant, but it didn't matter.

"Hattie," he said as he closed his eyes. "Can you sing?"

She smiled slightly through her tears. "A little. Someone I love recently taught me an old Irish song. I think I can remember it."

The last words he said were: "Hattie, sing to me."

Hattie swallowed hard, giving in to the tears she'd held back for so long. There were tears for her husband who had lost his way, for her children who she may never see again, for the life she would never have, and for this man who wasted his precious life. Her voice was broken, but she remembered the words and sang softly as Hayden left the world. She placed her head on his chest to hear his last heartbeat as she sang the last chorus of the song.

It became very quiet, except for the sounds of the closing of the doors.

Hattie lay in a deep stupor for some time, neither speaking nor communicating with anyone. It was as if her mind preferred no stimulation and required none. She stared blankly at the ceiling when in her room, or upon the lawn when she was in the solarium. She neither heard anything nor required anything. Her nurse was quite concerned as Hattie did not eat properly or consume fluids unless someone was there with her to constantly coach her.

"Mrs. Baker," the nurse began as she knelt next to Hattie's bed on the solarium. "This is a doctor from the lab. He works with the new medications and is interested in you."

Hattie looked blankly at the nurse and then the man standing next to her.

"Mrs. Baker," the nurse continued. "I'm worried that you are not progressing well since the death of Mr. Smith. I spoke to the doctors about this, and apparently Mr. Smith requested the doctor to ask you to take his place with the new medications."

The doctor knelt beside the other side of Hattie's bed. "Mrs. Baker. I've looked at your history, the x-rays, and your prognosis. I think you would make a good trial patient for this medicine. Would you be willing to work with us on this?"

Hattie remembered her promise. Somewhere between the letter from Martin and Hayden's death, she'd lost herself. She had become that mist of fog again. Waiting for the morphine because noth-ing else mattered. Oblivion was comfortable.

"Yes," she answered, hardly believing she had any voice with which to speak.

"Wonderful," the doctor said as she stood up. Speaking to the nurse, he said, "Please take Mrs. Baker back to her room and I'll come right back with the streptomycin." He faced Hattie before he left the solarium. "I believe she is a wonderful candidate. Her lungs are diseased, but they show great resiliency. There is scarring, but no cavitation. At least she was spared that much."

The nurse did as she was ordered. There was paperwork to be read and signed. A list of possible side effects was handed to Hattie which she looked at vaguely, especially since the last line read, "and others unknown including death." The doctor returned with the new medication. Hattie was surprised how painful this injection was. It felt like he was pushing jelly into her arm.

This routine was continued daily. Hattie wasn't expecting much. She thought most of her disease process was beyond her anyway, but she did notice a change. It started slowly at first. She was so very tired, which was nothing new, but the coughing was less violent. She found she could speak an entire sentence without stopping to breathe. The coughing itself was less and very seldom pro-duced blood. She was able to eat more. Her breathing was not as labored. She no longer had night sweats , and the burning pain in her chest was less. She was able to get out of her bed, no longer required a wheelchair, and was able to walk by herself on the grounds of the sanitorium. In all the time she'd been here, she did not know of all these buildings. There was a women's building and men's building to house the sick, but there was a school for the children with TB. They had their own building in which to live. There was a dairy, a barn, orchards, laundry, and newspaper. She saw the building where the doctor's office was located. He worked in the building where guinea pigs were raised. Their purpose was to test the medicine before it was given to humans. Hattie real-ized she was now the human guinea pig.

Her strength gradually returned, but she was tied to this place. Short periods without the medica-tion resulted in the return of the disease. Slowly creeping back into the fragile cells of her lungs. The tuberculosis inched its way to overtake other organs, including the bones and brain. So, while Hattie was improving, her tether was short. She needed to continue treatment, but she did not re-quire 24/7 care as she previously did when she first arrived. Without a home or family, her future was uncertain, and she felt at loose ends. She truly didn't think she'd live this long and had no plans, but she would need to make decisions. She would not be allowed to stay here free of charge forever.

There were a lot of benches in the garden where Hattie walked. She liked to sit in the garden. It re-minded her of her home. It was quiet, and she could hear the wind in the trees, smell the leaves, and feel the warm earth on her bare feet.

"Mrs. Baker," came a familiar voice from across the garden. It was the red-haired nurse. She sat down beside Hattie on the bench. "Do you have any plans for what you will do when you are re-leased?"

"No," she replied, somewhat ashamed that she had no options. "I'm not sure what I should do. I can't go too far away because I need these treatments so much, and I have no skills to get a job up here. My family's gone, and..."

Her voice trailed off.

"Then I have a proposition for you." The nurse smiled. "Since you are not able to be totally re-leased and must continue your treatment intermittently, but you are technically not contagious, would you be interested in working here at the sanitorium?"

Hattie was skeptical. "Doing what?"

She could picture all sorts of terrible, repulsive jobs, but she may have no choice. If it paid the bills, she would have to take the job, repulsive or not.

"We need someone who can help with the children. Many of them will be able to be managed out-side this facility, but they will have no skills. They have school every day, but no real-world expe-rience. They have spent their entire lives on this property, sheltered, and we need someone to help them assimilate in the outside world. Do you think you could help with this?"

Hattie thought about the proposition. "...And I can stay here?"

The nurse nodded, smiling. "Yes, you can live here and be an employee. You can also continue your treatments here."

Hattie wasn't sure what to say. It sounded good, but surely there was a catch. So far in her life, everything had a catch, and sometimes the catch was deadly.

"Mrs. Baker," the nurse continued. "You would be helping these children, and I think they would be helping you, too."

Hattie nodded. She knew exactly what the nurse was saying. Since Hattie lost everything, she lacked a purpose. She had no goals and no dreams, no reason to get up in the morning, nothing to look forward to.

"All right," she answered. She smiled. It felt strange to smile.

The nurse hugged her.

"But..." Hattie said as the nurse rose to leave. "I need to do one thing before I begin."

"Of course," the nurse answered. "You may come and go as you please. You are not a prisoner. You are an employee with a chronic illness, who must have continued intermittent care. Your dis-ease does not define you. You are not the illness."

The nurse leaned over and touched her forehead to Hattie's forehead. "You are free."

"I am free," she heard herself say. "Thank you."

The nurse stood up, straightening her dress and wiping a few little tears from her face.

"I do ask one thing. Is there anyone who can drive me?"

"Of course," the nurse replied. "I would be glad to do it myself. Give me a few minutes, if you

could. I'm admitting a new patient. A doctor's sister. She's bad off. I don't think there is much that can be done for her. So, we will just try to make her as comfortable as possible."

Hattie nodded. "I'll go put on my shoes."

Hattie got out of the car and walked towards the little church. It overlooked a beautiful, crystal clear lake. All of this valley was now underwater. The only building left standing was this church. Through the still water, she could make out the shadows of old houses, cabins, sheds, and barns. There were a few abandoned vehicles still parked outside the buildings, as if waiting for someone to start them up and drive them away. But it was all beneath the water, like the dreams of the life she once had. She went to the church cemetery. Kneeling down at a little grave, she placed yellow yarrow.

She traced the letters of the headstone: B-o-n-n-i-e I-z-e-l-l

She stood back to admire the little angel carved into the stone. She would be remembered. She was loved. It seemed so long ago. It was hard for Hattie to even remember that time. Hattie kissed her fingers and pressed them hard against the little angel. She walked away, pulling a small knife from her pocket. She continued to the largest tree she could find. It towered over the cemetery and church. Its shade reached from one end of the property to the other. She began to cut into the trunk of the tree, carefully carving the letters, making them deep and intricate. After a few minutes, she stood back and placed the little knife back into her pocket.

She admired her work. It was perfect. It said everything she wanted it to say; that is, "Hayden amatum."

It was carved so carefully, so that every person going into or out of the church would see it. Any-one who came up here to look down on the lake would also see it. She thought of him a lot. He saved her life. He gave her another chance. She would not waste it. She smiled a tearful smile as she walked away. A song she remembered came into her mind, and she began singing aloud an old Irish tune. She walked away from the lake with its flooded houses, abandoned cars, lost dreams, and abandoned lives, singing to herself.

J. Kenkade
PUBLISHING®

J. Kenkade
School of Publishing

Bring Your Story.
We'll Help you Write it!

For School inquiries or to hire a writing coach:
www.jkenkadepublishing.com
(501) 482-1000

Also Available from
J. Kenkade Publishing

ISBN 978-1-944486-87-7
Purchase at www.amazon.com or www.barnesandnoble.com

All who hear tales of Madam MaRooska's world-renowned yet exclusive specialty resort at Bellingfast Estates clamor to be granted attendance every year. One of the most compelling events in this two-week excursion is an elaborate masquerade ball in which guests can disappear into the personas of any historical figures they wish. However, Constance Stallings knows firsthand just how quickly this game of illusions can turn nefarious. Born into wealth and privilege but determined to make a name for herself as an author, she embarks on a second trip to Bellingfast with her family in the hopes of finishing her novel, The Angel Doll, and perhaps even uncovering the tragic mystery that looms over her last encounter with the seemingly cursed estate.

Also Available from
J. Kenkade Publishing

ISBN: 978-1-955186-20-9
Purchase at www.amazon.com

The goddess of water, Reina rules her country with an iron fist, enforcing her view of peace with great ruthlessness. She was not always so cruel; however, at one point, she ruled her people justly, with her friend Clara by her side. When a nation of humans decided to not heed to the authority of the gods, a war broke out. It was man vs god, a true David vs Goliath situation. In the heat of battle, Reina bore witness to her friend's last moments, sending her into a dark spiral. This twisted version of herself that we see today is what came of her after the war, a reclusive leader that rarely shows herself to her people. What do the threads of fate hold for Reina? Will she reopen her country and spare her people from their agony? Or will her nation stay in a state of limbo forever?

Also Available from
J. Kenkade Publishing

ISBN: 978-1-955186-23-0
Purchase at www.amazon.com

Winters is a captivating and passionate Christian suspense novel about a powerful, spiritual family who is anointed and ordained by God Almighty. You will feel love, pain, heartaches, compassion, grace, mercy, suffering, and God's spirit, all in one story. Find out why Winters is about the coldest season of the year in more ways than one. Come and live in the minds and hearts of Stella, Abe, Mr. Perkins, The Langley family, Hattie, Benjamin, and Minnie. So much more awaits you in this powerful Christian suspense novel. Both fiction and nonfiction, Winters will give you a chill like never before.

Also Available from
J. Kenkade Publishing

ISBN: 978-1-955186-18-6
Purchase at www.amazon.com

A collection of poems inspired by one man's story of love, pain, loss, and newfound hope and joy.

www.ingramcontent.com/pod-product-compliance
Lightning Source LLC
Chambersburg PA
CBHW020801250626
47155CB00003B/1169